THE GIRL LOCKED WITH GOLD

THE CHRONICLES OF MAGGIE TRENT, BOOK TWO

MEGAN O'RUSSELL

Ink Worlds Press

Visit our website at www.MeganORussell.com

This book is a work of fiction. Names, characters, places, and incidents either are products of the author's imagination or are used fictitiously. Any resemblance to actual persons, living or dead, events, or locales is entirely coincidental.

The Girl Locked With Gold

Copyright © 2019, Megan O'Russell

Cover Art by Sleepy Fox Studio (https://www.sleepyfoxstudio.net/)

Editing by Christopher Russell

Interior Design by Christopher Russell

All rights reserved.

No part of this publication may be used or reproduced in any manner whatsoever without written permission, except in the case of brief quotations embodied in critical articles and reviews. Requests for permission should be addressed to Ink Worlds Press.

Printed in the United States of America

DEDICATION

To the friends I trust to join me on the greatest of adventures

THE GIRL LOCKED WITH GOLD

CHAPTER 1

The weight of the smoke seared her throat as it pressed down into her lungs.

"Ber—" her hacking cough cut off his name. "Bertrand!"

The roar of the flames swallowed her shout.

The world is on fire, and I'll burn with it.

A scream carried down from high above, the voice too shrill to be Bertrand's.

"Hello?" Maggie stumbled toward the sound.

The dense smoke hid the form of whatever landscape burned around her, but the flames danced higher in the direction of the scream, reaching far above Maggie's head with no sign of something she might climb to reach the terrified person.

"I'm coming!" Maggie gagged on a burst of sour smoke. Something in the haze burned her eyes, blurring her vision.

Sparks whirled around her as she swayed, retching black that tore painfully from her throat.

"Bertrand." Her lips formed his name as she fell to her knees.

The heat of the ground burned through her pants, searing her flesh.

"*Primurgo.*" The spell took the last bit of air she had. The shield shimmered to life around her, blocking the waves of smoke, but not the terrible heat of the flames.

Her palms blistered as she pushed herself to her feet, squinting through the smoke.

No figure stumbled toward her. Not Bertrand or even a poor victim of the devastation in this unknown land.

"Bertrand!" Maggie shouted, coughing up more of the black goo. "Bertrand, we have to go!"

A *crack* rent the air, and the ground shook a moment later. Shield or not, they were running out of time.

"Bertrand Wayland, if you've led me to my death—"

"I have not led you to your death, Miss Trent." Bertrand tore out of the darkness, embers licking the tails of his black coat. "Nor have I ever assured your safety."

"Where the hell have you been?" Maggie dropped her shield, and Bertrand grabbed her wrist, dragging her straight toward a tower of fire.

"*Hell* seems a fairly accurate assessment, Miss Trent." Bertrand ducked as a wall of embers collapsed in front of them. Not pausing, he veered around the flames. "It took you so long to arrive, I didn't know if I would be able to wait for you much longer."

"Thanks for not abandoning me." Maggie leapt over a crack in the ground, her toes landing an inch from Bertrand's heels.

"Of course. Now, if you would." With two giant strides, Bertrand plunged into a black pit that consumed the center of the path.

Flat, scorched walls leading to darkness far below were the only details Maggie managed to see before overwhelming nothing consumed her.

The void squeezed every inch of her being. Her lungs couldn't have expanded to pull in air even if there had been any present for her to breathe. A whirling sense like rushing through a vast river tingled her toes, but there was no way to know how fast she moved in the nothing, if she was even moving at all.

As questions she would never get to ask trickled through her mind, a green light flashed into being around her, and pain shot through her knees.

"Ow." Maggie flopped to the side, not caring who might see her lying on the street. "Ow, ow, ow."

"Are you all right, Miss. Trent?" Bertrand hovered over her, silhouetted by the sun.

Maggie took a deep breath, testing her lungs as she rubbed her fingers over her unburnt palms. "No smoke inhalation or third degree burns, so I'd say the Siren worked her magic again."

"Then why are you lying on the ground?"

Maggie shielded her eyes so she could properly see the furrowed lines on Bertrand's brow. His hair was perfectly slicked back in its customary low ponytail. His white shirt and coat tails showed no signs of burns. Even his buckled shoes hadn't been scratched by their brush with fire.

"I'm on the ground because I, unlike perfect you, am not used to jumping back into the Siren's Realm from a land of fiery doom."

"As long as the Siren hasn't decided not to heal all wounds upon entering her realm, I suppose we're all right." Bertrand offered Maggie his hand, helping her to her feet as a gray-speckled centaur rounded the corner.

"How's it going?" Maggie waved, letting an overly-bright smile fill her face.

"As the Siren wills it be done." The centaur nodded and trotted past them without waiting for further conversation.

"Have a nice day." Maggie brushed the dust from the street off her clothes. "So, how long until you find another stitch for us to slip through?"

"Find another stitch?" Bertrand strode down the narrow street, not looking back to see if Maggie followed.

Allowing herself the luxury of rolling her eyes, Maggie trotted after him. "Maybe this time you could find a path out of the Siren's Realm that doesn't lead to Hell."

"The most interesting thing about fire, Miss Trent, is how very temporary it is." Bertrand cut down a wide road lined with tall tents. A gentle wind swayed the colorful fabrics. "Even the worst of blazes will burn out in time. We need only have patience while the flames run their course."

"Wait a second." Maggie dodged around a beautiful woman in red robes to match the tray of wine she carried. "Are you actually saying you want to go back there?"

"Of course, Miss Trent. There are a hundreds, perhaps thousands of tiny stitches joining the Siren's Realm to other worlds. Of all the stitches that exist, the Siren has only allowed us to find a tiny portion. She would not have left a stitch open for us to slip through were there not something interesting and wondrous on the other side. We should not deny ourselves an adventure simply because of a little poor timing."

"You know, that's what I think every time I almost burn to death. As smoke fills my lungs, making it impossible to breathe, *Wow, what a bit of poor timing.*"

"Sarcasm is rarely becoming, Miss Trent."

A wide square opened up in front of them, revealing a platinum fountain flowing in the middle of it all. A statue of a beautiful woman, her nakedness barely concealed by thin fabric, stood at the center of the pool.

A man had climbed up on the edge of the fountain, blocking the crowd from swimming in the sweet liquid. "The Siren's time is shifting away like sand. Her ways are beyond our ken, and times worse than storms are nipping at all of our heels."

"What?" Maggie grabbed Bertrand's sleeve to stop his momentum.

The people in the square were watching the man as he paced the rim of the fountain.

"For in light and peace, there must still come shadows, and it is only the will of the Siren that holds the darkness at bay."

"Let the Siren's will be done," a woman shouted, "and leave us in peace."

A cheer sounded behind the woman, then another.

"Those who do not read the winds shall be eaten by the storm!" the man warned as the crowd surged forward.

"Come along, Miss Trent." Bertrand cut out of the square and down a narrow alley lined with bright red tents.

"Shouldn't we help him?"

A roaring shout sounded from the square.

"Those people could really hurt him," Maggie said.

"A madman who's decided to speak on behalf of the Siren?" Bertrand said. "I don't think there is anything within our power to be done."

A wide lane opened up in front of them. Tables laden with goods from fine silks to fresh baked cakes were open for business. Maggie's stomach turned as a woman shook hands with a silk dealer. Her clothes shimmered for a moment as their colors twisted. Her plain green dress vanished, replaced by a red gown woven through with gold.

Maggie's hands tingled, remembering the feeling of magic zinging through her skin—the shock of it as it left her body in payment for goods, leaving a tiny hole that didn't refill. But if the woman hated the feel of it, her face showed no sign as she gleefully spun in her new gown.

"What do you think they'll do to him?" Maggie averted her eyes as a man paid for a diamond-accented pocket watch.

"I think what the crowd will do to him is the least of that man's concerns." Bertrand kept his voice low as they passed a woman tending a flowerbed filled with bright blue blooms in front of her matching blue tent. "He dares to speak for the Siren. It is never wise to make assumptions of one who provides all that is needed for survival."

"Because you've never tried to tell me how the Siren works?" Maggie whispered.

"I happen to have an uncanny understanding of the Siren and the wisdom to know that sometimes speaking the truth is best done quietly."

The road beneath their feet changed from dirt to cobblestone as they reached the fortress. Weathered and stately houses rose up around them. A lone gondola paddled down the canal, the boatman humming a slow tune. Iron barred windows stared down at them from above, and heavy wooden doors protected against unwanted visitors.

Maggie shuddered at the tingling feeling of dozens of unseen people glaring at her for intruding in this exclusive and intentionally private section of the Siren's Realm.

"I don't think we need waste our time as we wait for the smoke to clear." Bertrand's voice bounced off the stone houses. "You really should work more on your swordplay and hand to hand combat, and this provides an excellent opportunity."

"Remember that time when I was going to live out my days in the Siren's Realm in peace?" Maggie said as Bertrand stopped at a thick wooden door, barely visible beneath the stone overhang of a house. "I was going to fish and live on the rocks by the sea. Enjoy my time not almost dying."

"Let time drift by with nothing to show for it but a bit more wear on your shoes?" Bertrand heaved the wooden door open. The *creak* of the door had become too familiar to startle Maggie. "You would be miserable. If not now, then in a few years."

"Fine." Maggie followed Bertrand into the stone entryway, shoving the wooden door shut behind her and fixing the lock with a dull *clunk*. "But can we both at least agree this morning was not the kind of adventure we want to repeat?"

"But why? Isn't any adventure one survives a worthy undertaking?" Bertrand opened the door at the far end of the tiny, windowless room and strode up the steps to the main house, leaving Maggie barely able to hear his words as she chased him. "We'll give it a few days. By then, the inferno should have died, and slipping into a world of embers should be safe enough. Perhaps we can even discover the source of the blaze."

Bertrand stopped in front of the wide fireplace, lifting a teacup off the mantle and breathing in the sweet steam.

"Unless, of course, you'd like to stay behind and focus on your booming career in the fish trade."

Maggie exhaled, forcing her teeth to unclench. "I'll come with you." She took the second cup from the stone mantle, letting the herbal fragrance melt her frustration. "But only because I don't want you to burn to death."

"How very kind." Bertrand raised his cup to her.

A painting hung above the fireplace. Shadows crept in on either side of the frame with only a dull ray of sunlight peering through at the center. Hints of texture played in the background, but not enough to decipher what exactly the painting was meant to depict.

"You really should get some new art." Maggie sipped her tea. "Something a bit more cheerful."

"In time." Bertrand nodded. "But I'm still enamored of this piece for now."

Maggie shook her head, not setting her cup down as Bertrand dragged all of the furniture to the bookcase that lined the far wall.

"Would you like to begin with swordplay or boxing?" Bertrand removed his jacket, carefully folding the dark material before draping it on the arm chair.

"Do I want to punch you or try and stab you?" Maggie downed the rest of her tea. "Decisions, decisions."

"Swordplay it is." Bertrand knocked three times on the wall. A panel no more than a foot wide slid aside, revealing two swords and two daggers nestled in red velvet.

"How much magic did the secret compartment cost you?" Maggie asked.

Bertrand grabbed one of the swords, tossing the blade to Maggie.

Maggie caught the hilt and wrapped her fingers around the soft leather.

"I would rather pay the magic to the Siren to keep the blades safe than consider the possibility of weapons ever drifting into the Siren's Realm."

Bertrand lifted the other sword, examining the gleaming blade before bowing to Maggie.

Maggie bowed back, mocking Bertrand, though she knew he wouldn't respond.

"Besides, Miss Trent. We venture out of the Siren's Realm for adventure and riches. What good is bringing more magic into this place if we don't spend it?"

"Touché." Maggie lifted her blade.

"The term is *en garde*." Bertrand lunged, his sword bouncing off Maggie's with a satisfying *ting*.

CHAPTER 2

"Ouch, ouch." Maggie's legs throbbed their fatigue as she scrambled up the rocks by the Endless Sea. "Ouch."

A fine layer of sand coated the rocks, blown up from the stretch of beach where the waves gently lapped at the toes of the residents who preferred to bask in the sun. But the red of evening had begun to take hold of the sky, clearing the beach and leaving Maggie in peace to climb the rocks to her home.

Cracks split the giant stones. Each gap as familiar as the streets she walked every day.

"Learn to fight, Miss Trent," Maggie mumbled as she slid down the edge of an outcropping that hovered over the sea. "It'll be useful, Miss Trent." Blood trickled from the cut on her shoulder. "I'm not just being an ass who wants to jab you with a sword, Miss Trent."

A giant fluke broke through the sparkling water.

"I could just refuse to go with him, Mort," Maggie called to the whale as he lazily rolled in the water. "Tell him I'd rather not jump back into the fiery death world and just wait for the next round."

A plume of water shot into the air.

"I could do it. I could sit this one out. Don't doubt me, Mort. I might prove you wrong."

Maggie turned her back on the Endless Sea and smiled despite the blood on her arm. A tiny, stone house hid nestled on the rock outcropping. There were no seams between the walls and the rocks above and below. Only the thick wooden door and large window with heavy shutters hanging open showed the greatness of the Siren's magic hidden within.

At a touch from her hand, the door swung open. The lamps flickered on before she reached for them, lighting the tiny room with their warm glow. A bed rested in one corner, and a table with one chair in the other. The curving gap where the two rocks that formed the back wall met held her fishing net, a spare fishing net, and three books Bertrand had lent her.

"Home, sweet home."

~

The morning sun hadn't warmed the Endless Sea, but Maggie welcomed the chill on her sore limbs. Catching the fish came easily. The Siren provided plentiful fish in the Endless Sea for anyone who had the will to catch them.

Fill the net, bring the fish to town, sell the fish, purchase supplies, go to Bertrand's, come back home.

Maggie sank under the water, letting the gentle waves lift her hair and sway her limbs.

It had seemed like enough. Before she knew slipping out of the Siren's Realm into other worlds was possible, the routine had seemed like enough. Then having the magic to ask the Siren for her tiny stone house seemed like enough.

Enough is never enough.

Maggie kicked up to the surface, gasping for air.

Fish. That was the first step. Catch the fish, sell the fish…adventure.

Maggie yanked on her boots before her feet had properly dried. Her arms didn't ache as she pulled the net of fish up the rocks. She had done it too many times before.

"You were right, Mort," Maggie turned and shouted to the Endless Sea though the whale was nowhere in sight. "You always are, buddy."

The people on the lanes moved quickly in the mid-morning light, giving Maggie space to haul her net without having to worry about darting around dawdlers.

"Veils for the covering of faces," a woman shouted, her own face draped with a lilac veil. "Worth every drop of magic for a cloth this fine."

"No thanks," Maggie said before the woman took two steps toward her.

"But, my girl—"

Maggie dodged under the woman's arm, knocking her with the net of fish.

A splatter of seawater soaked the front of the woman's gown.

"Sorry." Maggie held one hand up, keeping the other tightly on her net. "I'm so sorry."

"You vagrant, little fish monger." The woman dropped her basket of veils, curling her hands into fists.

"Sorry!" Maggie ran down a narrow alley between two rows of tents.

"I will beat you with your fish, you insolent little Derelict!" The shriek followed Maggie as she weaved through a group of towering trolls and out into the market square.

Heart pounding, Maggie ducked into a sweets stall.

"Do not drip fish on my cakes." The old man who owned the stall wagged a flour-covered finger at her nose.

"No problem." Maggie smiled broadly. "Just looking for a snack. This one is great."

Without truly considering, Maggie lifted a purple circular pastry, holding it in her teeth as she offered her hand to the man for payment. As his flour-covered palm met her sea salt-covered skin, a tingle buzzed in her arm. A shock flew through her, leaving a tiny hole where her magic should have been. The unpleasant feeling lasted only a moment before the man let go.

"Thanks," Maggie murmured through her mouthful of pastry.

The market square was filled with its usual array of shoppers and people watchers. Some moved stall to stall, inspecting the wares though they hardly changed from day to day. Others lounged in the sun, watching the people inspecting the wares that hardly changed from day to day. No one ran into the square looking for the girl who had hit someone with her net of fish, so Maggie headed to the fresh food stalls at the far corner of the square.

The sweet jelly filling of the purple pastry coated Maggie's throat. The taste was something between blueberry and pear, but not quite either. Or maybe both. Good food had never been an expectation at the Academy.

"Mathilda," Maggie called into the shadows behind the counter of her tent. "Mathilda, what sort of fruit is in this?"

Maggie held the pastry out as Mathilda appeared from the shadows, her white mobcap bouncing as she ran toward her.

"It's good, I'm just not sure—"

"Maggie, child, where under the Siren's sun have you been?" Mathilda threw her arms around Maggie, knocking the rest of the pastry to the ground.

"What?" Maggie said as Mathilda took her face in her hands.

"I thought you were dead!" Mathilda grabbed the net from Maggie, tossing the contents on the back table. "Terrible things sweeping through the Siren's Realm, and you decide to just not turn up for a while?"

"What terrible things?"

"I ought to kick you out of my stall and never buy from you again." Mathilda grabbed a knife, lopping the head off a fish.

"Mathilda, what are you talking about?" Maggie leapt aside as Mathilda gutted the fish so enthusiastically, slime spurted from the scales.

"Consistency is important in commerce, and if I can't count on you—"

"Mathilda!" Maggie grabbed Mathilda's knife-wielding hand. "I don't know what you're talking about."

"You don't, do you?" Mathilda looked up to the ceiling of her tent. "Have you been hiding under a rock for the five days you've been gone?"

"Five days?" Maggie balled her hands into fists, tucking them behind her back to hide their shaking.

Five minutes. Maybe ten. That's all we were gone.

"Were you hiding on that rock you call home? Lost track of time?" Mathilda turned back to butchering the fish. "Perhaps it would be better if you lost yourself by the Endless Sea for a while longer."

"Why?"

"I wish I didn't have to be the one to tell you." Mathilda kept her eyes to her task as she spoke. "A sickness has come to the Siren's Realm."

"A sickness?" Maggie rolled the word around in her mouth, searching for a meaning that made sense. "People can't get sick in the Siren's Realm. She keeps all of us healthy."

"She also keeps the sun shining, but that doesn't keep her from bringing the storms."

"What kind of sickness?" Maggie looked out to the shoppers in the square. They were keeping a larger distance between themselves than usual. Diners sat one to a table, not clustered together in groups.

"First heard of it right after the last time I saw you. Man came running into the square, begging for help for his lover who'd taken ill. We all thought he'd gone mad." Mathilda shrugged. "Body was found in the Siren's fountain the next day. Black sores on her skin."

"Someone died? In the Siren's Realm?"

"Stone cold dead." Mathilda accented each word with a chop of her knife. "Folks had quite a time trying to figure out what to do with the body. People have started asking the Siren for protection, but there's no way to know if that's working until it doesn't."

"Have more people gotten sick?" Maggie's mind raced back to all the things she'd touched.

The veil seller, the baker's hand…

"Two more have been buried, but there could be others sick, or dead, and no one's found them."

"That's terrible."

"It is what it is when there's no one in charge to keep things running save the Siren, and she doesn't seem too fussed about it. That's why I thought you were dead. People falling ill, and you just disappearing." Mathilda wiped her forehead with the back of her hand. "Maybe it would be better if you had stayed holed up on your own."

"Is anybody fixing it?" Maggie asked, hating herself for sounding so childish. "I mean, aren't there any doctors in the Siren's Realm?"

"None have come forward." Mathilda wiped her hands before reaching for Maggie. "Do yourself a favor and lie low for a while. I can make do without the fish, and you should have enough magic stored up by now you can ask the Siren to provide for your belly."

"What about you?" Maggie took Mathilda's hand. Her skin itched as Mathilda paid her in magic, but the feeling stayed on her hand like a tight-fitting glove.

"I'll not abandon my shop." Mathilda shook her head. "I don't know if my soul could survive it. I nearly languished to nothing when I lived a life of leisure here, and I don't fancy drooping back into nothing again. I won't risk it. Work is the best way for me."

Maggie took hold of Mathilda's hand again. "Promise you'll be careful and take care of yourself?"

"As the Siren wills it." Mathilda smiled, but the wrinkles around her eyes didn't scrunch up as they should have.

Maggie nodded, her throat too tight to speak.

The weight of the net kept her from tucking her hands behind her back as she walked through the square, carefully avoiding touching anything. A chair pushed out too far into the walkway. A centaur who took up most of the lane.

Heart racing and cheeks flushed, she cut between two tents with their flaps tied tightly shut.

"Don't panic, Maggie Trent, you are fine."

Her heart didn't slow as she weaved deeper into the Textile Town. In a battle, she could defend herself. Even without magic, at least she could see the danger coming toward her and fight for her survival. But with illness…

It could already be on me. It could already be killing me.

"Meat fer sale!" a familiar voice barked in the distance. "Fresh roasted meat fer sale! Don't let yerself get weak with hunger! Good food'll keep the body strong."

"Gabriel!" Maggie shouted from the far end of the street, relief chipping away at her panic.

"I thought you'd still be alive." Gabriel smiled broadly at her, leaning on the side of his cart. "Some I'd think rotting if I didn't see 'em fer a few days when death's come knockin'. But I knew you'd turn up in time."

"I didn't even know anything was happening." Maggie resisted the urge to throw her arms around Gabriel's neck. "I stayed in by the sea for a few days. I only came back into town this morning."

"Probably better if you head back out by the sea." Gabriel handed Maggie a leg of fowl. "I'm not so worried about you gettin' sick, but when people start to panic, it's best to stay out of the way."

"But for how long?" Maggie took Gabriel's hand, still speaking even as he drew magic from her for payment. "A few people have gotten sick, but if whatever this is spreads, it could be a long time before it's over."

"Perhaps. But stayin' safe won't make it move faster or slower. Besides"—Gabriel glanced up and down the empty street—"I think you and I'll come out of this just fine. None of us want to go screamin' about it, but all of them who've fallen with the blackness, they've all had magic. Powerful amounts of it. Maybe they hoarded so much it rotted them from the inside out. But us who come in here with nothing but our boots, none of us has so much as sneezed."

"Is sneezing a symptom?" Maggie asked, a sudden tingle growing in her nose.

"No one knows. Don't think anyone's been found with it who's still able to speak to tell how it started. But us without magic, we'll be just fine. Keep our heads down, keep quiet, and we'll make it to the other side of the Siren's wrath sure as sunrise."

"You think the Siren's killing people because she's mad?" Maggie looked instinctively to the sky as though an angry face would appear to smite her.

"Read that law of the Siren again, girly. No one could wish this hurt on another. It's come from the Siren herself."

"Excuse me," a man with a pink cloth over his mouth spoke from ten feet away. "I'd like to purchase some meat."

"Get on with you. And keep tucked in someplace safe." Gabriel waved Maggie away before speaking to the man. "I've got meat fer you, but yer going to have to touch me to pay me."

Head down, Maggie walked up the lane. A few brave folks still walked through the Textile Town, but the pattern of their move- ment had a strangeness to it, as though each person were carefully considering who to pass nearest to, checking each face for signs of illness.

That woman looked like she might be ill, or perhaps she'd had too much wine. The young man was hunched over as though fatigue had sapped his will to stand upright.

But I'm hunching, too.

Maggie squared her shoulders, holding her head up high. She wanted to walk home. To curl up in her little stone house and wait for the Siren to end her purge. But if something horrible had found its way into the Siren's Realm, she couldn't just sit back and wait for death to pick people off at will.

"Bertrand Wayland," Maggie whispered to the air. "I want to find Bertrand Wayland."

Tingles flew through Maggie's chest as a little void formed. Closing her eyes, she turned slowly on the spot, tipping her face up to the sky. The sun warmed her skin, beaming its brightness through her eyelids.

How can anything be awful when the sun is shining so brightly?

"Has the blackness taken your mind, child?" a woman snapped.

Maggie gritted her teeth, biting back her retort at being called *child.* "Just looking for someone."

Maggie headed down a wide street, ducking around a woman with a scrap of fabric tied over her face. Tents large enough to house several people sat safely behind long strips of grass. Voices carried through the canvas, but the path was empty.

In the square ahead, groups of people crept past, staring at something Maggie couldn't see, as though unable to look away. Maggie jogged forward, letting her net flop at her side. The Siren's fountain came into view, though Maggie had no idea how the warren of paths had led her there.

The fountain sparkled in the sunlight, but the clusters of people all held back, watching one man who stood on the ledge of the fountain, staring down into the sweet waters. The man turned his face to the side.

Maggie yelped at the awful profile. A long black beak had taken the place of his face, and black gloves covered his hands.

"Bertrand Wayland, what the hell are you doing?"

CHAPTER 3

"*M*iss Trent." Bertrand's voice came out muffled through the thick leather of his mask. "I was hoping you'd see fit to find me. I would have attempted to find you, but I had rather more pressing matters to attend to."

"Like a costume party, because that's pretty—" the thin thread of Maggie's mirth snapped as she looked down into the fountain.

A body lay drifting face up in the water. Black tinged the unshaven face, creeping out from his nostrils and coloring his ears.

"That's the man who was ranting about the Siren's will." Maggie fought the urge to look away. Death was not a foreign beast to her, but death in the sparkling pool seemed somehow obscene.

"Perhaps the Siren didn't appreciate him speaking so freely on her behalf." A silver rod appeared in Bertrand's hand. Keeping one fist tucked behind his back, he used the rod to push the man's collar aside. More black crept up the corpse's collarbone.

"Do you have to poke the dead guy?" Maggie looked up to the sky. "He's dead. Shouldn't we be burying him?"

"This is the first of the fallen I've managed to find, Miss Trent. I can't let them bury him until I've examined him."

"Examined him for what? He's dead!"

"I am quite aware this man is no longer alive, Miss Trent, but if something foul is sweeping through the Siren's Realm, I'd like to know as much about it as possible. I should assume you would feel the same way with your hatred of suffering."

Maggie squeezed her eyes shut, wishing the lights flashing in her vision would spark sense into her. No inspiration came.

She turned her gaze to the fountain instead, carefully keeping the corpse out of her line of sight.

Etched into the base of the fountain, the words of the Siren's Decree glimmered in the sunlight.

In the Siren's Realm a wish need only be made.
Her desire to please shall never be swayed.
But should those around you wish you ill,
the Siren's love shall protect you still.
No two blessings shall contradict,
so be sure your requests are carefully picked.
Wish for joyful pleasure to be shared by all
of the good and the brave who have risked the fall.
But a warning to you once the wish is made,
the Siren's price must always be paid.

"The Siren demands a hell of a price," Maggie whispered.

"I understand death is terribly unpleasant and to be avoided whenever possible. However, if you weren't curious as to what is happening in the Siren's Realm, why did you find me, Miss Trent?"

"Fine." Maggie stepped up onto the ledge of the fountain.

"Excellent." Bertrand nodded, the beak of his mask bobbling with the movement. "You must ask the Siren for a mask and gloves. Until we know if this is a disease or purely the Siren delivering a specified death sentence, we must use every precaution."

"You really think a Halloween mask is going to help?"

"The finest plague doctors of my time wore them, Miss Trent." A second sliver rod appeared in Bertrand's free hand. Carefully, he began prying the man's shoes loose.

I wish for a mask and gloves just like my good friend Bertrand's.

The words sounded grimly sarcastic even in her mind.

The scent of lilac and orange blossom filled her nose as a mask appeared on her face, and a sting of magic left her chest.

"These masks are expensive." Maggie's words carried dully to her ears.

"You have the magic to spare, Miss Trent. Get rid of the net. We can't afford to be dragging useful things through filth."

I wish to send my net back to my house.

"Investigating death is really expensive." Maggie flinched as a fresh wave of magic left her.

Revulsion replaced the hollow in Maggie's chest as the dead man's shoes slid off.

He wasn't wearing socks.

The thought punched a hole through Maggie's lungs that had nothing to do with magic. The man had woken up and gone to rave about the Siren…without his socks.

Maybe he hated them. Maybe he didn't have the magic to ask for a pair.

Either way, he didn't dress to end up like this.

"It's not just affecting the faces." Bertrand poked at the man's blackened toes. "It's hitting the extremities."

"It looks like bad frost bite." A tear leaked out of Maggie's eye, wetting the leather of her mask. "Bertrand," Maggie said as quietly as the mask would allow, "did we bring this thing in with us?"

"How do you mean?" Bertrand rolled the body over with a sickening slosh.

"We were just in a faraway land where everything was fiery death. What if the people of that world lit everything on fire on purpose? What if there was a terrible disease and they were burning everything to get rid of the germs but we walked into the contamination and carried the germs back with us and now people are dying of the horrible fire world disease and we're the rats carrying the plague?"

"Impossible." Bertrand slid the back of the man's shirt up. "The Siren cures all who enter her realm. Besides, the disease began before we returned."

"That's the other thing." Maggie smacked Bertrand's arm.

"Miss Trent—" Bertrand finally turned to look at her.

"It's always supposed to be more time on the outside than in here. That's what you said. Ten minutes here could be an hour through one of the stitches, maybe even a year. But it's always more out there than in here. We were gone for a few minutes, and five days passed."

"First of all, Miss Trent"—Bertrand leapt down onto the street—"I specifically remember informing you that, though it had been my consistent experience, different stitches could work differently. Second, and I am sure this will be quite difficult to follow, I believe the Siren sped things up."

"I'm sorry, what?"

"You said you were only a moment behind me when we slipped into the fiery world?" Bertrand walked so quickly, Maggie had to jog to keep up.

"Right on your heels."

"Yet, I was battling the smoke for a full ten minutes before you arrived." Bertrand turned down a side lane. The few people in his path scattered at the sight of their masks. "Therefore, time at that point was, as expected, greater on the outside than on the inside."

"Right."

Bertrand rounded on her, his eyes glinting as they peered over his mask. "Then something happened in those few minutes we were absent. Something that made the Siren decide to speed time up."

Bertrand turned and strode down the lane, moving more quickly than he had before.

"Is time still sped up?" Maggie asked as she caught up to him.

"No idea."

"Why did she decide to play with time?"

"I doubt we'll ever know."

"Then why are you walking so fast?" Maggie gagged on the heat of her own breath mixed with the fresh scent of the flowers.

"Because if there are secrets to be discovered and depths of information to delve into, I know of only one place to start." Bertrand stopped in front of an enormous green tent bordered in violet. Threads of gold wove through the fabric in an intricate design Maggie didn't quite understand.

On every other day, a line of people waited outside the tent, but today, only a minotaur blocked their path.

"You've got to be kidding." Maggie stopped two feet behind Bertrand, perfectly willing to let him take the brunt of the minotaur's withering glare.

"We're closed."

Maggie bit back a grin, grateful for the beak covering her face as the minotaur spoke. With the head of a bull on top of the body of an enormous man, his innate intimidation couldn't be denied. But the lips of a bull forming the rumbling words held a hint of comedy Maggie couldn't ignore.

"I'm quite positive that is the best course of action." Bertrand nodded with no hint of humor in his voice. "However, I am not here to give patronage to any who work in your fine establishment. I am simply here to see Lena as a concerned friend seeking to discover the root of the despair that currently wracks the Siren's Realm."

The minotaur glared at Bertrand for a long moment. "Lena, you've company."

A beautiful, pale face surrounded by a cascade of platinum hair appeared at the flap of the tent. "Bertrand?" Lena's perfect mouth twisted into a pout. "Why under the Siren's sun are you wearing that awful mask?"

In an instant, Bertrand's mask and gloves disappeared. "Protection from the dangers we now face. Though I am sure I will be exquisitely safe in your care." Bertrand bowed, and Lena grinned.

"You may bring in your pet, but only if she shows her face." Lena examined Maggie from her worn boots to her horrible mask. "I don't care how much danger there might be, the rules of the palace must be obeyed."

"As you wish." Bertrand bowed to Lena. "Send the mask away, Miss Trent."

Hey, Siren. Wanna magically store this mask and gloves for me? Maggie gulped in fresh air as the mask evaporated.

"Are you sure you wish to bring the child in, Bertrand dear?" Lena beckoned them forward with one finger. "She might decide she likes the palace life and abandon you."

"I'm not a child." Maggie stepped in front of Bertrand. "And I really doubt you'll have anything I want in there."

Raising one blond and perfectly sculpted eyebrow, Lena drew back the flap of the tent.

"After you, Miss Trent."

Maggie's breath caught in her chest as her mind raced to make sense of the scene in front of her.

Glistening lights shimmered from the top of the tent as though bouncing off an invisible chandelier. A fountain at the center of the space shot jets of twisting and arching water into the air. Moss coated the ground, begging for bare feet to nestle in its depths.

Tables laden with food and wine dotted the space, some in groups, some hidden in dark corners. And all around the vast tent, different colored swatches hid entrances to places Maggie wasn't sure she wanted to see.

"See? Naïve, like a child." Lena's low voice drew Maggie out of her wonder.

"Not what you thought it would be, Miss Trent?" Bertrand held his arm out to Lena. "This place holds many wonders. Pleasures of the flesh are but one small item to be found."

"And what is it you crave today, sweet Bertrand?" Lena cooed as she led them toward the back of the tent. "You've never brought a friend into our midst before."

"Eww." Maggie shivered. "Just eww."

"I'm seeking information of the type only you can provide," Bertrand said.

Lena stopped in front of a table set with wine, chocolates, and berries. She draped herself on the fainting couch in a way that would have seemed absurd from anyone less graceful.

"Don't tell me," Lena purred. "The great Bertrand Wayland has decided to delve into the depths of the Siren's Realm to discover the root of the mysterious blackness and save us all."

"You really do know him well." Maggie sat on a plush, purple chair.

"I am not attempting to save all." Bertrand's voice betrayed only a hint of annoyance as he glanced from Lena to Maggie. "I would never assume myself so great as to raise the dead."

"Pour us wine, Bertrand." Lena waved a hand at the table. "I refuse to discuss death and terror without wine."

Bertrand picked up the decanter of red wine, breathing in its scent before pouring three glasses.

"Miss Trent." Bertrand handed her a glass.

I'm not old enough teetered on Maggie's lips for a moment. But Earth's time moved at a different pace than time within the Siren's Realm. She could be a hundred by Earth's standards. And what did it matter how old she was anyway? Drinking the wine wouldn't go against any of the Siren's rules.

"To the greatness of the Siren." Lena raised her glass to the sky.

"To the Siren." Bertrand and Maggie chorused.

The wine had a taste of wood in it Maggie hadn't expected, and a bitterness that clung to the back of her tongue.

"So what do you want to know, sweet Bertrand?" Lena trailed her finger along the rim of her glass.

The wood taste wasn't bad exactly. More like forest than pencil. Like freshly cut trees.

"I was taking a bit of time away from the Textile Town when the blackness came," Bertrand said. "I'm not even sure who's died."

"A bunch of stuffers." Lena made a disgusted noise. "You know the kind. Finding ways to hoard masses of magic and never spending it on anything. The first one, the man, he came in here all the time. The lot of us were terrified he had spread something horrible in here with him. Most of them are still afraid." Lena spoke loudly enough the people hiding behind the nearby curtains would be able to hear.

"If he frequented the palace, he can't have truly been hoarding," Bertrand said. "Though well worth the cost, the services here carry a heavy price."

"Not for what that one wanted," Lena said. "He'd wait in the line just to come in and stare at people. Would never pay for anything, just sit and stare."

"Creepy," Maggie said.

Lena and Bertrand turned to her as though they'd forgotten her existence.

"It is a little creepy." Maggie took another sip of wine. The taste of the second sip wasn't as shocking as the first.

"What about the others?" Bertrand sat by Lena's feet.

A smile like that of a cat who had just cornered a juicy mouse curled Lena's lips. "The floating woman was much the same. Worked her way up to a fine jewel trade. Knew how to ask the Siren for jewels beyond what anyone else could think to wish for and sold them for an astronomical price.

Then two men who worked in the spice trade, partners in a business at the far end of the Textile Town. Their *spices* had a way of doing something marvelous to the mind." Lena's smile turned to a pout. "Them I might actually miss."

"And the man from this morning?" Bertrand took a slow sip of his wine.

"Completely unlike the others," Lena said. "A madman really. I'm surprised he made it through the last storm without being swept away with the Derelict."

"And who would you say is next?" Maggie asked, letting the faint warmth of the wine wash away the fear that had gripped her since her meeting with Mathilda.

"I suppose that depends on how the blackness spreads." Bertrand tented his fingers under his chin.

"Well, it could be airborne," Maggie said. "Or foodborne, or only move through bodily fluids…" Her words trailed away as Bertrand's eyebrows climbed his forehead. "Germ theory? The spread of infectious disease? Do you not know about that?"

"I doubt the blackness spreads like a normal disease," Lena said. "No matter how the vermin you think control diseases might work. A man died, but not his lover. A woman died in the fountain, but not anyone who swam with her. Before I ran from my world, a terrible illness spread. When it took one, it took a family. A few people fought their way through the sickness, but it didn't skip about town pulling people down one at a time."

"But what if the blackness isn't skipping around?" Maggie leaned forward. "What if they all sat at the same table in a restaurant, or drank from the same bottle of wine. Or were a part of a secret club? What if"—Maggie stood up—"what if they all traded magic, and the magic was contaminated?"

"A distinct possibility," Bertrand said. "But we live in the Siren's Realm, and all that happens is by the Siren's will."

"So, the Siren herself caused it." Lena raised her glass to the sky.

CHAPTER 4

" $\mathcal{L}$ ena!" A beautiful girl with dark skin and a sapphire robe ran toward them from the far side of the tent. "You were right. The centaurs can get it. A cart just rattled past carrying one. He's as dead as the other type."

"Is there more than one type of dead?" Lena asked.

"If there is an outbreak in the centaurs' section of the city, then I'm afraid we must depart your exquisite company." Bertrand placed his half-finished wine on the table.

"Do you think you'll discover something more from the four-legged dead than the two?" Lena asked.

"There were two wizard deaths on the first day, correct?" Bertrand gestured for Maggie to stand. "I can only hope whatever forces the Siren has employed to purge her realm are consistent. If we can find the one on the verge of death, perhaps they will have more of a story to tell."

"Thanks for the wine." Maggie followed Bertrand across the soft moss toward the minotaur-guarded entrance.

"Of course," Lena said. "Should you ever tire of Bertrand's company, you may always visit us here."

"Thanks," Maggie called over her shoulder.

"Mask on, Miss Trent." Bertrand waited for her next to the minotaur, his face already covered by the giant beak.

May I please have my mask and gloves back?

Even though Bertrand couldn't hear her polite query to the Siren, Maggie's cheeks burned in embarrassment as the leather of the mask pressed against her face.

But if the Siren really is just killing people who make her mad…

"This way, Miss Trent." Bertrand strode down the street, not pausing to peek down alleys or ask the few who braved the Textile Town where the centaur had died.

Bertrand squeezed between two fuchsia tents with red embroidery. Maggie turned her beak over her shoulder as she sidled between the tents.

"What makes you think seeing someone in the process of dying of the blackness is going to tell us anything other than the Siren has decided to pick people off and didn't want to bother whipping up a storm to blow them away?" Maggie's words resonated through her cheeks, as though trying to find a clear path out of the mask.

"Nothing," Bertrand said, stepping aside as a cluster of three men jogged past, each clutching a cloth to his mouth. "In all likelihood, this is purely the work of the Siren, and there is absolutely nothing we can do about it."

"Then why are we creeping through side streets with freaky masks on? Masks won't stop the Siren. You said yourself the blackness probably doesn't travel like germs."

"Because"—Bertrand rounded on Maggie—"pragmatic as I may be, there is a glimmer of optimism in me that has yet to be squashed."

"What is that supposed to mean?"

Bertrand took Maggie's arm, dragging her into a gap between tents barely large enough to fit one person, let alone two.

"If the blackness is a disease similar to those that have so often plagued our world, then we would have a chance to stop it."

"And if it's not?" A faint tingle of panic hummed in Maggie's chest.

"Then we who live in her paradise have somehow angered the Siren, who has taken it upon herself to purge her realm, and we are powerless to stop her."

Maggie tore off her mask, willing the fresh air to slow her heart. "And if she has decided to purge her realm?"

"Then we hope we have not lost favor."

A high keening sounded from the street beyond their view. "Siren, let this not be your will. All the magic I have I offer you! Spare me, sweet Siren."

"Mask, Miss Trent."

Maggie took one last breath of fresh air before pulling the heavy mask back on.

On a normal day in the Siren's Realm, a crowd would have gathered at the sound of someone screaming so loudly. But the street beyond the fuchsia tents was bare, save one centaur standing in the center of the dirt lane.

"Please, Siren, I beg of you." The centaur swayed on his dappled legs. His face dripped with sweat, and the red of a fever colored his cheeks. A tinge of black crept out of the centaur's nose and stained the tips of his ears.

"Excuse me, sir?" Bertrand stepped toward the centaur.

"What do you want with a dying man, you foul, beaked beast?" Black tears trickled down the centaur's cheeks.

Sour soared into Maggie's mouth.

"I am investigating this illness to understand its form and attempt to save the people in this realm from its horror." Bertrand bowed.

"Thank you, Siren!" The centaur raised two shaking hands toward the sky. Black touched his fingertips and trickled down like rain. "Please, help me quickly."

"There are some things I must know." Bertrand stepped back

as the centaur reached for him. "Have you had contact with any of the others who have fallen ill?"

"No." The centaur's breath rattled in his chest. "As soon as I heard of an illness, I hid in my home. I only heard the names of those lost through the canvas of my tent."

"And they aren't people you associate with?"

"I stay within the centaurs. I do not roam where the two-legged ones play." The centaur's legs collapsed beneath him.

"Is there an industry you partake in to earn large amounts of magic?"

"Please help me." The centaur sagged toward the ground.

"Your industry." Bertrand leaned over the centaur. "I must know."

"I create the designs for the centaur's tents." The centaur coughed, spattering Bertrand's boots in black. "The Siren cannot replicate our designs from vague wishes alone."

"And do you have much magic stored from this venture?"

"More than you can imagine—please." The beast gagged on his words. "I'll give you every drop of magic for a cure. Please help me."

"Of course." Bertrand held out his hand, and a glass appeared in his grip. "Drink this."

He passed the cup to the centaur, who drank as well as he could with his hands trembling.

"Thank you," the centaur mouthed before lying still on the ground.

Silence filled the street.

"Did you just kill him or save him?" Tears streamed down Maggie's cheeks, her nails threatening to break through her gloves as they dug into her palms.

"Neither." The black disappeared from Bertrand's shoes. "I put the poor creature to sleep. There was no need for him to suffer any longer."

"Right."

"Come away, Miss Trent." Bertrand started down the street, walking as though he'd already run ten miles.

"It really isn't spreading like a disease is it?" Maggie choked on the words. "She's going after the stuffers."

Bertrand's mask disappeared. His face had grown pale. Sadness filled his eyes.

"Are you sick?" Maggie wished away her own mask.

"No, Miss Trent."

"I've seen you charge into death, and you've never looked like this before." Maggie resisted the urge to reach for him. Comforting people had never come naturally to her, but the hopeless look in his eyes was too painful to bear.

"Forgive me if I am being presumptuous in my understanding of the Siren's ways, but I believe they are *rotting*." Bertrand sounded ill from disgust. "They hoard magic, keeping it trapped inside themselves. Away from the Siren, away from the rest of us. Never using, just packing more and more into their bodies. And the Siren…the Siren—"

"The Siren let their magic rot like spoiled fruit." Maggie turned away just quickly enough to vomit onto the side of the street instead of Bertrand's shoes.

"Indeed."

Bertrand waited while Maggie emptied herself of the scant breakfast she'd eaten.

"Why?" Maggie took the glass of water Bertrand passed her. "Why would the Siren do that to people?"

"I could guess a hundred things, and we'd never know if any of them are right."

Maggie gulped down the water. The liquid was clear and cool, its magical making obvious in the taste. "Okay, then what do we do? How do we stop this?"

"No one but the Siren can stop the Siren's will." His words sounded hollow, hopeless.

"There has to be something we can do!" Maggie's shout

carried over the tents. But there was no one to stare at her. No passersby to glower.

"My sweet Siren." Bertrand turned his face to the sky. "We are but humble servants, seeking refuge in your realm. As you will it, your will be done. But sweet Siren, if there is a way we might ease the suffering of those who have allowed their magic to decay, show us the path. Guide our steps to ease theirs. Allow Miss Trent and me to be your hands in healing. And above all, if it suits your will, protect that which I hold most dear."

A shiver ran down Maggie's spine as she waited for either all her magic to be drained or for the blackness to creep inside her.

The sky didn't open and swallow them in darkness. Her stomach didn't curdle with rot.

"Thank you, Siren." Bertrand smiled wearily as he gazed down at a bird that had landed on the lane ten feet in front of them.

"The bird is the cure?" Maggie whispered as the bird hopped away before looking back over his shoulder, as though making sure they would follow.

"I asked the Siren to lead, and she has granted my wish." Bertrand started after the bird.

The faster he walked, the faster the bird moved. First, hopping forward, its white tail feathers fluttering, then spreading its black-tipped, gray wings and soaring over a patch of tents only to wait on the next street as Bertrand and Maggie ran to catch up.

"Are we really following a bird right now?" Maggie asked as she ran by Bertrand's side.

"The Siren sent us a sign as requested." Bertrand rounded a corner so quickly, the tails of his coat slapped against a tent. "If you have a brilliant idea you have yet to share—"

"The bird seems great." Maggie skidded to a stop an inch shy of trampling on their guide bird.

The bird looked up at Maggie, cocking its head to the side to stare at her with one black eye.

"Is this the end of the line?" Maggie asked, instinctively glancing around to be sure no one but Bertrand would witness her speaking to a bird.

A narrow slit between two tents caught Maggie's eye. A shadow that looked horribly familiar.

"Bertrand"—Maggie's words came out in a conversational tone, though her heart beat as though trying to burst from her chest—"is that the stitch to the fire and death world?"

"I believe it is, Miss Trent." Bertrand leaned toward the narrow gap, examining the darkness. "Is this where the Siren wished to lead us?" Bertrand asked the bird.

The bird did nothing but stare resolutely at Maggie.

Bertrand lifted his face to the sky. "Thank you, Siren."

"Are we just supposed to jump through and hope everyone we know isn't dead when we get back? We were gone ten minutes and missed five days. Who knows how much time will pass if we go back through?"

"Will staring at those you care for while their lives are in danger make you feel better?"

"Or course not, but—"

"Do you believe there is anything in this realm that holds the possibility of stopping the blackness?"

"No, but—"

"Are you willing to entirely dismiss the possibility that the key to our salvation may be through this stitch?"

"No, but—"

"But what, Miss Trent?" Bertrand stepped closer to the shadow.

"We think the Siren is rotting people's magic, but we don't know. We're making assumptions about the Siren, and I think we both know how dangerous that is. Especially after the guy in the fountain died. What if the disease really does travel with magic-rotting germs? What if we leave and I never see any of my friends again? What if they wander around looking for me and end up getting hurt? What if everyone who knows my name is dead when we get back?"

"As the Siren wills will be done, Miss Trent." Bertrand inched closer to the shadow. "We asked for her help, and she led us here. She sees more than we see, knows more than we know. If this is the path to finding an end to the blackness and we refuse to take it, will you be strong enough to survive the deaths of those you care for, knowing you turned your back on the opportunity to help?"

"Do you really think we're going to find something that can help us through this stitch?"

"I adamantly believe there is nothing in this realm that can save anyone from the blackness. We asked for the Siren's help, and she delivered. Will you refuse her?"

"Sometimes, I really don't like you, Bertrand Wayland." Maggie's teeth clenched together so hard it seemed they might crumble.

"I am glad you do not blindly follow." With a nod to the bird, Bertrand stepped into the shadow.

Maggie covered her face with her arms as a flash of green light shot from the darkness.

"Please take care of them," Maggie whispered to the sky before stepping into the alley.

She didn't raise her arms against the flash that swallowed her. They had already been pinned to her sides by the squeezing nothing. Squishing the air from her lungs, just as the blackness had stolen the breath of its victims.

Magic, or the universe, or a vast nothing, or whatever it was kept rushing by, not caring that Maggie wanted to scream and cry. But the terrible pressure of the black stole even that comfort from her.

How poetic. Blackness killed them, and blackness takes me away.

Maggie tumbled to the ground in the fiery world, laughing. But coals didn't scorch her stomach or burn her hands.

Coarse grass surrounded her, blocking everything from view save the sea of green.

"If you're able, please stand, Miss Trent." Bertrand's voice came from a few feet away.

"Party pooper." Maggie wiped the tears from her eyes and stood.

The grass reached up to her ribs and stretched out toward a chasm at the base of a towering ruin. Rushing water thundered far below, carrying above the sounds of the waving grass.

Bertrand stood ten feet in front of her on a stretch of stone wall that had long since fallen to the ground. Before them leaned a great tower, four-stories high, that had been crumbled by time and blackened by long-extinguished flames.

Bertrand beckoned Maggie toward him without looking back at her. He gazed forty feet up, his eyes fixed on a man who teetered on a crumbling ledge, arms stretched out to his sides as though poised to leap into the chasm.

"Please accept me, Siren!" the man screamed into the abyss.

CHAPTER 5

"Pardon me, sir," Bertrand called up to the man, "but if it truly is the Siren you seek, I am afraid you are about to make a grave error."

The man looked down at Bertrand, his gangly arms pinwheeling as a rock slipped out from under his foot, tumbling into the chasm below.

"I will take to the Siren's Realm," the man shouted. "You cannot dissuade me!"

"I wouldn't dream of it," Bertrand said. "I am quite fond of the Siren's Realm and believe it to be an excellent place in which to reside. However, jumping off that ledge would lead only to your death, and, I believe, your body being swept down the river below."

Maggie tramped forward through the grass, letting the blades scratch her arms in her haste.

"This is the path to the land of peace." The man pointed to the river below.

"It's really not," Maggie said. "Trust me, Bertrand would know. We've just jumped out of the Siren's Realm."

"You've been to paradise and returned to torment?" The man

looked wildly between them as though trying to decide if he'd lost his mind or if Bertrand and Maggie were the insane ones.

"Paradise is a loose term," Maggie said.

"Miss Trent," Bertrand warned under his breath before turning back to the pinwheeling man. "We are adventurers come to explore the wonders of this land. If you'd like, I would be happy to assist you in finding the entrance to the Siren's Realm. It would be far preferable to watching you die."

"You're wrong!" The man's tears glinted in the sun as he looked from the chasm below to Bertrand. "Hundreds have traveled to the Siren's Realm by this path. They'll be waiting for me."

A lump the size of a fist settled in Maggie's chest.

"I'm afraid no one who attempted that path has found their way to the Siren's Realm."

At Bertrand's words, the man collapsed to his knees, sending more stones tumbling down.

"Bertrand," Maggie whispered, "if he doesn't come down soon, the whole wall is going to fall. And unless you've already figured out how magic works here, we're not going to be able to save him."

"I appreciate how devastating this must be for you." Bertrand inched closer to the wall. "But you really do need to come down."

"What does it matter?" the man said. "There is nothing but suffering in this world. Even the promise of escape has been a lie."

"Not a lie," Bertrand said. "The instructions are simply wrong."

"Simply wrong?" The man dug his fists into his eyes. "How many are dead because of *simply wrong*? Unless you're lying." The man studied them, his gaze darting between Bertrand and Maggie. "Unless you're purra trying to keep me from escaping."

"I am not lying, nor do I know what a purra is." Bertrand stepped closer to the tower.

The man leapt to his feet, leaning out over the chasm.

"Don't!" Maggie screamed. "Look, I don't know why you think your world is so awful. I don't know what a purra is or why you need to escape them. I've only been in your world for about ten minutes before today. Ten minutes, and it looked like your whole world was on fire. There was nothing here but smoke and flames, and I thought I would choke to death before I could slip back home to the Siren's Realm. But I didn't.

"Bertrand led me to the way back in. And it was a jump down, but not into a river. Whoever told you the way out got part of it wrong. It is a leap down, but that's the wrong down."

The man's breath came in heaving gasps.

"I know what it's like to lose people." Maggie reached up toward the man. "I know jumping down to be with them might seem like the best idea, whether it leads to the Siren's Realm or not, but you're wrong. There is a path out of this world that leads to the Siren. In her realm, there's a long stretch of beach by the Endless Sea where you can lay in the sun all day. There's food from a hundred different worlds, and the wind carries the scent of all of them."

The man leaned against the wall.

"We all come from different worlds, but some wonderful magic has made it so we all speak the same language."

He sank to his knees.

"I don't even know how many worlds are attached to the Siren's Realm, but they all hold magic in them. I don't know if all the worlds are spread out or sitting right on top of each other. I doubt anyone but the Siren really knows."

"Is everyone escaping from worlds as dark as this?" the man asked.

"The darkness in worlds tends to be cyclical in my experience," Bertrand said. "A dark and horrible world one century might be a near utopia in the next."

"Then I was born at the wrong time." The man nodded.

"What's your name?" Maggie kept her hand in the air, reaching for him.

"Alden SicBurnis." Alden looked up to the sky. "Can you leave your name behind when you reach the Siren's Realm?"

"Of course," Maggie said. "There isn't a roll call when you get there, Alden."

Something in Alden's face changed at the sound of his name.

"Come down, Alden," Maggie said. "If you want to learn about the Siren, learn from down here. You're giving me a crick in my neck, and the wall's about to collapse anyway."

"What if you're lying?" Alden said. "What if you aren't from the Siren's Realm at all? What if you've only come to capture me and take me back?"

"We haven't," Bertrand said. "I give you my word I will help you reach the Siren's Realm through the proper entrance."

"Please, Alden, give us a chance," Maggie said.

Alden stared into Maggie's eyes, examining them as though searching a miniscule map.

"Fine." Alden scrambled down the back side of the wall and out of sight.

Maggie let out a huge breath she didn't know she'd been holding and dug the heels of her hands into her eyes. "Did we really just stop someone from killing himself trying to get into the plague-ridden place we just left?"

"It would seem so."

"Should we have told him about the blackness?" Maggie said as Alden appeared around the back of the ruin.

"I don't believe it was the appropriate time." Bertrand strode over to Alden, holding out his hand. "It is a pleasure to meet you on level ground."

"Yes." Alden took Bertrand's hand, but rather than shake it, he twisted it to be wrist up before lifting the cuff of Bertrand's sleeve.

"What are you—"

"It's all right, Miss Trent." Bertrand cut across her while Alden examined Bertrand's other wrist.

"You say you're a magician?" Alden said.

"We use the term *wizard* at home," Bertrand said, "but I suppose *magician* will work just as well."

"Prove it." Alden took two steps back, folding his gangly arms over his chest.

"*Primurgo*," Bertrand said. A shield blossomed into being, starting as a shimmering point over Bertrand's head and growing to surround him.

Alden stepped forward and poked the shield. The spell stopped his finger from reaching Bertrand. Maggie hid her smile as Alden winced at the shock the shield delivered.

"And you?" Alden stepped toward Maggie, who presented her wrists for examination without argument. "Show me your magic."

"*Inexuro*." A tiny flame appeared in Maggie's palm.

"They haven't trapped you," Alden whispered, something like joy dancing in his eyes. "They haven't tagged you or cuffed you. You are the ones we've been waiting for. Praise be to the Siren for sending hope when our world abandoned us!"

"I'm sorry, what?" Maggie clenched her fist, extinguishing the fire.

"We have to go." Alden seized Maggie and Bertrand's wrists, dragging them along behind him. "If they catch you untagged at this age, there would be no way to avoid a massacre."

"Tagged for what?" Maggie asked as Alden led them away from the ruins and the river toward the hills far beyond.

"You don't know?" Alden looked up to the sky, shaking back his unkempt brown hair. "Of course you don't know."

"I do beg your pardon," Bertrand said, "but I'm afraid I really must ask where you intend to lead us before we follow you. I've no doubt you're a fine gentlemen, but caution is necessary when following someone who leads with such fervor."

"It's only an hour before the sun sets." Alden didn't slow his pace. "The sniffers come at dusk. If they catch wind of magicians in the open, we'll be caught and hauled to Histem. Finding two adult, untagged magicians would be the making of their career and the end of your lives."

"Okay, sniffers bad," Maggie said, ignoring the hundreds of tiny scrapes as the tall grass lashed her bare arms. "But where are we going? Are we hiding from the sniffers?"

"Of course." Alden laughed.

Maggie looked to Bertrand.

He's crazy, Bertrand. We saved a crazy person, and now we're following him.

If Bertrand understood Maggie's silent warning, he didn't heed it as he raised one eyebrow and allowed Alden to keep leading.

"Where are we hiding from the sniffers?" Maggie asked as they started up the hill. "Isn't high up on a grass-covered hill usually a bad hiding spot?"

"We have to go up to go down," Alden said. "The Mira is deep belowground where the sniffers can't sense us."

"Sense us?" Maggie quickened her pace as images of great beasts with sniffing noses over snarling teeth flooded her mind.

"The ore in the walls and depth of the tunnels protect us," Alden said.

They reached the top of the hill, and Maggie forgot how to walk.

A wide valley opened up in front of them, reaching out toward a plain in the distance. Trees and grass dotted the valley. The river cut through the far end before twisting out of sight to become the place where the Siren seekers met their end.

But it was the plain beyond that stole Maggie's ability to reason.

A great glimmering mass rose up in the distance. A wall surrounded the base of the city, and soaring towers reached toward the sky. Things flew through the air as high as the tallest towers, some moving evenly like slow airplanes, some swooping around like giant birds.

As Maggie watched, the front portion of the wall sank away, disappearing into the ground, making way for a dozen dots to race forward.

"We have to run." Alden let go of Maggie and Bertrand's wrists. "Run. Now!"

He weaved down the slope of the valley, his destination impossible to predict.

"Quickly but carefully, if you please." Alden leapt over a fallen tree. "If someone has to be carried, it slows everything down exponentially."

"Why did they let those dots out of the city?" Maggie puffed as they reached the valley floor and started up the far slope. "Are those the sniffers?"

"Yes."

Maggie's heartbeat skipped at the deathly finality of Alden's tone.

"Not too much farther." Alden angled his path toward the city.

"You have confidence in the Mira's ability to hide us?" Bertrand asked.

"A little late to be asking that now." Maggie ducked under a low branch, wincing as it tore out a chuck of her hair.

"When the Mira falls, all of magic will die." Alden circled around the back of a giant stone and disappeared from view.

"Alden?" Maggie stumbled to a stop.

A hand reached up from the crack where boulder met earth and grabbed Maggie's ankle. Before she could scream, the ground had swallowed her whole.

Pain shot through her spine as she landed on her back, but she was still moving, traveling through the darkness at an alarming rate. But the blackness surrounding her didn't squeeze with the same terrible pressure that stopped her breath when she slipped in and out of the Siren's Realm.

This blackness had a scent. The wind that flew past her smelled of damp earth and old smoke. And there was texture to the travel, bumps and divots that knocked into her spine as she shot ever downward.

I'm on a giant slide, falling into the earth.

Just as she opened her mouth to shout to Bertrand, the slide disappeared out from under her, and she freefell for half a second before landing on something soft and cold.

CHAPTER 6

"Bertrand?" Maggie's spine ached as she sat up. "Bertrand?"

Something flew toward her with a rumbling *whoosh*.

Maggie rolled sideways, gritting her teeth and hoping she wouldn't fall down another chute.

With a *thump* and a grunt, the something landed next to her.

"Bertrand?" Maggie said. "*Inexuro.*"

A tiny flame flickered to life in her palm. Bertrand lay on the ground next to her, blinking at her light.

"You didn't land on your feet." Maggie scrambled to stand. "I am obscenely happy you didn't land on your feet."

"I am glad to provide you entertainment, Miss Trent."

"Look out below!" Alden's voice echoed from above.

Maggie yanked Bertrand to his feet with her fire-free hand as Alden shot off the end of the slide and landed on his back, a huge smile lighting his face.

"So this is all according to plan?" Bertrand helped Alden up. "It is always good to know one means to be in the darkness underground when one ends up in such situations."

"Of course we meant to take the chute." Alden shook his head.

"How would it have gotten here if it wasn't meant to be used? The magicians of old made the chute and the soft place to land."

Maggie's gaze followed Alden's pointing finger down toward the soft ground. Moss covered every inch of floor her light touched. This moss didn't hold the rich emerald green of the kind that graced the palace floors. Darkness had stolen its color, leaving the ground a dull gray. The floor was also thicker and spongier than any moss Maggie had ever seen. It gave her step a bounce as Alden led them away, almost as though she were walking on rubber.

"Why did the magicians of old want slides into the dark and rubberized floors?" Maggie asked as Alden led them to a thick, wooden door braced by gold bars. "And why did they put gold on the doors?"

"You don't know?" Alden looked up to the ceiling, invisible in the darkness, his eyes lit with wonder. "Of course you don't know. You're pure! Untagged."

Alden pulled back his sleeve. Gold glinted on his wrist. For a moment, Maggie thought he wore an intricately crafted bracelet, but there was no chain reaching from one bit of gold to the next. The metal had been woven into his skin in a pattern that seemed to mean something, though Maggie couldn't tell what.

Alden pressed his wrist to the gold of the door. A light flashed, flooding the room, revealing walls ten feet apart with no other exit, a slide that began seven feet in the air, and gray moss covering the whole floor.

The light faded as the door swung open with a *creak*.

"Please do keep up." Alden trotted into the darkness. "As you've no tags, I'm not sure if you'll be recognized as a friend."

"Recognized by whom?" Bertrand asked as the door slammed shut behind them.

"The nics." Alden loped along in front of them.

Maggie jogged to keep up with his long stride.

"What's a nic?" Maggie searched the walls for creatures

peering out from the darkness. Her light didn't show anything but stone.

"The purra made them to track us and keep us in line, but we've managed to befriend a few of them." Alden paused, furrowing his brow. "Well, I don't know if it could really be called *befriending* as they've no proper brains, and we did take them apart to make them stop hunting us." He started down the hall again. "Either way, I'm not sure if they know we're friendly because they can scent our magic or because they see the inlaid bonds and know we've been contorted by the purra the same way they have."

They reached a chamber with five tunnels leading off in different directions. Alden licked his finger and held it up in the air. After a full minute, Maggie glanced to Bertrand, who did nothing more than raise his eyebrows and continue to look on patiently.

Finally, Alden took a deep breath, as though reveling in the scent of a fresh baked pie, and started down the second tunnel to the left.

"You always have to be careful with those passages," Alden said. "They change all the time, and if you choose the wrong one, you'll be dead lucky if someone finds your bones in the next century."

"The tunnels change?" Maggie dragged the fingers of her non fire-bearing hand along the wall, trying to sense something in the stone walls that would make them capable of movement.

"It's all in the safety of the Mira." Alden glanced back over his shoulder. "I keep forgetting you don't know. Everyone in Alondra knows the legend of the Mira, even if they don't believe the truth of it."

"I'm afraid you'll have to start from the beginning with us," Bertrand said.

"Of course." Alden leaned against a wall, beckoning Bertrand and Maggie to do the same. "It all started with the forming of the

Convocation more than a thousand years ago, though no one is quite sure of the exact date as it started out as such a secret thing. Back then, people who were born magicians mostly hid their powers to stay safe."

"Were they hunted by the humans?" Bertrand asked.

"The purra didn't hunt the magicians. I think they were too afraid to try."

Something hard pressed on the front of Maggie's arms. "No, no, no!" Maggie screamed, trying to wriggle free of the wall as the flames in her hand disappeared. Stone formed around her arms and legs as she sank into the wall as though falling very slowly into water.

"Best not to fight it."

Maggie fought harder at the calmness in Alden's tone.

"The purra were afraid of magicians?" Bertrand asked over the sounds of Maggie's struggle to break free as the stone closed around her chest, threatening to crack her ribs.

"They called the magicians 'mistakes made by the sky.' Anyone who showed any magic became an outcast."

Stone swallowed Maggie's face. Before she could panic over the lack of air, she'd fallen butt first through the other side of the wall. Bertrand and Alden emerged beside her.

"This is not okay," Maggie muttered as three torches burst to life, valiantly fighting to light the cavern they had tumbled into.

The ceiling reached five stories above them with towering columns of stone made by years of aging rock. Some of the columns appeared untouched by anything but time, but in the center of the space, a circle of seats had been carved into the surrounding stone.

"Magicians grew tired of being outsiders and decided to form their own place." Alden beckoned them to the circle of seats. "They formed the Convocation, and the Convocation built the Mira." Alden spread his arms wide. "Once, this place was full of magicians learning their craft. Our knowledge wasn't passed down in alleys anymore. There were proper teachers and classes. It was a beautiful time."

Alden sank down onto a stone seat.

"What happened?" Bertrand sat across from Alden, his hands tented under his chin.

"Too many things," Alden sighed. "The magicians got tired of living in the darkness and marched into Histem, the capital of Alondra. They showed their newly-honed skills to the king. The weapons they could forge and buildings they could mold were more than enough for the king to greet them with open arms. With magicians and purra working together, there was a time of light as had never before been seen."

Maggie bit her lips together at the wistful tone in Alden's voice. Such longing only came from something lost.

"How did the age of light end?" Bertrand asked.

Maggie glanced over at him. She recognized the danger in his tone. The darkness in his eyes matched the tension in his jaw.

"I do wish I could lie and say the king became unbelievably greedy and ruined everything." Alden shook his head, his floppy brown hair tumbling into his face. "But you're untagged, and it would be wrong to ask you to help people who lie to you."

"You would be amazed how many people ignore that nicety," Bertrand said.

"At first, the magicians were happy to simply be accepted for their magic." Alden picked at the worn fabric of his pants. "But the king and the purra began making money off the magicians. Selling magician-made wares and not paying them a fair price for their labor. Labor a purra couldn't do. Putting magicians on the front lines of battles and letting them be slaughtered in mass for a country that only accepted them when they discovered how much they could use their magic."

A hole formed in Alden's pants, but he didn't stop picking at the threads.

"That's when the Convocation denounced the king's rule.

Decided they would set their own prices for labor and goods. The king was furious and attacked the Convocation. But he couldn't defeat the magicians he'd trained for war."

"And the magicians took control." Maggie tried to picture it. A wizard sitting in the White House, granting entire national parks as range for the centaurs. Giving wizards the freedom to live in the open.

A beautiful dream with an inevitably horrible ending.

"With the Convocation in control, things went well for a while," Alden said. "The magicians ruled, and if the purra wanted their services, they could pay the Convocation-set price for them. But most couldn't pay. They grew furious knowing magical answers to their problems existed but weren't freely given. The purra gathered all the magic-made weapons and goods they could find and staged an uprising. They even figured out how to dampen our powers so they're mostly useless."

Alden held out his wrists, the inlaid gold glinted in the light, and his cheeks blushed in shame. "They tag every magician baby. If you aren't tagged as an infant, the consequences are too terrible to consider. The only place the sniffers can't find us is in the Mira. And hiding down here isn't much of a life."

"I suppose that depends on who you ask."

Maggie leapt to her feet, fists ready to fight.

The woman standing behind her cocked her head to the side and smiled. Her gaze drifted from Maggie to Bertrand, finally settling on Alden.

"I thought you'd finally decided to join the Siren." The woman slunk into the circle of seats, her skirt trailing along the ground.

She, unlike Alden, didn't have a hair out of place, and her dress was made of well-kept, if plain, blue fabric.

"Decided to make new friends instead of chancing the fall? I had nearly thought better of you," the woman said. "I'm so glad I didn't bet on you jumping."

"There was betting?" Alden twisted his hands together.

"If you'll allow me." Bertrand bowed to the woman. "I am Bertrand Wayland, adventurer, resident of the Siren's Realm, and very new to your world."

Maggie snorted a laugh.

"And this is Maggie Trent," Bertrand said without acknowledging Maggie's laugh.

"Adventurer and resident of the Siren's Realm." Maggie mocked Bertrand's bow.

"We arrived just as Alden was attempting to leap into the Sir—" Bertrand began.

"They are untagged." Alden seized Maggie's wrist, displaying it for the woman.

"Stop grabbing me." Maggie wrenched her hand back. "If you want me to show off my gold-free wrists, you can ask."

"May I?" The woman stared pointedly at Alden.

"Of course." Maggie held up both her wrists.

The woman twisted Maggie's wrists in the torchlight.

Bertrand stepped forward, presenting his arms as well.

"And we're both magicians. *Inexuro.*" The ball of fire reappeared in Maggie's hand.

"They arrived just as I was about to jump," Alden said. "You may be happy ignoring the world and living in darkness, but if this isn't a sign that we should move into the light, then whatever the skies may send you, I doubt you will ever believe me. They are the opportunity we have been waiting for."

The woman crossed her arms, staring up at the top of the cavern. "Fine. This may very well be the end of what little there is left of the Convocation, the Mira itself may fall, but we might as well try to save the world. I'm bored tonight."

"May I ask your name?" Bertrand bowed deeply.

"Call me Lara." Lara winked. "And keep up."

Lara turned and sauntered back in the direction from which she'd appeared.

"Bertrand," Maggie whispered, walking as close to him as she could, "we are following people who really might not be the good guys who want to use us in some plan we don't know about."

"We are, Miss Trent."

Lara stopped at the edge of the cavern, but rather than falling down a chute or sinking into a wall, she slipped sideways into a shadow and out of sight.

"Just through there." Alden hurried them toward the shadow.

"Do you really think it's a good idea to go deeper into this thing?" Maggie said. "We've got our own people to save."

"And the Siren sent us here when we sought her help," Bertrand said.

Maggie clenched her teeth as they passed through the shadow and into a long tunnel that swept down at a steep angle.

"And what if they want us to murder innocent people?" Maggie whispered, letting Lara get as far ahead of them as she dared. "Or want to use us as untagged magician sacrifices?"

"Under normal circumstances, I would agree that extricating ourselves from our current company as quickly as possible would be the wisest course of action," Bertrand murmured. "However, as we have very little hope of finding our way out of the Mira unassisted…"

"We smile and play untagged hero," Maggie finished for him.

Lara stopped at a solid wall.

"Is it a chute or sinking?" Maggie's voice sounded too bright in her own ears. "Maybe a sensible secret knock?"

Better.

"Not everything needs to be so dramatic." Lara clapped her hands, and the little section of floor where they'd all gathered began to sink.

Maggie widened her stance, waiting for the floor to tilt and send them all careening into the darkness.

"I do appreciate a lack of drama," Bertrand said. "It gives things a sophisticated air."

"Really?" Maggie spoke through gritted teeth. "I thought you lived for drama. Extravagant displays, jumping off cliffs into battles…"

"I embrace drama when it becomes necessary, Miss Trent." Bertrand didn't look away from Lara as he spoke.

As they sank, the ceiling above them sealed with a stone slab that looked as though it had always been there. At the same moment, a sliver of light appeared around their feet.

Maggie squinted against the brightness.

Maybe we're in the open air.

Her faint glimmer of hope disappeared as stone walls set with wavering lights came into view.

A mechanical whirring came from ahead of them. Maggie studied the walls, searching for a section grinding open that would lead them along their path.

The sound came closer as the panel they had been riding down melded with the floor of the room they'd just entered.

The whirring sounded again as three knee-high things rolled toward Lara's feet.

"I told you I'd be right back," Lara cooed, patting each of the mechanical things on the head in turn. "The nics really have become too attached to me."

CHAPTER 7

"So these things are nics?" Maggie said.

As if the things had understood her words, their heads swiveled toward Maggie.

Not really heads.

Three little wheels supported a teardrop-shaped body with a second teardrop facing the wrong way perched precariously on top. A floppy collar made of dangling bits of metal hung around the nics' necks. One circle of light that dimmed and grew, as if in time with a heartbeat, shone in the middle of the nics' heads. All three lights had swiveled to stare at Maggie.

At least they don't have fangs.

"Now, nics"—Alden stepped forward—"these two are untagged, but they are magicians just like Lara and me. They're friends. Give them your wrists, Maggie."

"Why not?" Maggie leaned forward, holding her palms up, expecting the nics to sniff her like dogs.

A *whir* sounded from all three of the nics as the metal hanging around their necks moved, twisting and unfurling into spindly arms that reached for Maggie's hands.

"If those things attempt to harm Miss Trent, I will have to

destroy them." Bertrand stepped up to Maggie's side, his brow furrowed with something between fear and intrigue.

"As though you'd be able to," Lara laughed as Maggie said, "Thanks, Bertrand."

Pinchers formed on the arms of the center nic. It seized Maggie's fingers, dragging her wrist down to press her skin to its circular eye.

"Miss Trent?" Bertrand asked.

"It's fine," Maggie said, carefully keeping her tone friendly and calm. "A little warm but nothing to worry about."

The center nic turned his eye up to Maggie, clicking and whistling to the other nics, both of whom reached out to grab Maggie's hand.

"One at a time, boys," Maggie said.

The center nic whistled louder as the other two's arms spun to life, reaching over the middle's head to swat at each other.

"Nics!"

At Lara's shout, all three froze.

"You may each examine her in turn."

The first moved on to checking Bertrand while the other two gave each other one more good swat before patiently taking turns pressing their eye to Maggie's flesh.

"Well, now we know they sense magic not tags." Alden bounced on the balls of his feet.

"It lessens their worth." Lara pursed her lips. "If *our* nics sense magic not tags, so will the Regent's."

"Then we avoid the Regent and her fleet of nics. They have full use of their magic. We can find a way in." Alden tore his hands enthusiastically through his hair, leaving it standing up on end.

"There's quite a bit more we need to learn about your people and Alondra before we can know how best to help you," Bertrand said.

"A man of reason." Lara gave Bertrand coy smile that only

lifted one corner of her mouth. "Perhaps there is something worth seeing aboveground. Are you done with your inspection, sweet nics?"

All three nics spun to face her, each whistling a different note of apparent assent.

"Then let us not hover waiting for Alden to bring disaster when we ourselves might be the cause of it." Lara started down the corridor, the nics barely avoiding her heels as they followed her like eager puppies.

"Those things were designed to keep magicians in line?" Maggie asked. "Don't they seem a little too adorable?"

"They are rather nice to have around if you're one of the ones they like." Alden nodded, his puffed up hair bobbling with the movement. "If you're on the wrong side, they can take you down and make you beg for death while they wait on the sniffers to haul you away."

"Mini death bots?" Maggie shrugged. "Not what I was expecting. A little weird, and not something I ever thought I'd see in real life, but pretty cool."

"Miss Trent."

Maggie stepped aside to walk next to Bertrand.

"Miss Trent, do they have things of this sort where"—Bertrand glanced from the nics to Maggie—"where we come from?"

"Have you never found robots and machines in any of the worlds you've slipped into?" Maggie swallowed her laugh. "We have machines back home that can hold thousands of books' worth of information. And cars—well, wagons with no horses, I guess. We have boxes that project people acting out stories, and planes that fly across the ocean in a few hours."

"You led me to believe wizards were not in power in our world when you departed," Bertrand said.

The corridor angled to the right. The walls in this portion of the hall had been delicately carved in a curving pattern, and the lights were set closer together, giving the stone a homey glow.

"Wizards aren't in charge," Maggie said. "It's just technology."

Bertrand's eyebrows scrunched even closer together.

"Things that look like magic but really aren't." Maggie stopped in front of one of the lights, squinting into its brightness. A wavering like that of gentle flames had been trapped within the glass but with nothing visible for the flames to burn. "We have light bulbs in our world. Lit by electricity. A sphere of glass holds filaments that glow really brightly when an electrical current flows through them."

"The humans have learned to do magic of their own." Bertrand touched the light.

"Pretty much," Maggie laughed. "But I still prefer real magic. I'll take levitation over a jet pack any day."

"Perhaps your world is much like ours," Alden said, his face looming over Maggie's shoulder.

"Don't do that." Maggie clutched at her heart.

"The purra twisted our magic and used it to banish us below-ground," Alden said, his face still right next to Maggie's.

"Being banished underground isn't the worst fate." Lara waited fifty feet down the hall, the three nics circling around her feet.

"Dare I ask what the worst fate might be?" The lines of concern on Bertrand's forehead smoothed out as he smiled at Lara.

"Spending your life trapped underground with Alden."

Alden blushed. "I'm not as terrible as being tagged above-ground. Believe me, Lara, there are depths of horror you cannot understand until you've lived in Histem."

"Poor you." Lara started down the corridor.

Alden followed, head tipped forward so his hair hid his face.

Maggie glanced at Bertrand before running to walk by Alden's side.

"Has Lara never been aboveground?" Maggie asked.

"She has," Alden said. "Everyone has to be taken aboveground to get their tags. Some of us just get stuck aboveground for much longer."

A door as tall as the wall in front of them came into view, blocking the end of the corridor. The nics sped forward, whistling and whirring their delight.

"A few rules before we enter Lowgry." Lara rested her fingers on the handle of the door and turned her sparkling gaze to Bertrand. "If you wander and the others kill you, I'll congratulate them. If you get out of line and they kill you, I'll thank them. If you speak out of turn and they kill you, I'll give them all wine. And if you displease me and they kill you, I will give them a feast and mark a day in honor of your demise. Any questions?"

The nics purred as Bertrand shook his head.

"Wonderful." Lara smiled and opened the door.

The door itself seemed to grow as it opened. By the time it had swung aside, the wood had reached fifteen feet tall and twenty feet wide.

"Lara!" a low, masculine voice called, followed by the squeals of twenty children who rushed forward, petting the nics and shouting Lara's name.

"Yes, I adore all of you, really I do. But we have very important guests, and I really must take them to the Convocation." A little girl scrambled into Lara's arms despite Lara's warning. "Fine, fine." Lara carried her into the cavern. Firelight burned behind glass domes, which peppered the ceiling high above, casting their light like a thousand dazzling stars.

A wide yard swept out in front of Maggie, the ground covered in the same gray moss that had caught her at the end of the slide. Homes that seemed to have been stretched up out of the stone beneath them dotted the cavern. Peering between the houses, Maggie caught a glimpse of trees bearing jewel-colored fruit that seemed out of place so far underground. Vines climbed the walls far beyond, reaching up as though aware sunlight waited far above through countless layers of stone.

"Welcome to Lowgry." Alden bowed, ushering Bertrand and Maggie on as the children continued to swarm Lara.

"This place is"—Maggie glanced up to see an older woman staring at her as she munched on a piece of cake—"amazing."

"The Mira was built to be self-sustaining." Alden picked at the edge of his sleeve. "Which is really quite remarkable. No sunlight, the only water provided by runoff from the rocks, and the magicians of old built an entire city."

"How many live in Lowgry?" Bertrand asked.

"About seven hundred," Alden said. "Really six-hundred-and-ninety-two. Would have been six-hundred-and-ninety-one if I'd gone to the Siren's Realm."

"Is that all that's left of the magicians?" Maggie's chest tightened at the thought.

Six-hundred-and-ninety-two to carry the weight of magic.

"Yes and no," Alden said. "There are many more who carry magic in their veins, but they toil aboveground, fighting to survive in Histem. Some have tried to escape, to reach the Mira, and failed. It may sound cruel to keep the entrances to our haven a secret, but if everyone knew how to find it, the Regent would slaughter us all in a week. I've heard rumors about clusters of people living far out of reach of the city, but I don't know if they can be believed since I've never met a person who's actually been to a colony. Or even met someone who's met someone who's been to a colony."

"So the entire magical population of Alondra consists of six-hundred-and-ninety-two magicians hiding underground, people fighting for their lives, and myths?" Bertrand asked.

"Yes." Alden pulled a thread free from his sleeve. "Though I suppose that's as well as can be expected when war comes and you're on the losing side."

A building with lights hung around the roofline in a festive fashion came into view between the houses. Glass-paned windows blocked out the impossible rain, and a slanted roof stood guard against snow that would never come.

"The Convocation will want to see you before we can get you settled in." Lara spoke to Bertrand, her hair still perfect even as she balanced a child on her hip. "If they've decided to keep you around once you've spoken to them, I'll help you find a place to rest your weary head."

And I'll sleep on the moss.

Maggie plastered a smile on her face. "We look forward to seeing you shortly. I'm sure Lowgry has much to offer."

"More than you can imagine." Lara didn't look away from Bertrand.

A wooden door in the stone building creaked open.

"I look forward to rejoining you," Bertrand said.

Lara ignored his bow as she led her flock of children away.

"Best of luck." Alden bobbled.

"Thanks," Maggie said. A chill wind from the doorway lapped at her neck, raising goose bumps on her arms. "Don't go too far, okay? And definitely don't try to get into the Siren's Realm without our help." The wind grew stronger. "Even if the Convocation decides to eat us."

"Of course, Maggie." Alden settled himself onto the moss. "I'll wait here."

"Perfect."

"Shall we, Miss Trent?" Bertrand stepped into the doorway.

"Right." Maggie nodded and pulled herself to stand up straight, ignoring the knot of worry gnawing at her chest. "Let's meet the Convocation."

Together, they stepped into the empty hallway.

Maggie shuddered as the door closed behind them with a *creak.*

Wooden benches lined the stone walls. Grooves sank into the

wood as though many people had sat on the benches for many hours.

Tapestries hung high on the walls. It wasn't until she'd reached the third panel that Maggie realized each image was a continuation of the same story.

A man turning his back on the city and digging deep below the earth. Others traveling through the darkness to join him. A woman carrying gold to a man in a palace. That man bowing to the woman and presenting her with jewels. Then men fighting. A man standing on a throne of gold, light shooting from his hands. A giant black bird swooping down upon the man, tearing apart his chest.

Then the tapestries stopped. The benches along the hall continued lining their path, but the stone walls above were bare.

"They just stopped recording," Maggie said.

"Very few cultures memorialize their defeats," Bertrand said.

A set of double doors waited for them at the end of the benches.

Maggie didn't even flinch as the doors swung open, revealing the four members of the Convocation.

CHAPTER 8

Four wrinkled faces peered out at Maggie. With sunken bags under their eyes and cheeks drooping beyond definition, she couldn't tell if the four were male or female.

"Are you why Alden came back?" The first of the Convocation squinted at Maggie.

"We met him just before he jumped in his attempt to reach the Siren's Realm." Bertrand bowed.

"Then Lara didn't deceive us," the second said, their voice so crackled with age, Maggie still didn't know what gender they might be.

"Come in." The first flung out an arm so enthusiastically they wobbled precariously for a moment.

"How did Lara tell you we were here?" Maggie asked.

"Nic." The third pointed beyond the circle of finely upholstered chairs that took up the center of the room to a lump of metal in the corner.

Banged up into a nearly unrecognizable shape, the thing's metal had tarnished so it blended in with the wall. The nic gave a weak whistle in greeting, sounding as ancient as the members of the Convocation.

"Then you know we're untagged magicians." Maggie tucked her hands behind her back. "Good to have that part out of the way."

"I'm not sure I agree with Lara or Alden." The fourth sank into a chair. "We have long dreamed of destroying the pacel, but to bring outsiders into our fight seems not only foolhardy but selfish beyond redemption."

"I am willing to forgive our selfishness if it grants our people freedom," the third said after all the Convocation settled into their seats.

Twelve chairs in the circle were left empty.

"But at what cost?" the second said, waving a finger in the air. Their sleeve slipped to show a swatch of scattered gold an inch wide. The skin around the inlaid metal had wrinkled and sagged, puckering in a painful fashion.

Maggie winced at the sight of it.

"Have we so very much left to lose?" the first said. "Those aboveground are as good as lost to begin with. Either they cower or perish. And we belowground…the Regent herself could cut into the stone, and I firmly believe the Mira would stand."

"The Regent has new weapons," the second said. "Things more terrible than what the purra had in the war. It's not just men riding rammocs against us anymore. They have intets stories high that could rip through the rock above us!"

"And how would they know where to dig?" The first tapped a finger on their knee. "And would the rock even allow itself to be moved? I say the Mira will stand."

"The Mira will fall!" the second's voice cracked as they shouted.

"Pardon me." Bertrand bowed.

All four turned to him with varying looks of apparent surprise at finding Maggie and Bertrand standing in the room.

"I do hope you'll forgive my interrupting"—Bertrand stepped into the circle—"but I would hate for you make plans for us to which I cannot agree. I'm afraid Miss Trent and I cannot be involved in destroying anything that does not need destroying."

"And our standards might be a little different from yours," Maggie said as the first opened their mouth to speak.

"Do you believe the enslavement of a people is wrong?" the first said.

"Of course—"

"Do you believe a child should be punished for the sins of their great-grandfather?"

"No, but—"

"Do you believe the gifts born into one should be abused and molded into something unnatural by another?"

"Never, but—"

"Then you will agree—"

"But what would happen to the children of the purra?" Maggie cut across the first. "If everything you say is true, then you're right, we should help you. But if we help you, will you try and live in peace with the purra? Will you do horrible things out of revenge? Sometimes doing the right thing now makes things a lot worse later."

"Worse for whom?" the fourth asked, their hands tented under their chin.

Maggie's heart melted a little. She could be staring at a centuries old Bertrand. Not that Bertrand wasn't already centuries old.

"What is the pacel?" Bertrand asked.

"A terrible place. A place of unnatural horror." A tear dripped from the second's eye, catching in the creases of their face. "The metal they set into all our people not only acts as a tag to mark us, but also as a damper to block the best of our powers, and a conduit to drain them."

"Drain them?" The room swayed. Maggie focused on the

second's eyes, breathing deeply to keep from being sick on the floor.

"The ones who are disobedient to the Regent. Who have tried to run or refused to work. They are sent to the pacel. Every day they are marched into that terrible place, and their magic is drained. All so the Regent can power her intets."

"She's using people to power her machines?" Maggie swallowed the sour that rose into her throat.

"We've sent dozens to try and destroy the pacel," the second said, "but with the tags blocking their magic, there is no hope of success. If they manage to make it past the nics and soldiers, they can't do enough damage to stop the pacel from working."

"Even if we agreed to destroy the pacel, what would stop the Regent from building a new one?" Maggie asked.

"Once broken, it could never be rebuilt," the third said. "The materials are irreplaceable."

"If you refuse to help us," the first said, "you are condemning generations of magicians to slavery and suffering."

"Well, when you put it that way…" Maggie squeezed her eyes shut. "Bertrand?"

"We've no idea how the city is built, where the pacel is, or who the Regent's allies are." Bertrand tented his fingers under his chin. "While I wish for freedom for magicians, I don't believe we have any hope for success if we go alone."

"Alden can accompany you," the fourth said. "He's familiar with the city and knows as much of the pacel as any living magician."

"I'm sure he'll be thrilled," Maggie said.

"The Siren sent you to him for a reason," the third said, "and what better reason can there be in this life than service to the greater good?"

A shiver wiggled up Maggie's spine.

"Rest." The first stood shakily, a wince of pain flitting through their eyes. "Rest now, and leave tomorrow."

"When it is done," the second said, not attempting to stand, "we will hold a feast in your honor."

"I look forward to the celebration." Bertrand bowed.

Maggie wasted no time in heading for the doors, which opened as she reached for them.

"May magic grace your steps," the third said.

"And may understanding and forgiveness grace your hearts should you ever rise above the purra," Bertrand said.

Without waiting for the Convocation to respond, he strode out into the hall.

Maggie didn't dare look back as she jogged a few steps to catch up to Bertrand.

"Did we really just agree to do something that tons of people have died trying to do?" Maggie whispered. A tingle like dozens of eyes watching her kissed the back of her neck.

"We did." Bertrand matched Maggie's low tone.

"Do you really think they'll be forgiving and understanding if they manage to break out of the Regent's control?"

Bertrand stopped at the end of the corridor, examining the first tapestry of the man digging deep into the darkness.

"One sad truth I have learned in my travels, Miss Trent—scars of the flesh die with the bearer. Scars of the soul and heart may haunt the spirits of generations."

"What if we help them and then the Convocation attacks the purra and kills thousands of people and we're responsible for the massacre?" Maggie balled her hands into fists to keep them from shaking.

"Righting one wrong does not a new wrong fix," Bertrand said, "but to ignore suffering is just as bad as to cause it."

Maggie dug her knuckles into her eyes. "So, we destroy the pacel and hope a massacre doesn't happen."

"No." Bertrand pressed open the door to the main cavern. "We make sure we haven't been deceived and work from there."

"Still time for a way out. I like it."

"Maggie, Bertrand." Alden loped toward them. "What did the Convocation say? I'm glad they didn't decide you were purra spies and kill you. Have they convinced you to help us?"

"They have." Bertrand gave a tiny bow. "And you will be accompanying us on our journey to the pacel."

The scant color in Alden's face drained away. "That's what they said? They want me to go with you to the pacel?"

"We don't know anything about the city," Maggie said. "We don't know how to slip in without being caught by sniffers and nics. We wouldn't know how to get to the pacel even if we made it into the city."

"Right." Alden worried his lips. "Right. It would be necessary, wouldn't it? And what's necessary must be done."

"Exactly." Maggie shot a sideways glance to Bertrand.

The way Alden unraveled bits of his sleeve, he'd be naked by the time they made it to the city. If he even survived that long, which Maggie doubted considering his splotchy pallor.

"Is there a convenient place we can rest?" Bertrand asked. "It's been a rather eventful day for us, and sneaking into cities to destroy evil devices can be terribly tiring."

"Of course." Alden perked up, a bit of color returning to his face at the more pleasant task. "I have plenty of room in my home. Well, my practice and home. It's supposed to be for a whole family. But I needed the office, so I got the house even though I haven't any family."

Alden led them past the first row of houses and out toward the vine-covered walls. The lights in the ceiling had dimmed in their time with the Convocation, casting the leaves into shadows that seemed to twist with every step.

"Here we are." Alden stopped at a house too large for one person. "I'm sure I can find something to eat as well."

Alden pushed the door open. A little nic, smaller than those that had circled Lara, raced up to the door, its eye light blinking enthusiastically.

"I know I said I wouldn't be coming back." Alden petted the nic on the head with a dull *clunk*. "But I am happy to see you again as well. And you'll be going on a journey with my new friends and me."

The nic whirred and rolled deeper into the house.

"Right this way." Alden led them past a large, waist-high table with padding on one end like a pillow. Jars of every size lined four long shelves against one wall, while dried herbs hung along another.

"Alden," Maggie said as they left the front room and entered a kitchen. A fire sparked to life in the wide fireplace at a glance from Alden. "Alden, what is it that you do exactly?"

"I'm a healer," Alden said.

Maggie knocked into the kitchen table, sending pain shooting up her shin, but she couldn't pull her gaze from Alden's face.

"Well, not really." Alden shrugged.

"What do you mean *not really?*" Maggie hobbled to a chair.

"I was training to be a healer." Alden turned to the fire, hiding his face as he threw vegetables into a pot. "But the healer I was training under started pushing the bounds of magic allowed with the tags. He might have been onto something, you know. The Regent got wind of the work he was doing and had him taken to the pacel. I barely got away to come here myself."

"How much of your healing knowledge relies on spell work?" Bertrand tented his fingers under his chin, casting eerie shadows across his face in the firelight.

"None of it really," Alden said. "The healer didn't let me in on the experiments. He thought it would get me killed. I suppose he was right in the end." A gray potato-like thing slipped from Alden's hand and rolled across the floor. He didn't seem to notice. "They think I'm useless here in Lowgry. I studied for years, but all I can do is work with herbs and poultices and the like."

"But that's a lot." Maggie scooped up the gray potato. "Being able to do that sort of thing is perfect!"

"Not to them." Alden held up the pot for Maggie to drop in the potato as though afraid he wouldn't be able to do it right on his own. "I…I'm the first healer they've had in the Mira since the fall. The healers who used to have this house could work amazing magic to heal people of all sorts of things. Broken bones mended in a heartbeat. Terrible illnesses cured with an incantation. That's what they thought they'd be getting when I made it to the Mira. They thought I'd be like the healers of old, but I'm not. All I've got are some herbs."

"But that's infinitely better than nothing." Maggie took the pot from Alden. "You don't understand, the Siren sent us here to—"

"To have a great adventure," Bertrand said, "and the adventure of the day is destroying the pacel. Whatever they might have believed of you before, everything is about to change."

Alden opened his mouth, then closed it firmly, freezing for a moment before speaking. "Everything changes in the end."

A knock sounded on the door.

"Pardon me." Alden ran from the room.

"I must urge caution, Miss Trent." Bertrand sat in one of the worn kitchen chairs, which had probably been in use since the healers of old had lived in the house. "Enthusiasm is vital when dire troubles are about, but enthusiasm at the wrong moment can set things two steps back."

"You know, I'm really getting sick of the platitudes today."

"Then I suppose you won't mind if I borrow him." Lara appeared in the doorway. This time, only one of her nics trailed behind her.

Alden's smaller nic rolled out of the corner, whistling a greeting.

"Borrow him for what?" Maggie asked as Bertrand stood.

"If you're going to go fight your way through the city to the pacel, I think it only fair you know what you're fighting for," Lara said.

"True enough, and a very generous offer." Bertrand headed for the door.

"Where are you going?" Maggie said.

"To learn what wonders we venture to protect, Miss Trent," Bertrand said. "I'm sure Alden will keep you safe in my absence."

"Of course." Alden dropped another potato.

"Remember, Miss Trent, caution is paramount when exploring new avenues. Especially when one has a particular goal in sight."

"Thanks for that." Maggie put every bit of frustration she could muster into a withering glare.

"Shall we?" Bertrand held out his elbow.

With a grin to Maggie, Lara took his arm, leading Bertrand through the office and out of sight.

"Well," Alden said.

Maggie turned slowly, her feet telling her to run, common sense telling her to find a soft place to sleep.

Alden held a wooden spoon in one hand and yet another potato in the other. "Would you still like some soup?"

CHAPTER 9

*A*t least the bed is soft and clean.

The feather mattress looked to be as old as the members of the Convocation, but no dust puffed from it as Maggie twisted to her side. The plain furniture in the bedroom had been freshly and meticulously cleaned, not a thing out of line nor a spec of dirt in sight.

He cleaned it for the next person.

A hollow sadness trickled into Maggie's stomach.

He wanted to make everything nice for them. Keep them from thinking badly of him.

The soft *thumps* of Alden moving about the kitchen carried up from below. Maggie rolled over in bed again, willing time to freeze so she could get just a little more sleep. She didn't know when she'd get a chance to rest again. Maybe not until they returned to the Siren's Realm.

If the Siren's Realm will even be worth returning to.

Images of bodies lying in the street swam unbidden into Maggie's mind. Gabriel dead. Mathilda dead. Everyone who knew her name dead.

Will the Siren leave them to rot in the sun or call up a storm to wash them away?

A knot of panic seized Maggie's chest, squeezing the air right out of her. Flipping the thick blankets aside, Maggie stumbled out of bed, bracing herself against the stone wall as she forced her lungs to accept air.

We need to go back. We need to grab Alden and take him into the Siren's Realm. Kicking and screaming if we have to. The Siren sent us to him because she wants us to drag him in.

Just like she did to me.

Maggie slid down the wall, letting herself hit the floor with a *thunk.*

Alden's people needed help. They couldn't ask him to leave until he'd done all he could to save the magicians.

"So let's go in, destroy some shit, and get home."

A timid knock sounded on Maggie's door. "Maggie, I've made breakfast."

"Is it potatoes?" Maggie opened the door. "I'd really love some more potatoes."

"You're in luck!" Alden smiled, the expression ridding his face of its usual painfully thoughtful lines. "I have made potatoes."

"Perfect." Maggie bit back her smile as she followed Alden down the stairs.

"Miss Trent." Bertrand sat at the kitchen table, a plate of roasted potatoes already in front of him. "I was beginning to think you'd sleep forever."

"At least I slept." Maggie sat down opposite Bertrand.

"There are some things more productive than sleep when adventure is on the horizon," Bertrand said.

"Eww. Just eww."

Alden placed a plate of potatoes in front of Maggie. Their taste was duller than what she remembered from childhood. Her mother had always made potatoes with lots of butter and salt.

"We can't bring too much into the city." Alden placed two satchels between Maggie and Bertrand. "If we bring in large bags, they'll stop us for a search, and that'll give the soldiers a closer look at you than we want. And I'm afraid you'll have to change your clothes as well. Our best hope for making it to the Asty is for no one to give us a real look."

"What's the Asty?" Maggie shoveled down her last bite of potato.

"A safe place." Alden nodded before shaking his head. "What I mean is I have friends there who will be willing to help us get into the palace."

"Excellent," Bertrand said.

"Good." Alden gave a quick smile. "Here are your clothes. I scrounged them up from the others. They should be the right size." He held out two neatly folded piles.

A pale purple dress for Maggie, and a brown shirt, pants, and coat for Bertrand.

"I've never seen you in anything but tails and black buckled shoes," Maggie laughed as Bertrand accepted his pile.

"I am capable of being a chameleon when the occasion arises, Miss Trent."

"Yeah right."

Maggie slipped into the office to yank on the dress. The material held more weight than her clothes from the Siren's Realm, the coarse fabric woven for wear rather than basking in endless sunshine.

The skirt draped down to her ankles, covering most of her boots, but whoever had donated the dress to the cause was built smaller than Maggie up top.

"Just great." Embarrassment flushed her cheeks as she fastened the last button. The dress scooped low, and the tightness pressed her chest out beyond the point of being ignored.

"Slip through a city unseen," Maggie muttered. "With your boobs out."

Maggie folded her clothes, regretting having mocked Bertrand.

He's never going to let me forget this.

Maggie strode back into the kitchen, keeping her head down, and went straight to her satchel to tuck her own clothes away.

"I'm so glad the dress fits," Alden said.

Maggie turned to face him, and his cheeks flushed red.

"And what a lovely dress it is." Alden's voice squeaked as he spoke.

Maggie turned to Bertrand, gritting her teeth in preparation for his mockery, but a laugh escaped from her before Bertrand could say anything.

The brown pants were a different shade from the brown shirt, and the brown coat was a third entirely different, and unattractive, shade of brown.

Whereas Maggie's clothes had come from someone a size too small, Bertrand's appeared to have come from someone four sizes too big. The pants bunched awkwardly at the waist, the shirt and coat had been rolled several times at the sleeves, and all of it hung so loosely from his frame, he looked like a child playing dress up.

Maggie glanced down to see his black buckled shoes and doubled over in laughter, struggling to pull in air against the tightness of her dress.

"We are traveling incognito in a foreign land, Miss Trent," Bertrand said. "Disguise is no laughing matter."

"I beg to differ," Maggie giggled.

"We should go then." Alden grabbed his satchel and headed for the door, pointedly looking anywhere but at Maggie. "Don't want to waste any daylight. We'll be lucky if we make it to the Asty before dark. Come, Nic."

The little nic whistled cheerfully and rolled away at Alden's heels.

Maggie grabbed her satchel. "Right this way scarecrow. We're off to see the wizard."

"They refer to themselves as magicians in this world. You'd do best to remember that, Miss Trent."

Maggie laughed all the way out of the house, through the field filled with potatoes and vegetables, and up to the vine wall where Lara waited with her three nics. Though her hair hung loosely around shoulders, not a strand had dared to stray from its perfect position.

"Leaving already?" Lara purred, her gaze steadfastly on Bertrand.

"When the future of magic hangs in the balance, time is of the essence," Bertrand said.

"And you thought you'd slip out without saying goodbye?" Lara pouted, the droop of her lips failing to make her any less pretty.

"I've never been fond of goodbyes," Bertrand said.

"I love them." Lara stepped toward Bertrand, seizing the front of his floppy shirt.

"Are you ready for an adventure, buddy?" Maggie knelt in front of Alden's nic, speaking more loudly than necessary. "It'll be lots of fun!"

The nic's head tipped as it watched Bertrand and Lara with its one glowing eye.

"Not even a whistle of joy?" Maggie leaned to block the nic's view, willing it to look at her. "I bet we'll be great friends in no time."

The metal ruffle around the nic's neck whirred to life, forming an arm that pushed Maggie's head aside.

"Rude." Maggie stood.

"May we meet again, Lara," Bertrand said.

"And he uses her first name," Maggie muttered.

Bertrand stepped around the still pouting Lara to stand by Alden.

Alden stared dumbly at Bertrand, his mouth open.

"Let's go destroy the pacel." Maggie smacked both men on the shoulders.

"Right." Alden's eyes found Maggie again. "Right." His gaze drifted out over Lowgry. "Of course." His voice faltered.

Lara's nics whistled, and Alden's buzzed a response.

"This way then." Alden walked up to the vines, his hand held out like a divining rod. He swept his fingers back and forth across the leaves for a moment before sidling ten feet to the left and pulling a thick cluster of vines aside.

A tunnel barely taller than Alden himself and too narrow for two people to walk abreast had been sliced into the rock.

"This path isn't as beautiful as the way we took in," Alden said, "but it'll take us to whatever exit is closest to the city."

"Perfect," Maggie said.

Lara's nics whistled again.

"Let's go." Maggie shooed the men into the tunnel, not relaxing her jaw until the vines draped shut behind her.

She hadn't noticed the sounds of life from Lowgry until the vines silenced them. Silenced everything but the footstep and breathing of the three magicians and the dull grinding of the nic moving forward.

"*Inexuro.*" A fire flickered to life in Maggie's palm, casting slanting shadows in the corridor.

"It must be wonderful," Alden said from the front of the line, "having such magic in the palm of your hand."

"You lit the fire in your house," Maggie said.

"But I can't touch it without being burned," Alden said.

"I never really thought about it. In my world, I could do a lot more." Maggie tossed the fire from one hand to another, reveling in the joyful tingle of magic that thrummed through her skin. "I could crack the ground beneath your feet. Shoot blazes of fire and streaks of lightning at you. Conjure up a wind that could tear all the vines in Lowgry down."

"That's magnificent," Alden breathed.

"It was pretty cool." Maggie smiled, shaping the fire in her hand into a prefect sphere. "But you can't use spells in the Siren's Realm, and I don't know how magic really works here."

"Miss Trent," Bertrand said warningly.

Maggie poked him in the back to keep him walking.

"See, magic works a little differently in every world," Maggie pressed on even as Bertrand shook his head. "So only a few of the spells I know from home work the same here."

Alden stopped short, turning around to face Bertrand and Maggie. "How are you going to destroy the pacel if you don't know how to use magic here?"

"I was given a bit of a tutorial by Lara last night." Bertrand shooed Alden on.

"Really? I thought you'd been sleeping." Maggie's tone dripped with sarcasm. "You seemed so well rested this morning."

"Understanding can be quite invigorating, Miss Trent," Bertrand said. "If magic back home were the life blood pumping through your veins, magic here is the electricity of a thunder bolt coursing through your flesh."

"Sounds dangerous. I like it." Maggie balanced the fireball in her left hand, focusing all her energy on trying to feel electricity zinging through her right. "Is there a spell language?"

"There was," Alden said. "A long time ago when the Mira was built, there were whole books of spells meant to be used to focus magic. With those words, magicians could accomplish greater feats than could be done through mere instinct and luck."

"Dare I ask what happened to the books?" Bertrand said.

"When the Convocation held Alondra, they moved all the books aboveground to the library of Histem," Alden said.

"And where are the books now?" A zing of energy touched Maggie's fingertips but didn't take any form.

"As soon as the purra took charge, they hauled all the books out of the library." Alden's voice crackled. "They burned them in the streets, then used the building to house the pacel."

"Those filthy little sons of—" Sparks of light flashed from her fingers. Maggie squealed and let the magic go.

"Are you all right, Miss Trent?" Bertrand seized her hand, examining her fingertips.

Maggie rubbed her fingers together. She had felt magic surge from her flesh, but it hadn't left a mark. No burn blemished her skin. No pain lingered. "I am. It's good to know anger can make the magic click."

"Be careful with magic born of anger," Alden said. "Rage burns, and fire cares nothing for what it destroys."

"Well said, Alden," Bertrand said.

"I don't think I like the two of you together." Maggie waved them on.

Alden stopped twenty feet down the tunnel.

"If we don't keep moving, we'll never get to the Asty before…" The words faded from Maggie's lips as the corridor in front of Alden began to shift.

What had seemed like more of the long tunnel had suddenly become a slanting wall, which formed a steep incline in front of them. A crackling blue light shot from above for a split second before a humming started high up and out of sight. The *buzz* sounded like a thousand bees all swarming together.

"Bertrand." Maggie took a step back.

The sound drifted closer, but the buzzing had turned into a whirring like a dozen nics preparing their many arms to attack.

"Alden, what is up that shaft?" Bertrand held both his hands in front of him, preparing to do what, Maggie didn't know.

"It's the fastest route." Alden glanced up into the opening. "The magicians of old left themselves a path for quick escapes. Keep your elbows tucked, and best to close your eyes if you're one to get dizzy."

The whirring shifted again into a rush of wind, like a tornado whipping through the narrow shaft.

"Just lean into it, and don't fight where it wants to take you."

Alden stepped up to the slanted rock and tipped forward. In a second, his feet left the ground, and he twisted up and away.

"You've got to be kidding me," Maggie said.

The nic rolled up to the opening, whistling shrilly as the wind carried him up the chute.

"If you don't mind, Miss Trent, I'd prefer to go first." Bertrand stepped toward the opening.

"Afraid I can't handle whatever's through the twister?" Maggie extinguished the fire in her hand, leaving only the dim blue glow from above to light the corridor.

"Nothing of the kind. You are simply wearing a dress, and I wish to protect your modesty."

The wind sucked Bertrand into the air, twisting him out of sight.

"Great, just great." Maggie tucked her skirt between her knees, crossed her arms over her chest, and leaned into the spiraling wind.

CHAPTER 10

Maggie's hair whipped into her mouth as she spun through the vortex. Her elbow struck stone as the tunnel twisted. The rushing air stole the gasp of pain from her throat.

The tunnel curved again and again, arching around obstacles Maggie couldn't see through the churning wind. Her stomach rolled, and she shut her eyes against the movement, willing it to be over.

You've survived the Academy, and battles, and Bertrand Wayland. You will not vomit on your own cleavage.

The air around her changed, spinning her at a slower rate. Maggie dared to open her eyes just in time to see a bright light flash above.

Instinct told Maggie to brace herself to be shot into the sky, but she didn't know what bracing might help. Before she could decide if throwing her arms out would save her life or break her wrists, the brightness engulfed her.

Maggie screamed as she flew ten feet into the air before tumbling down onto something soft.

"That wasn't so bad, was it?" Alden asked, his cheeks pink as Maggie scrambled to her feet. "And it did save us quite a bit of time."

"Time in getting to where?"

The tunnel hadn't led them aboveground as the brightness had seemed to imply. The light shone from a dome above them. Bright blue sky filtered through, twisting as the glass distorted the scene. The walls and floor were made of the same gray moss that had softened their landing once before. The opening to the tunnel below and a stone square on the wall were the only other breaks in the moss.

"It's an emergency egress, if you will." Alden shrugged and stepped below the dome. The moss under his feet bulged, lifting him to be eye level with the glass. He made a slow circle, peering in every direction. "Not a sniffer or a nic in sight."

The small nic whirred.

"I know *you're* here." Alden jumped off the mound. "But you're meant to be here."

The nic whistled.

"Shall we?" Bertrand looked toward the square of stone.

"Of course." Alden frowned at the exit as though the last thing he wanted was to crawl through it. "If anyone stops you and asks why you're going to the city, say you're farmers, visiting family. If they ask you anything more than that"—he picked at the end of his sleeve—"I'd say just run."

"Great." Maggie took Alden's hand, lifting it away from his cuff. "Let's go."

Alden placed one finger on the stone square. From the look of fear on his face, it seemed as though the stone were about to bite him, or at the very least demand a small blood sacrifice.

The stone slid aside with a faint *rumble*. Alden crawled through and onto the grass without looking back.

Bertrand followed, leaving Maggie alone with the nic.

"After you." Maggie bowed to the nic.

With a whistle, he rolled up to the square, which started a foot off the ground.

"Do you need help?" Maggie reached to lift the nic, but his collar spun to life, forming arms that dragged his body through the opening. "Or not."

Maggie crawled through the square and out into the open air.

They were nowhere near where they had entered the Mira. That much was clear from the hills surrounding them. Maggie searched the grass for the glass dome Alden had peered through. An odd, perfectly shaped mound cut through the ground.

Maggie crawled toward the mound, running her fingers through the sun warmed grass that had been invisible from the other side. A faint tingle flowed through her fingers. The grass was real, but only from one side.

"An elaborate exit." Bertrand knelt next to Maggie, his floppy sleeves billowing in the breeze.

"The magicians of old had plenty of magic, time, and reasons to be afraid." Alden stood ten feet away, his face pinched with worry. "If you don't mind, I'd rather not linger."

"Of course." Bertrand stood. "Lead on."

Maggie let the tingle of magic hum through her fingers for another moment before following the men, the nic wheeling along behind her.

Not a single cloud marred the bright morning sky. The only things in the air were birds circling in the distance, flitting around each other as though in dance. The gentle breeze carried the soft scent of grass.

Plotting destruction seems wrong on such a pretty morning.

"We should head to the trees." Alden pointed to a strip of woods a few hundred feet away.

The trees reached off into the distance toward the city, weaving a path through the valley in a meandering way.

Maggie opened her mouth to argue for a straighter route, but the men had already headed toward the trees.

"Sure, leave the one in the dress behind," Maggie muttered.

The nic knocked its head into her knee.

"Thank you for staying, Nic."

Maggie and Nic chased after Bertrand.

"Histem is larger than it looks." Alden stopped just inside the tree line. "We really must keep together. If you get lost in the city, we might not find each other for months."

"Are there so many who wish to crowd together when such a fine valley waits right outside their gates?" Bertrand asked.

Alden sighed and started through the trees. Though their branches dripped with bountiful green leaves, there was something about their bark that made the trees seem young. The thinness of the woods was strange as well, as though the trees hadn't had time to expand their territory.

"Was this part of the valley burned with the ruin?" Maggie asked.

A stream bubbled in front of them. Alden stopped before stepping over it.

"Everything in the valley burned." Alden dipped his toe into the water. "The purra had heard of the Mira. They burned the valley to destroy it."

Nic rumbled through the stream and stopped on the far side. He turned back to the group, staring at them with his one eye.

Maggie leapt to a stone in the center, wobbled for a moment, and leapt again, landing on the other side.

"Were there no people living in the valley?" Bertrand followed Maggie's path.

"Oh, plenty." Alden stayed on the far bank, again dipping his toe into the water. "The wealthiest of the magicians had taken over the valley. There were estates large enough to employ fifty purra. But they burned it all."

"That's terrible." Maggie tried to picture the fallen down

tower. It could have held a rich young girl's bedroom or hidden the stairs to the servants' quarters in the attic.

"No one's lived out here since. Not aboveground, at least. It's not allowed, living outside the city." Alden stared up through the leaves. "Not without a farmer's permit, and you have to have a lot of money or an ally in the Regent's court to get one of those. You can apply to be a worker on a farm, but the work is hard and the pay is bad, so few choose that life."

"So basically you're saying the entire population of Alondra, except for a few farmers, live in Histem?" Maggie tried to picture a city that large. To have thousands, maybe even millions of people trapped in the great, walled capital.

"You can leave during the day." Alden slogged through the stream, not bothering to step on the stone to keep his feet dry. "You've got to be in by sundown, though. That's when the sniffers come out. If anyone's caught out of the city, it's not a pleasant sight."

"For the purra as well as magicians?" Bertrand asked, following Alden as he weaved through the trees.

"The purra get fines or a few days locked up," Alden said. "Magicians get sent to the pacel. If they make it that far."

"And the purra just agree to live all crowded together in the city?" Maggie asked. "I mean, I understand the magicians might not have a choice, but if the purra are in charge, shouldn't they be able to decide where they live? I mean, isn't that the point of winning a war, to gain more freedom?"

Alden walked in silence for a few minutes, glancing behind several times as though preparing to answer Maggie, before turning back around.

Just when Maggie had decided the answer would never come, Alden spoke, keeping his face steadfastly forward.

"They hate magicians. They call us the impi. It's a foul name and one I'm certain our ancestors earned. They spent a long time hating us when we were in power, and now they hate us while they're in power. The Regent promised them we'd never rise again if they follow her orders, so they do. They stay in the city because spreading out would make it easier for rogue impi to hide. They're so afraid of us sneaking off to live in the woods, they stay packed together to prevent it.

"Even if they did want to leave, they'd have to give up all use of intets. No nics or lights, no way to travel but walking. Intets draw power from the pacel, and that can only be done within the city walls. Farmers have to be very careful about making sure their intets draw enough power when they come to the city, and sniffers have to be careful, too. I heard of a sniffer who got stranded in the mountains for two weeks once because his intet ran out of power."

"How does this little guy keep going?" Maggie asked. "Do nics just have a super long battery life?"

"Battery?" Bertrand asked.

"He runs off of me," Alden said. "He draws from my tags, as Lara's do from hers."

"But what would have happened to him if you had jumped into the Siren's Realm?" Maggie asked.

Nic growled.

"He would have slept," Alden said, "until someone else from the Mira linked him to their tags."

Nic growled again.

"I'm sure it wouldn't have been long."

Nic formed a prong and poked Alden in the leg. Maggie laughed. Alden ignored it.

They traveled in silence for a long while. The trees surrounding them made it impossible to tell how far they were from the city, but Alden kept leading on, his shoulders creeping closer and closer to his ears as the time passed.

"What's the Regent like?" Maggie asked when her hands had begun to sweat in anticipation of what might await them in Histem.

Alden stopped walking but didn't look back. "A murderer who enjoys torture."

"No reason within her?" Bertrand asked.

"She is full of reason." Alden dug his muddy toes into the dirt. "All of her reasons simply lead back to the destruction of magicians. She's beautiful and terrible. Horribly intelligent and utterly merciless."

"Great." The sweat on Maggie's palms doubled.

Alden started forward again.

Maggie didn't ask any more questions.

A shadow passed above the trees, barely showing through the leaves.

Maggie peered up through the branches, willing something beautiful to burst into view. Anything to distract her from the high walls of Histem still hidden from sight.

Dink, dink, dink. Nic tapped quietly on his chest.

Alden's head snapped back, his gaze fixed on the trees high above.

A question balanced on Maggie's tongue, but something in Nic's eye as it swiveled toward her kept her from speaking.

Bertrand took a step closer to Maggie, his palms raised as though poised to release magic.

A *screech* pounded into Maggie's ears. A rush of air throttled the tops of the trees as a massive something blocked out the sun.

Maggie raised her hands, wishing for the thousandth time her magic would work as it had on Earth.

Another cry rent the air. An answer sounded in the distance.

Maggie looked to Alden who remained frozen, his head tipped toward whatever flew above.

Nic lengthened an arm, beckoning Maggie forward.

Maggie poked Bertrand's arm.

Nic beckoned him, too.

With a nod, Bertrand started toward Alden, carefully

choosing each footfall. Maggie followed, placing her feet exactly where Bertrand had trod.

Alden didn't look away from the sky until Maggie took his elbow.

Sheer terror filled his eyes. Sweat dripped from his forehead.

What's up there?

Maggie wished she could ask the question as the shadow circled overhead.

Alden's shoulders crumpled as a triumphant *caw* sounded from straight above.

Nic whistled, darting off the way they'd come. At the same moment, Alden seized Maggie's and Bertrand's hands, dragging them toward the city. Maggie glanced back long enough to see Nic dart out of sight as great talons wrenched a tree out of the ground by its roots.

Maggie swallowed her scream, keeping as close to Alden's heels as she could.

The light changed ahead of them. Brighter, without the shade of hanging leaves.

Instinct told Maggie to keep to the trees. But the great talons struck again, ripping up a tree not three feet behind her.

Maggie ran faster, pulling past Alden and Bertrand. There was no point in hiding the sound of their footfalls from the beast as it followed them, tearing up trees like they were no more than blades of grass.

An open field peeked through at the end of the forest.

Maggie waited for a jerk on her hand, or a spell from Bertrand. Anything that might mean someone had a plan other than running as quickly as possible and hoping the monster didn't catch them.

Bright sunlight burst around them as they broke free from the last of the trees.

Histem loomed at the end of the valley, its walls impossibly high, towers soaring toward the sky.

Black and scarlet wings large enough to engulf a house blocked the sun from view. Black talons reached toward Maggie as deep red breast feathers pulsed with the creature's cry.

"*Primionis!*" Bertrand screamed the spell the instant before talons reached for Maggie's face.

CHAPTER 11

The shimmering shield blossomed to life, bowing as the beast clawed at Maggie.

"Don't move," Bertrand warned, holding Alden's arms pinned to his sides.

"Can it hold the rammoc off?" Alden whispered, huddling close to Maggie's back.

"Do you have a better idea?" she said.

"Not that's immediately applicable," Alden whimpered.

A *hum* echoed through the shield as the monstrous bird clawed at Bertrand's spell.

"We can't just wait here." Maggie's mind raced through a hundred impossible options. "Where did the other one go?"

"Nic led one off." Alden glanced back through the trees. "I'd hoped both would follow him."

"Then we need to move before the other one comes back, or we're spotted by the purra, or sniffers come to check out what the evil bird wants for lunch."

"You're not helping, Miss Trent." Bertrand squinted toward the city.

"Well, if I knew how to help, I would try that instead." Maggie spoke through gritted teeth as the beast pecked at her head.

The shield shimmered as it stretched toward her.

"Let the beast take me." Alden strained against Bertrand's grip. "You'll have time to run."

"Run and do what?" Maggie asked. "You've said yourself we wouldn't be able to make it through the city without you."

"I also don't fancy watching your evisceration," Bertrand said.

"Better one than all three." Alden flinched as the rammoc tore at the shield with its great talons.

"Do you have anything metal?" Maggie dug in the satchel at her side.

A leather skin of water, some food wrapped in cloth.

"Do you have anything metal!" Maggie shouted.

"Nothing." Alden dug through his own sack. "I only packed food."

Maggie snatched Bertrand's wrist, yanking off the thin silver bracelet he always wore.

Pinching the loop, Maggie lengthened the metal into a silver tube.

The beast screeched its fury, and the shield hummed, struggling against the monster as though the spell were a living thing.

"Miss Trent!"

Maggie didn't look to Bertrand as she pressed the cylinder through the shield, funneling all her fear and frustration into magic that stung her skin as it flew from her palm into the metal. The rammoc's grip closed around the tube, its sharp talons piercing her flesh before her magic surged into the beast.

The rammoc's scream burst through the air in a terribly human way, but it couldn't let go of the prize it had fought so hard to win.

A cry tore from Maggie's throat as the spell burned her and the talons ripped her flesh.

The rammoc's gaze locked with Maggie's as she pushed the magic further.

A *crack* echoed through her chest as the rammoc fell from the sky, landing with a *thud* that knocked Maggie from her feet as the beast's talons ripped free from her hand.

Maggie lay panting on the ground as the shield faded, leaving only empty sky above her.

"Miss Trent, are you all right?" Bertrand's face blocked out the sun, concern crinkling his forehead.

"How did you do that?" Alden dropped to Maggie's side, wrapping her hand in pale blue bandages before she could think of getting to her feet.

"We need to move." Maggie stood, leaving her hurt hand in Alden's grip. "We don't know how far the other one went."

The downed rammoc lay still on the grass, its black wings bent in a grotesque way.

"I've never seen one this close." Alden stepped toward the thing.

Maggie hadn't realized he'd let go of her hand.

"I don't think any magician in the last hundred years has and lived to describe a close view of the beast." Alden leaned over the creature, his eyes wide with awe.

"Well, let's go before we get an even closer look at the other one." Maggie took Alden's hand, dragging him toward the city.

"How did you stop it?" Alden's gaze stayed on the monster as Maggie jogged forward, keeping her hurt hand close to her chest.

"Electricity," Maggie said as Bertrand moved to her other side, his gaze scanning the horizon. "If magic here is like electricity, then metal is a conductor. It was just like sticking the rammoc's finger, well talon, into a socket."

"I have no idea what you're talking about, Maggie, but you are brilliant." Alden pulled Maggie to run faster as a distant *caw* carried through the valley.

"What about Nic?" Maggie asked, wanting to think about anything besides the walls of Histem growing higher as they neared the city.

"If he's functional, he'll find me," Alden panted. "He can track me wherever I go. He's connected to my tags."

"Will they ask about Miss Trent's hand at the gate?" Bertrand said.

Maggie chanced a glance at her hand. Red had replaced most of the blue. Seeing her blood on the bandage suddenly made the wound seem more real, doubling the her pain as her pulse raced. "Sorry. I'll just tear my hand off and leave it out here, okay?"

"Don't be absurd—you injured yourself saving us all. I only fear showing up at the gates of the capital injured will bring unwanted questions."

"She'll have"—Alden gasped—"to hide it."

Sweat poured down his brow, whether from fear or running, Maggie didn't know.

As they neared the end of the valley, details of the outside wall became clearer.

Reaching six stories high, jagged ridges like teeth protruded from the top of the wall. While at a distance it had seemed to be made of one solid sheet of metal, up close, lines where heavy blocks had been welded together broke through the perfection.

Toward the center of the wall, gears larger than a person sank into the surface, bordering the shining section of the gate the ground had swallowed the evening before. A road led from an opening in the gate two stories tall and half as wide. A few figures came into view, wearing bright jewel tones as they strode down the dirt lane. More colorfully clad people lined up in a clump at the entrance to the city.

"Don't run." Alden stopped so suddenly, Maggie toppled forward, catching herself on her bad hand as Alden kept a vise-like grip on the other.

"Ow, ow, ow," Maggie groaned as Alden dragged her to her feet.

"We have to walk calmly onto the road give her your coat." Alden spoke as though both thoughts were one. "We should have walked more slowly for a while now. But the rammocs are nearly as terrifying as the soldiers who guard the gate, so it was a bit of a gamble either way."

Bertrand passed Maggie his oversized, brown coat.

"If they ask why we were running, say we were afraid of missing the gate for the night," Alden said. "Not that they'll have seen. They don't look so closely at the ground these days. Honestly, if magicians could turn into worms, they'd never notice us at all."

Maggie pulled on Bertrand's coat, letting the sleeves flop over her hands.

"I wish I could think of something else to tell you." Alden ran his hands through his sweaty hair, leaving it standing on end. "Or another way in. Or a reason to give up on this entirely."

"Procrastination rarely improves one's situation." Bertrand strode toward the road, his chest puffed up and his arms swinging lazily at his sides.

"He's right." Maggie looped her arm through Alden's. "Waiting is always the worst part. Best to jump right in and get it done."

"Of course." Alden's face paled as they cut toward the road. "Of course, you're absolutely right."

"Then stop looking like we're walking to our deaths," Maggie said. "We're here for a visit, remember? If I can look like my hand isn't throbbing and dripping blood, you can look like you're having a good time."

Alden took a deep breath and pushed a smile onto his face.

"Better." Maggie laughed.

She hummed to herself as they walked the rest of the way to the road, changing the tune every time Alden's smile faltered.

She didn't remember the words to most of the songs. Music hadn't been allowed at the Academy. Every once in a while, students would sing quietly to themselves for comfort, or the new ones would share some fresh bit of the outside world. Anything to prove life carried on beyond the Academy walls.

But once they were in, they weren't allowed out. Not unless, by some miracle, someone claimed an unwanted child. Then the chosen one would disappear forever.

Aging out. Turning eighteen, that was the real path to freedom. Years and years of waiting. Trapped within the walls of the Academy with no hope of escape.

Maggie's breath hitched in her chest as they stepped onto the road, the great city wall looming above them.

This isn't the Academy. They won't keep you trapped behind this wall.

"Are you all right?" Alden scrunched up his brow.

"Yeah." Maggie's voice came out with a foreign brightness.

"You're not." Alden kept his arm looped through Maggie's as they walked steadily toward the gate, Bertrand slipping into step beside them.

"You're also a terrible liar," Alden whispered. "Not that that's a bad thing."

A line of people waited outside the gate, some standing and chatting in groups, some riding machines ten feet high.

"Incredible." Bertrand peered through the group in front of them, scanning a low riding machine.

The thing had three metal wheels, like the nics but on a much larger scale. Rather than holding a tear-shaped torso, a long body like a canoe sat perched on top of the wheels. Five red leather seats were occupied by passengers basking in the sun as they waited for their turn to go through the gate.

"Whoever owns that has money." Alden spoke through the side of his mouth.

"It's like a clockwork gone mad." Bertrand inched forward as the line moved.

"That's one of the simplest types of intets in Histem," Alden whispered. "Once the purra harnessed magic, they let their imaginations run wild."

"If they weren't torturing magicians to do it, the whole intet thing would be pretty neat," Maggie said.

"There are many things in many worlds that would be wonderful were they without consequence," Bertrand said.

The line surged forward again as a towering intet trundled into the city. Blades ten feet long glinted on either side of the machine.

"Tell me that's for farming," Maggie murmured.

"It is."

A booming voice cut short Maggie's sigh of relief.

"I will not have impi wandering in and out of Histem like they own the place!"

A scuffle sounded from the front of the line. Maggie craned her neck but couldn't see anything as everyone backed away from the gate.

"No, I'm tagged, I'm tagged!" a woman pleaded. "I didn't do anything wrong."

"Just decided to leave the city?" The man shouted, as though wanting to be sure everyone nearby could hear. "Wanted to fill your impi lungs with fresh air? Think you have a right to take up my time trying to get back into Histem?"

"I've broken no laws," the woman sobbed.

"And I'll break none by keeping you out of the city."

"Please!" Thumps and scraping carried from the front of the crowd. "Please, please, let me in!"

"Go hide under a rock, and see how you fare when the sniffers come."

The crowd laughed as two large men in black and gold uniforms dragged the woman off the road, dumping her onto the neatly trimmed grass.

"Isn't she disgusting?" a girl in a sapphire dress with a matching parasol giggled. "I expect Histem will smell better without her."

"Please, I have children," the magician begged.

"We should help her," Maggie whispered.

"We can't," Alden said. "Just keep moving."

"You bred impi children?" A soldier loomed over her. "Pity that's not a pacel offense in itself."

Both soldiers turned and strode back toward the gate.

"I think I really hate these people." Maggie's jaw seized as she bit back the urge to scream. "You couldn't help her get to the Mira?"

"She'd never survive the tunnels." Alden kept his eyes fixed on the gate.

Maggie looked up to the gears overhead, tearing her gaze from the woman who sobbed twenty feet away.

The portion of wall that made the entrance had been raised high above like a guillotine, waiting to kill them all.

"I can't understand why they don't just keep them all locked up," the soldier with the booming voice said as they reached the gate. The man wore a black uniform with a leather chest plate. Unlike the two who had hauled the woman away, the only trace of gold on his uniform was a golden cog embossed over his heart.

Maggie's stride faltered as they drew level with the soldiers, her mouth sandpaper dry as she tried to remember what Alden had told her to say.

Visiting from the country. Workers from the farm.

Alden squeezed her arm, leading her forward without a hint of hesitation.

Maggie kept her eyes to the ground, watching her boots hit the cobblestone street as she waited for the soldiers to chase them. Thirty feet of dim tunnel led them to the far side of the wall. No voices bellowed at them to stop, no hands roughly seized them.

Light and sound waited for them at the edge of the wall as the road widened, stretching out to the heart of Histem.

CHAPTER 12

inkling music carried under the sounds of the crowd, like the glittering buildings around them were all part of a giant music box. The shortest building on the main street was tall enough to peer over the wall, and some reached so high, Maggie couldn't begin to guess their height.

The buildings hadn't been built of brick or stone either. They were all constructed of metal. One shaped like a unicorn horn seemed like it had swirled seamlessly up from the ground, its striations twisting as the tower grew. Another had folds and angles that glinted in the light of the setting sun, as though a giant had created the largest piece of origami of all time.

"This way." Alden led them down the main road.

Side streets branched off in either direction at regular intervals, as though someone had set the roads up in concentric circles with the cross of the two main thoroughfares cutting through it all.

"Absolutely marvelous." Bertrand squinted up at the tops of the towers.

"Don't do that." Maggie forced her eyes to scan the purra

meandering the streets. "If you look up, they'll know you're a tourist."

"How did you come to that glorious conclusion?" Bertrand kept his gaze high to the tops of the buildings.

"Because that's what they say back home," Maggie said. "If you go to New York City, don't stare at the skyscrapers. It's how everyone knows you don't belong."

"Are the buildings in New York City as high as they are here?" For a split second, a bit of dew glistened in Bertrand's eyes.

"Maybe." Maggie shrugged. "Probably. I don't really know, I've never been."

"Then how do you know not to look up?" Alden asked.

"It's just what everybody says, okay?" Maggie poked Alden in the shoulder, wincing as pain surged through her torn hand.

"Fresh meat for sale!"

Maggie's heart leapt at the familiar call, but the voice was too high and the words too crisply spoken.

Steam puffed from a cart that wheeled down the center of the street, the meat seller perched comfortably on top as he offered his wares. "Don't forget to feed your belly as the sun sets."

Alden steered them out of the path of the cart to the side of the street. Stalls selling flowers that sparkled like jewels and toy figures that flew sat next to booths filled with fancy gloves and a woman weaving braids into ladies' hair.

"Nearly there." Alden dodged around a man offering to clean the mud from their shoes.

The man's clothes were nearly as worn as the ones Alden had given Maggie and Bertrand. He had a fear behind his eyes as he bobbed from person to person, seeking work.

Is he a magician?

Maggie tossed the question aside. What did it matter if he had magic in his blood or not? They had come to the capital to help the magicians. If all went well, that man would be better off in a few days anyway.

Or we'll have started a war that will get him and a thousand others like him killed.

A glittering building made of metal so pale it rivaled the Siren's fountain came into view.

The structure was wide and far shorter than the towers surrounding it. Columns lined the walls, surrounding a staircase that swept up to an ornately engraved door. *And in learning, all things grow.* The words cut through the intricate swirls.

"The library." Maggie scanned the building, looking for any hint of the horror inside.

Soldiers surrounded the building, placed in front of each of the columns, spears in hand and swords at their hips. Six soldiers flanked the door, armed just like the others.

Above the windows, which glowed with a dim, golden light, turrets balanced on the four corners of the building. They were made of a different sort of metal than the rest of the structure and welded thickly on as though they'd been added in a hurry. Each turret held two men, bows in hand with arrows nocked and ready.

"An impressive guard," Bertrand said as though commenting on pleasant weather. "Is there another way in?"

"The way they bring in magicians to be used for the pacel." Alden's arm shook in Maggie's grip. "There are tunnels under-neath. From the prison where they're kept, from the pits where they're punished, from…whatever other horrors hide in the darkness."

"Sounds like a lot of tunnels." Maggie squinted, trying to peer through the high library windows.

"They run under most of the city," Alden said.

"Then down sounds like the way in," Maggie said.

"Better than fighting well-armed soldiers on a public street," Bertrand said.

"I truly hope you'll feel the same once we've found our way down." Alden nodded, leading them away from the library.

"Have you ever been in the tunnels?" Maggie asked.

"Of course not. I'm alive." Alden didn't say anything else as he cut onto one of the curving streets and away from the center of Histem.

Shops with fine dresses behind glittering windows took up the first arc. Fabrics Maggie longed to trail her fingers along, in every jewel tone a person could desire, filled the stores in an abundance to rival the Siren's Realm.

Maggie caught a glimpse of herself in the window. Her hair pulled back without care. The brown jacket covering most of her worn dress but still showing enough of her pale flesh to redden her cheeks.

"You look well enough," Alden said, setting her cheeks to blazing.

Maggie turned away from the window, grateful for Bertrand's silence as Alden led them on.

Bookshops, jewelers, and restaurants with tables under lavish awnings soon took over the street.

Maggie's mouth watered at the scent of savory food, but Alden turned onto another arc. They walked on and on as the sun sank in the sky.

Why isn't he leading us straight to the Asty?

The question balanced on the tip of Maggie's tongue, but the moment she thought it, the prickle of eyes on the back of her neck silenced her.

The buildings became gradually shorter as they worked their way toward the outskirts of the city. Out here, where the curved streets were long enough to stretch far out of sight, the buildings were barely four stories tall. The only shops were small and lacked the glittering wares of the center of town.

A low *rumble* sounded as the ground trembled beneath Maggie's feet. She froze, her gaze darting up and down the street, searching for whatever horrible thing had shaken the earth.

The people around her meandered by without seeming to have noticed the tremor.

"The gate." Alden tugged on Maggie's arm. "It's only the gate letting the sniffers out. You mustn't show any fear, or they'll know you don't belong."

"Yes, Miss Trent." Bertrand raised one, perfectly sculpted eyebrow. "Do not allow a look of amazement to cross your face or they shall know we are intruders."

Maggie clenched her fist and instantly regretted it as pain surged through her right hand.

"Fine," Maggie said, "but can we get where we're going so I can pretend the sniffers aren't going out to hunt for magicians in peace?"

The amusement slipped off both men's faces.

"It's just this way." Alden led them to the edge of an arc, stopping at the last building on the street.

The house had been made of metal, like the rest of the city, but built a bit sadder somehow, as though the metal itself had fought the construction. A dim light glimmered through the ground floor windows, but above that, heavy curtains had blocked out all chance of light.

Alden stared at the house, as though searching for a street number, but Maggie hadn't seen a single street number or name since they'd entered Histem.

"Are we lost?" Maggie asked after minute had passed.

"No." Alden continued to stare at the house.

Maggie followed his gaze, trying to find whatever it was he'd been searching for.

Contorted reflections of the people passing by played across the house in the dim light.

A woman in an emerald green dress pushed a bright pink pram behind them and rounded the corner, turning out of sight.

"In we get." Alden stepped forward, disappearing into the side of the house before Maggie could blink. Bertrand stepped up to the house, disappearing as Alden had.

"Okay then." Maggie took a breath and followed, her whole body tensing as sense declared she was about to slam into a solid wall.

A chill like cold mist licked her skin as the world flickered for a moment, resolving a breath later into the inside of a dimly lit dining room.

"If you wish to survive, move no farther."

Maggie stopped short, instinctively raising her hands. With Bertrand and Alden standing in front of her, she couldn't see whoever had spoken from the other side of the room.

"Has it been so long I've been totally forgotten?" Alden asked.

"Alden?" the voice said. "You…died."

"No, I ran." Alden stepped farther into the room and out of Maggie's way, revealing a muscular man with bright red hair and stubble to match. "I wasn't at the shop when they came for Remur. I fled to the Mira."

The man ran a hand over his stubble. "You should have come here before chancing the Mira. You would have been protected."

"I should have done a lot of things." Alden shrugged. "But life works out as it should, and when you hear what we've come to do, you'll be glad I ran."

The man walked to the polished table at the center of the room, leaning his weight on the back of a chair, but making no move to sit. "What brilliant thing makes your return to the Asty worthwhile?"

"*Inexuro.*" A ball of fire sprang to life in Maggie's palm.

"By the burning skies." The man stared in wonder at the flames. "They're untagged, and they've decided to enter the city? Have you dragged lunatics to the Asty? How have they survived this long? How did they escape tagging? Were they born in the Mira?"

"A bit farther out than that." Bertrand stepped forward,

holding his hand out to the man. "Bertrand Wayland at your service. Miss Trent and I hail, most recently, from the Siren's Realm. We slipped into your world searching for a bit of adventure and wish to lend our services in the aid of the magicians of Alondra."

"Lend your services?" The man ignored Bertrand's outstretched hand.

"We have a plan," Alden said. "Well, more like a goal really. But right now, I need to bandage Maggie's hand, and we need a safe place to sleep for the night. I promise, Ellic, once I've tended to them, I'll tell you everything you want to know."

Ellic kicked the chair, letting it fall to the floor with a *clatter*.

"Fine, Alden, I'll trust your word that far. Take them and wrap them up nicely for the night."

"Thank—"

"But if you've brought trouble to the Asty for nothing"—Ellic cut across Alden—"nothing that's come before will save you from the consequences."

"No worse than I deserve." Alden set the chair back up on it legs and waved Maggie and Bertrand to a narrow door at the other side of the room.

"Thank you for your hospitality." Bertrand gave a small bow and followed Alden.

Maggie said nothing as she hurried in their wake.

The inside of the house looked almost normal considering they'd walked through a wall to get inside. The room wasn't made of metal, or at least no metal showed through the painted decorations.

A teakettle hung in a fireplace in the room next to where they'd entered. If that would have been considered the dining room, this was a study. Solid and well fluffed couches cornered around the crackling fire, and bookshelves lined the walls.

"If everything in the library was burned, what's in these

books?" Maggie asked as Alden kicked the bottom of the wall, revealing a trapdoor.

"Everything we've tried to cobble together in the last hundred years." Alden swung the trapdoor open. "It's sad and feels utterly hopeless. Like blind children leading blind infants. But they're the best we have."

"It's how all great libraries begin," Bertrand said.

"But we don't have the luxury of waiting another century to build something great." Alden started down the steps. "If things continue as they are, if we don't succeed, I sincerely doubt there will be any magicians left alive in a hundred years' time."

"Not even in the Mira?" Maggie followed Alden down the stone steps. The air held the musty scent of a basement, though not a speck of dirt clung to the floor.

"The people in the Mira bring their children aboveground to be tagged." Alden twisted a knob, and lights flickered to life around the windowless room. "When the magician population in the city becomes too scarce, they'll start keeping the children who are brought in. Then there'll be nothing left."

A table much plainer than the one upstairs took up the center of the room. Mismatched chairs were neatly tucked in around it, and a stack of papers sat in the middle. Maps of Histem took up most of one wall, and three doors scattered about the others.

"I hate to sound insensitive to the traditions of other cultures—"

Maggie swallowed a laugh.

"—but why would magicians present their children to be tagged?" Bertrand continued. "Wouldn't it make more sense to hide the children, keeping their powers unbound?"

"Magicians did that for a while." Alden dropped his bag on the table and fidgeted with the clasp. "People would try and hide their children at home, or search for the Mira in hopes of refuge. But the purra found out. For every one, they will take twenty."

"What does that mean?" A knot of panic balled in Maggie's throat.

"If they find a one-year-old who is untagged, they will kill twenty children." Alden twisted the clasp of his bag. "For a two-year old forty. If a child reaches ten—" The clasp tore from the bag and clattered to the ground.

"Two hundred dead children," Bertrand finished for him.

"They start with those living closest to the family." Alden grabbed the clasp from the ground. "The only way to exempt a child is for their parent to turn in the untagged."

"Neighbor turned against neighbor." Maggie blinked back the stinging in her eyes.

"Tagging is the only way we can continue to survive," Alden said. "To refuse makes you a traitor to all magicians. It's a price few would pay, and none who move in magical society."

"What if they catch us?" Maggie asked.

Alden tucked the clasp into his satchel.

"We can't be here if it could mean them slaughtering hundreds of kids." Maggie took Alden's shoulders, twisting him away from the bag.

"They've already sentenced us all to death," Alden said. "We're only dying very slowly."

CHAPTER 13

M aggie didn't argue as Bertrand took back his coat and Alden led her to a seat at the table.

Three-hundred-and-forty. Just for me.

Bertrand studied the maps, noting the many variations of thick, black lines running through each copy.

"The location of the tunnels." Alden gave the maps a fleeting glance. "Or at least a dozen peoples' best guesses."

How many for Bertrand? Would they even be able to tell his true age?

Bertrand examined what lay behind each of the three doors. Beds, supplies, weapons.

Maggie closed her eyes against the clanging as Bertrand sorted through the stores of weapons.

"Ouch." Pain in her hand dragged her out of silence.

"Sorry." Alden unwrapped her bandages. "I wish I didn't have to fiddle with it, but with an animal wound, we really can't risk infection."

"What happens if they catch an untagged adult?" Maggie pulled her hand away from Alden.

"An untagged adult hasn't been caught in a very long time." Alden reached for her hand.

Maggie clutched it to her chest. "But if they do?"

"The last time, they raided a quadrant of the city. They say the ground was slick with blood."

Maggie forgot to fight as Alden gently took her hand, laying it on the table.

A gouge cut to the bone on the side of her wrist. The skin between her thumb and pointer finger had been punctured completely.

"Don't think about what will happen if they find you." Alden pulled a curved needle and spool of thread from his satchel. "The sniffers can't tell the difference between tagged and untagged. As long as you're with me, they'll think it's my scent they're after. They'd have to see you use magic for them to know you're like me."

"So, no magic then." Maggie jiggled her leg in a failed attempt at distraction as the thread pulled her torn flesh together.

"Not until we reach the pacel." Alden worked quickly, his hands so steady the movements were mesmerizing. "Then there won't be a choice."

"And if it doesn't work? If we don't destroy the pacel, and the purra are still in power?"

Alden paused for a moment before tying off the last stitch in Maggie's hand.

"I don't know a single magician who wouldn't gladly die for a world without the pacel. They're only too afraid to be the ones to make the change. You're doing them a service, Maggie. Don't think of anything but that. You are going to do what thousands upon thousands have dreamt of and none have dared. Hold onto that. The rest will only muddy the path ahead."

"Well, it sounds so easy when you say it like that."

"It does." Alden nodded then turned back to his bag, digging around for a moment before pulling out a little metal pot.

Maggie could smell the sickly sweet cream before Alden had twisted the lid fully off.

"What is that?" Maggie held her uninjured hand over her nose.

"It'll keep infection away." Alden dabbed the paste over the stitches. "It's fairly effective, much better than the options if infection does set in."

"Smother it on then."

A *thump* and a *creak* sounded above.

"It's all right." Alden shoved the medical supplies back in his bag. "If there were someone coming down who shouldn't be, we would know."

"How?" Maggie asked.

Alden stood, ignoring Maggie's question and fiddling with his sleeve.

"I've brought food and drink." Ellic appeared at the top of the stairs, a tray in one hand and a pitcher in the other. "If we had more people in the Asty tonight, there might not have been as much to spare."

"Where is everyone?" Alden took the pitcher from Ellic's hand as soon as he reached the bottom of the stairs.

"The usual." Ellic set the tray on the table. Two rolls tumbled off the side. "I assume you remember what the Asty stands for? What we spend all our time in this cursed place doing?"

"Of course I remember." Alden half-ran to a cupboard in the corner, fumbling as he pulled out plates and cups.

"I wasn't sure if you'd decided to forget everything about the Asty or just your place in it."

Alden blinked, his body frozen as though someone had cast a spell on him.

"What is the Asty?" Maggie asked, glancing between the two men.

"A place people abandon." Ellic turned and walked up the stairs, slamming the trapdoor shut behind him.

"Should you go after him?" Maggie whispered.

"No." Alden shook his head, his eyes still wide. "That would be a terrible idea. There are some injuries best left undisturbed. No good can come from prodding at them."

"What sort of injuries?" Maggie took the cups from Alden, pouring each of them a drink.

"I left." Alden poked the liquid in his cup.

Maggie sniffed hers before sipping. Chilled enough to leave a trail of cold down her throat, it tasted like water infused with a tang of fruit.

"During my apprenticeship, I discovered the Asty." Alden downed his whole cup. "Didn't discover it, truly. More like found my way to the place by gently pressing likeminded individuals."

"What is the Asty?" Maggie sat at the table, filling a plate with rolls and cheese.

"A well-constructed hiding place favored by those who seek to end purra rule." Alden sank into a chair.

"Rebel headquarters."

"Designed for safety against infiltration. The entrance from the street took ten years to construct working with only the magic allowable by the tags. The whole thing was desperately hard to do." Alden picked up a roll. He turned it over in his hand, examining every crack in the crust of the bread. "The books are hidden here, and the maps. What little magic is dared to be taught within the city has slowly been collected by those who have access to this sacred place."

"The Asty is sacred?" Maggie asked.

"As sacred as the freedom magicians hope to gain." Alden tore his roll in half. "I found a purpose when I found my way to the Asty. I had thought helping people by healing them would be enough, but it wasn't. I helped save a man from dying, and one week later he was taken to the pacel. I couldn't bear to spend my time trying to stop disease when the real plague killing my people is the Regent and all the purra."

"Sound reasoning." Maggie took a bite of bread. It lacked the sweetness of the Siren's Realm, but after the day they'd had, even gritty food was welcome.

"The work of the Asty gave my life meaning." Alden smiled, though worried creases still marked his brow. "I was the closest to happy I'd ever been."

"Why did you leave?" Maggie shook her head as Alden's smile disappeared. "I guess I mean, why didn't you run here when they took the healer you were training with instead of all the way to the Mira?"

"When the purra soldiers banged on the door, Remur told me to run. He wanted me to save myself to protect the bit of healing I knew. There aren't many healers left among magicians, and purra healers won't touch us."

"Then you did what he—"

"They killed him," Alden said. "They took him to the pacel and killed him in that demonic beast. He was like a father to me, and I ran while they hauled him away. It was always the same here at the Asty, too. The others would go around the city, searching for an entrance to the tunnels or weaknesses in the soldiers' barracks.

"I was always told to stay safely behind. Ready to patch up their wounds if they lived long enough to slip back through the wall. After running while they dragged Remur away, I couldn't face it anymore. So I fled for the Mira."

"I don't blame you," Maggie said. "I'm not great at letting other people take the risks either."

"You know what the worst part is?" Alden shredded his bread. Maggie didn't bother trying to stop him. "After leaving. After hiding in the valley, risking sniffers and rammocs and finally finding the Mira, I was an utter disappointment to them."

"Then I guess we'll just have to destroy the pacel and save all magicians to show Lara you're worth a hell of a lot more than she is."

Alden gave a faint smile. "I don't think Lara would ever believe that."

Maggie finished her roll, then moved onto another.

Alden finally took a few bites of cheese.

"Are all the people in the Asty going to be as mad at you as Ellic is?" Maggie asked. "If they won't stay in the same room as you, are they really going to help us?"

"Ellic will help as far as he's able once he knows what we've come to do," Alden said. "As much as I hurt him in leaving, he's in love with the idea of free magic, far more than he was ever in love with me."

"Oh." Maggie drummed her fingers on the table, wincing as the stitches stretched her skin. "I didn't know we'd showed up at your ex's house, that…that's…I'm sorry."

Alden shrugged. "It was a lifetime ago if you consider all that's happened in between. And Ellic is strong enough to understand."

"Still, I'm sorry."

"Nothing to fret over." Alden waved a hand through the air, a hair away from knocking over his cup. "I should go up and explain what we're here to do, though. He knows more about the theories of the tunnels than anyone else in Histem."

Alden stared at the trapdoor as though it led to the gallows.

"We'll have to make plans for tomorrow. Figure out which maps are best. I'll have to convince him he's not to come with us. It'll be an awfully long fight."

"Is there anything I can do to help?"

"Just keep that hand clean." Alden stood abruptly, knocking over his chair. "If we have to fight off an infection, we'll have to wait for you to heal, and that will only drag things out." He set the chair back up on its feet. "And now that we're going to the pacel, I'd rather get it done as quickly as possible."

Squaring his shoulders, Alden walked over to the stairs and up out of sight without another word.

Maggie ran her good hand over her face.

We're saving a world, and he's leading us to do it.

"Has he left?"

Maggie didn't even open her eyes. "Yep."

"While I admit I am enthralled with the weapons here in the Asty, and the spells on the front entrance are rather impressive given the restrictions on magic, I had hoped for a bit larger population from which to draw support for this endeavor." Bertrand filled his cup and plate.

"You mean you didn't want to choose between the almost doctor and his angry ex? Yeah, me neither. Alden did make it sound like there might be others who can help."

"Perhaps." Bertrand abandoned his food and moved to the maps on the wall. Each pattern of black lines was different. Some swirling, others created of jagged angles. One had only two tunnels running right under the main thoroughfares of the city, another had more tunnels than streets, as though the ground under the city were almost entirely hollow.

"What do almost all of these maps have in common, Miss Trent?"

Maggie joined Bertrand by the wall, swallowing her instinctive answer. *Most of them are wrong.*

"Right there." Maggie prodded a point on the map in the northwest quadrant of the city. All the maps except two had tunnels running through that intersection. "Pretty much all the map makers agree there's a tunnel right under there."

"But why?" Bertrand tapped the map as though sounding the ground to see if it was hollow. "What have they found there to make them so sure there's something beneath?"

"No idea. We can ask Alden when he comes back."

"When he's done speaking with his former lover?" Bertrand raised an eyebrow. "We might as well sleep while we wait. I doubt that will be a speedy reunion."

"I suppose you have a lot of experience there."

"I also have the wisdom to leave the past where it lies."

Bertrand unpinned a map, rolling it up and tucking it in the inside pocket of his awful coat.

"We're in the city and have a place to sleep for the night." Maggie sighed. "Can we just call that a win?"

"Absolutely, but I must urge caution." Bertrand walked back to the table and returned to his untouched food.

"Caution in what?" Maggie prompted when it seemed as though Bertrand would never continue.

"Alden ran from his lover and his friends," Bertrand said. "While his reasons seem legitimate, running from danger is a learned reaction. Alden was attempting to run from his entire world when we found him."

"You ran from our world," Maggie said.

A shadow passed through Bertrand's eyes. "I didn't run. I found a path to survival."

Maggie sat in the chair opposite Bertrand, afraid to say anything else, yet wanting to know what shadow had chased him from their world.

"I worry about an attachment forming between the two of you." Bertrand's demeanor returned to the cocky status quo. "I'm not sure it would be healthy on either end."

"Hmmm." Maggie pursed her lips and tapped her chin. "I'm not interested, and he likes guys. I think we're good on this one."

"If my instincts are wrong, I'll replace those torn up clothes of yours when we return to the Siren's Realm." Bertrand bowed.

"And if you're right?" Maggie folded her arms over her chest.

"You simply have to utter the phrase, *Bertrand Wayland, you were absolutely right.*"

CHAPTER 14

A tray of rolls and cheese sat on the table as the lights shone with an unwavering brightness. The only sign that night had passed was the jug of bitter brewed leaves replacing the pitcher of tangy water. Maggie didn't know which she liked less.

"Even if you get into the tunnels, there's no way to know what you'll find or where the path will lead you." Ellic tapped his finger on the map Bertrand had taken from the wall. "We know they imprison, torture, and kill, but we have no idea how or where."

"Someone must have escaped." Maggie clutched her mug.

Ellic shook his head.

"Been released then?" Maggie offered.

"Only purra have ever been released," Alden said. "The ones taken in on minor infractions, like vandalism, or disturbing the peace, and none of them will be willing to talk to us."

"From what we've surmised from the stories they've spread, the tunnels are vast," Ellic said. "Where they entered the tunnels and were kept before sentencing was far away from where they served their term of imprisonment."

"And the entrance is in the palace, which would be even worse to get into than the library," Maggie repeated the facts that had already been given.

"But of the places we believe the tunnels to reach, this is the most consistent." Alden pointed to the spot on the map Maggie and Bertrand had noticed the night before. The back of his pinky grazed Ellic's thumb. Alden snatched his hand away, tucking it into his pocket.

"Why have so many of your map makers decided on this point?" Bertrand asked.

"It's a fine dress shop," Alden said. "A place only ladies with huge amounts of money would frequent."

"When we first began searching for the tunnels, each of us went out, charting our suspicions without sharing with the group how we'd done the job until we'd finished the task. Some watched people, others felt for the hum in the ground when the gate closed."

"What happened in the dress shop to make you believe there's an entrance to the tunnels?" Maggie leaned over the map.

"Men," Alden said. "Men entered the shop, at least a few a day."

"Couldn't they just have been buying dresses?" Maggie asked. "Presents for wives and daughters?"

"Not all of the men would be able to afford such a purpose," Ellic said. "All were dressed in fine clothes going in. They'd stay, some for hours upon hours, up to whole days. When we followed them home, they went all the way to the outskirts of the city. If they could purchase a pair of gloves in that shop, they'd be able to live in the center of Histem."

"What would men in fine suits be doing in the tunnels?" Bertrand tented his fingers under his chin. "If they were prisoners or workers, they'd be going in through official entrances."

"I have no idea what they do." Ellic rubbed the back of his

neck. "There might not be an entrance at all. But you've asked for my guess on a way in, and that's the best I can offer."

Bertrand nodded, still staring at the map as though searching for a hidden message.

"All right." Maggie took another sip of the hot brew, regretting it instantly. "We've got to see if there's an entrance into the tunnels, so we wait until tonight and break in? Search while there's no one around?"

"That would be one way." Alden looked to Maggie, his gaze traveling from her hair hanging loose around her shoulders to her exposed cleavage. "Though there is a simpler choice with much less risk."

"What?" Maggie leaned back in her chair, wishing she'd changed back into her own clothes.

"We enter as shoppers," Alden said. "Take the opportunity to search without breaking in. If we break into the shop and there is a tunnel, it would be easy for the soldiers to guess why we'd chosen that business to plunder. But if a few shoppers disappeared without buying anything…"

"It is a far safer plan." Bertrand examined Maggie.

"Sure," Maggie said. "I'll just waltz into the fancy shop in my worn out dress like Cinderella searching for her fairy Godmother."

"They'd never let you in," Alden said. "You'd have to look the part to get past the door, we all would."

Ellic gave a low laugh, running a hand over his chin. "You're hitting all the marks, aren't you?"

"I'll make her understand," Alden said. "I'm not popping by for a chat, I'm trying to save us all. There has to be a little leeway that comes with it."

"You'll be lucky if she lets you in the door," Ellic said.

"You did," Alden said.

"If you don't mind, Ellic"—Bertrand stepped between Ellic

and Alden—"if we are to venture out into the world, I would prefer to do so well armed. Might Miss Trent and I borrow a few weapons from your stores?"

"*Borrow* implies returning," Ellic said, "and I doubt any of you will be coming back. Take what you want and get on your way."

Ellic turned toward the stairs.

"We need clothes as well," Alden said. "Miram won't have anything for Bertrand and me."

Ellic froze, his foot on the bottom step. "If you need a pint of my blood, you'll let me know, won't you?"

"Ellic—"

"Go try and save us all, best of luck to you, but don't expect me to mourn you again. I've done it once already." Ellic climbed the steps without looking back.

"I deserve that," Alden said. "I'm quite sure I do."

Maggie bit her lips together as silence hung in the air.

"You have clothing for the two of us?" Bertrand asked. "As much as I've enjoyed this charming dash into the realm of ill-fitting clothes, it would be a pleasant change to return to well-tailored attire."

"Right." Alden nodded. "Of course." He stared at the steps, pulling apart the sleeve of his coat.

"Where are the clothes?" Maggie asked. "If we're going to play dress up and break into the tunnels, we should get going."

"Right in here." Alden led Bertrand to the supply room.

"I'll pick some nice weapons." Maggie headed toward the weapon room, laughing as Bertrand's, "This is much more promising," followed her.

The walls of the weapons room were lined with shelves and brackets built to hold knives, swords, and bows. Most of the shelves were bare.

Maggie reached for a glittering sword. The narrow blade and hilt were nearly the same as the sword she'd used to practice with Bertrand.

"And where would I hide it?"

A shelf of daggers sat across the room. Most of the blades were old, dings made by who knows what marking their edges. One even had a touch of rust crusting it.

Maggie moved methodically, picking up each knife, testing the weight in her hands, checking the edges for sharpness, before settling on two for herself—a short knife that tucked easily into the side of her boot, and a longer blade with a belt attached to the sheath.

Wrapping the belt twice around her thigh, Maggie strapped on the long blade.

"Not as good as a spell, but it could be worse."

Grabbing the best of the other knives and one sword short enough to be hidden under a long coat, Maggie headed back out to the map room.

Bertrand waited by the staircase, fluffing the lace that lined his collar. The black silk jacket, pants, and cream, lacy shirt were eerily similar to his usual garb.

Alden had chosen a long jacket that hung past his knees and buttoned all the way up to his high collar, giving him the look of something between an undertaker and a pastor.

"Alden gets the sword then." Maggie passed him the blade.

"Are weapons allowed on the streets of Histem?" Bertrand asked.

"Not without a position that warrants their use." Alden struggled to buckle the sword under his coat as Bertrand grudgingly accepted a belt with two matching knives.

"Nothing else of use?" Bertrand asked.

"Not unless you have somewhere to hide a bow and arrows." Maggie grabbed her satchel from the table.

"You'll have to leave it behind." Alden reached into his own bag, choosing a few items and stuffing them into his pockets.

"Traveling light, I love it." Maggie dropped her bag back onto the table and headed up the stairs, pushing the heavy trapdoor aside.

The *thump* of footsteps headed out of the room as she entered it, catching a glimpse Ellic's boot disappearing from sight.

"Best to let me lead." Alden emerged from the basement, flinching as a door on the second floor slammed shut. "We mustn't look like we don't know where we're going."

"Lead away." Maggie hung back, letting Alden enter the dining room alone before turning to Bertrand. "Do we really think we should take him into the tunnels with us? He gets nervous and tears his sleeves apart around his ex. What's he going to do if we get penned in by soldiers?"

"I don't think we have a choice, Miss Trent." Bertrand walked into the dining room, leaving Maggie shaking her head behind him.

Alden waited for them by the front door. He glanced back and forth between Maggie and Bertrand several times, as though counting to be sure they were both there before opening the door to the street.

Maggie stepped out into the bright sunlight.

Even in the outskirts of town the buildings glistened more brightly than they had the evening before. The vivid blue sky reflected off the metal walls, bathing the streets in an ethereal glow.

"This way." Alden walked ahead of them, seeming to apologize for his existence with every step.

"Alden." Maggie ran up, catching his arm with her good hand. "Remember how I told Bertrand not to stare up at the buildings because someone would notice he was out of place?"

"Of course." Alden nodded, nearly knocking Maggie over as he dodged around a woman leading a pack of small children.

"A rich man wouldn't apologize for walking down the street."

Alden reached for his sleeve.

"Or pick at his expensive jacket," Maggie added. "You've got to hold your head up high. Show the world you're confident, and they won't question why."

"I wish it were so simple," Alden said.

"Just try it." Maggie nudged him with her shoulder. "Chin up, eyes steady, you'll be great."

"Chin up, eyes steady." Alden raised his eyes and held his head level. The grim set of his mouth didn't change, but in a few steps he'd transformed from a nervous fool to a solemn undertaker.

"Better." Maggie smiled.

They twisted closer into the center of town, Alden leading them on several switching spirals before they reached the center rings.

A prickle kissed the back of Maggie's neck as the terrible feeling of being watched overwhelmed her. She tightened her grip on Alden's arm, scanning the people around her. More than one person had their eyes trained on Maggie. A group of women whispered behind their fans.

"Bertrand," Maggie said in a calm voice. "People are staring at me."

Bertrand took a moment, his gaze sliding over the passersby. "I'm not surprised, and they don't seem menacing."

"Why aren't you surprised?" Maggie asked. "Isn't getting stared at usually a bad thing when you have the type of plans we have for today?"

"Miss Trent," Bertrand said, an ill-concealed grin on his face, "you are a poorly dressed yet very pretty girl in the company of two apparently well-moneyed men. I'm sure their suppositions will give them something to titter about for the rest of the day."

Maggie's face burned. "Sometimes I do not like you, Bertrand Wayland."

"It's an unfortunate truth, Maggie." Alden led them onto a new arc. "You are very beautiful. Even if we were all dressed in rags, I'm sure there would still be some staring at you."

Bertrand raised an eyebrow at Maggie, giving a little cough to be sure she'd see.

Maggie glowered the rest of the way to the glittering tower where Alden stopped. This street was nothing like the shabby section of town that housed the Asty. The building in front of them held hints of gold in its walls, weaving around in a mesmerizing pattern.

"No point in procrastination." Alden's Adam's apple bobbled in his throat.

"Let's go then." Maggie elbowed him in the ribs.

Swallowing again, Alden started toward the entrance.

The oversized front doors swung out as they approached.

For a moment, Maggie thought they had opened of their own accord, but two men in deep red uniforms followed the doors out, holding them wide to greet their party.

"Thank you." Maggie nodded.

Neither of the men looked at her.

The front doors of the building opened up into a wide courtyard with a fountain, surrounded by ferns and bright-colored flowers.

"Your friend lives here?" Maggie plastered a smile on her face as Alden led them through the atrium. There were more eyes following her inside than there had been on the street.

"She lives near the spire."

A wide arch cut through the back of the tower. A spiral staircase twisted up and out of sight, the steps rising constantly, carrying the finely dressed purra up to their homes.

"How miraculous," Bertrand breathed.

"Play it cool," Maggie muttered, her own heart racing in her chest.

A landing greeted the spiral stairs at every level, but the constant motion never ceased its twisting all the way up to the spire of the tower.

"Watch your hem," Alden cautioned as they stepped onto the stairs.

Maggie kept her face to a plastered pleasantry as she tried not to cling too tightly to Alden's arm.

She'd ridden escalators when she was little, before life had condemned her to the Academy, but unless she'd forgotten how they worked, the local mall had nothing like this.

Up and up they twisted. The glittering walls dizzying as they moved past.

The woman riding in front of them wore a dress dripping with white, purple, and blue feathers. She stepped off ten stories up, leaving the stairs in front of them clear as they continued to climb.

"All of this is powered by the pacel?" Maggie whispered.

Alden nodded.

"How did they invent such marvels?" Bertrand asked.

"Took the best of what magic had to offer and twisted it to their own purposes," Alden said. "When magicians were strong, they could fly to the tops of high buildings like birds soaring on the wind. They stole everything we had and manipulated it to glorify themselves."

Alden stepped off the stairs two floors from the top of the tower.

"Don't tell Miram what we're planning to do," Alden whispered. "She's always been sympathetic, but she's a purra. No amount of pity can change that."

"If we're not supposed to tell her why we're here, then what are we supposed to say?" Maggie asked.

Alden stopped in his tracks halfway down the curving hall.

"I..." Alden worried his lips together. "I think it's best to see how the greeting goes and move on from there."

"Great." Maggie looked over her shoulder, begging Bertrand to come up with a better plan as Alden led them to a shining red door.

Two jewel-inlaid pots of bright white flowers flanked the door.

"For the good of magicians." Alden nodded and knocked.

No sound carried through the red.

Maggie rocked back and forth on her heels as the seconds stretched on.

Finally, the door swung open. A woman with bright blond ringlets and a scarlet silk dress stood in front of them. Her eyes changed from cheerful, to surprised, to furious in the span of half-a-second.

"You," the woman growled.

"Miram," Alden's voice cracked. "You look positively radiant."

"You miserable, reprehensible—"

"Now Miram"—Alden held up a shaking hand—"remember, I wasn't the only one in the wrong. You had a proclivity for soldiers, I had a need to save the world. We couldn't have lasted forever. It's probably for the best I left when I did."

"Left?" Miram tipped her head back and laughed. "Left? What a simple way of saying *left me utterly heart broken and the sad sack of society*. People laughed at me, Alden. I despise being laughed at."

"I'm a wretch." Alden took her hand. "A horrible, worthless creature who doesn't deserve to look at you let alone touch your sweet hand."

Maggie fought to keep her eyes from rolling.

"But I've nearly been killed at least six times, there are soldiers after me, and we've got to be able to slip out of the city in good fashion, and, my sweet Miram, if you've ever cared a breath for me, please help us now. My friend's wife won't be allowed out of the city dressed in rags like she is, and you're the only one I know who might be able to save us." Sweat beaded on Alden's brow.

"You want me to help you sneak impi out of the city under the soldiers' noses?" Miram sniffed, tilting her perfectly-shaped nose into the air.

"She's a purra…and pregnant," Alden whispered. "They're striking out for lands far beyond the mountains. A purra and an impi together…" Alden's voice trailed away. "The poor child."

"By the glittering horizon, get the pregnant girl in here." Miram seized Maggie's wrist. "The last thing I need is an infant halfling's suffering on my conscience."

CHAPTER 15

"What a positively abysmal way to treat a pregnant young lady." Miram dragged a comb through Maggie's hair. "Forcing you out into the wilderness. What does that impi husband think you'll do? Spend your life in a cabin deep in the mountains? Teach your child to read by drawing in the dirt with a stick? Do you have any family in farming?"

"No." Maggie winced as Miram twisted her hair. Pins scraped across her scalp. "I've never been out of the city."

"Of course you haven't." Miram pulled free tendrils of hair to frame Maggie's face. "Why would anyone want to? A picnic can be charming, but having a guard to ward off the rammocs makes things utterly dull."

"Of course." Maggie kept her hands clasped in her lap as Miram flitted around her head, using hot irons and flower-scented spray to shape Maggie's hair.

"It really would be better if you had longer hair." Miram pursed her perfectly painted lips. "It's too late for that now, I suppose. What did you do in the city that you've...How did you meet your husband?"

"He worked for the family," Maggie said, the urge to shatter the giant mirror in front of her nearly irresistible. "He has a certain charm, but I should have known better than to love an impi." The word tasted foul in Maggie's mouth.

"I understand." Miram squeezed Maggie's shoulders. "Believe me, I do. Something about forbidden fruit. Or knowing the raw power that courses just beneath their flesh, it's an undeniable lure."

Miram stepped in front of Maggie, applying pastes and powders to her face.

"Do you know if the child is an impi or not?" Miram asked with no glee in her tone.

"No, how—"

Miram reached down, placing her hands on Maggie's stomach. "Some say you can feel it while they're still growing. A spark of unbound magic."

Maggie balled her hands into fists, waiting for Miram to let go of her.

"Maybe you're not far enough along yet." Miram snatched up a pot of deep red paste. "Or perhaps you're lucky and the child won't be born an impi. Then you can come back to the city. You and the child would be able to lead a normal life. Your husband might even be better off with a normal heir in the family. Either way, I'm sure Alden will be able to help you. He may be a scoundrel who left me broken hearted, but he is a terribly good man. I suppose that's why it hurt so much to lose him."

Miram stepped aside.

Maggie blinked at the reflection in the mirror for a moment, bewildered as to how another girl had taken her place. But the eyes were hers, even though they were lined with black and gold. The lips were hers, even though they were painted red. Her brown hair had been pinned up in an elegant twist, with ringlets framing her face, but the brown was the right shade.

"You're really quite beautiful."

Maggie reached up to touch her cheek.

"Don't fiddle with." Miram swatted her hand away. "It'll smudge and ruin the whole thing. Now, into a dress."

"Right," Maggie murmured, unable to tear her gaze away from her face.

"Something in blue, I think. Glorious but easy to move in. You'll be running across the valley, so nothing with a train." Miram took Maggie's hand, dragging her across the gilded dressing room to a wide wardrobe that took up nearly an entire wall.

Miram opened the doors, and a plethora of colors spilled out. She dug through the dresses, pulling out a sapphire gown and holding it up to Maggie before throwing it to the ground. A sky blue dress with a straight skirt and silver embroidery was the next cast off. A dark blue gown with purple sleeves flew through the air a moment later.

"There has to be something that will work." Miram flipped through more gowns. "I don't suppose you could wait for a few days. I could have Gitchem make something new."

"Any of these would be lovely," Maggie said. "It doesn't need to be anything special. I'd hate to take something too nice."

"Too nice?" Miram plucked a dusky blue dress from the wardrobe. Gray silk trim around the bottom matched the lace forming the neck and sleeves. "You really did grow up on the outskirts, didn't you? I can have another of these made in a few days' time. I could hire Gitchem to build me a whole new wardrobe." Miram held the dress up to Maggie. "A dress is only a bit of cloth at its heart, and all it takes is money and a skilled designer to make the fabric into something remarkable."

Miram shoved Maggie behind a modesty screen, tossing the dress in after her.

"Clothes are meant to be disposable. They aren't jewels or even intets. They'll be stained or ripped or destroyed by some other horror eventually. The purpose in fine clothes is to impress those around you so they go out and buy fine clothes to try and out do you. It goes on and on to wretched infinity."

Maggie undid the buttons on her purple dress and slipped into the blue silk, careful not to let the hilt of the knife strapped to her thigh catch the fine fabric.

"If you really think of it," Miram said, "all the finery in the world is just a waste of resources as we all compete to do our best impression of preening birds. But I'm rich enough that I have to spend my money on something, and it might as well be on something pretty that brings me a modicum of joy."

"Right." Maggie fastened the thin line of buttons hidden under her arm. The silk clung to her figure, but not nearly as tightly as the coarse cotton dress had. The neckline ended lower than the other dress, dipping past the point of reason. The thin woven lace climbing up to her neck was the only saving grace that allowed her to walk out from behind the screen.

"You look absolutely divine," Miram cooed. "A pair of silk slippers, and you'll be on your way."

"No!" Maggie said a bit too quickly. "No. I need to keep my boots for the journey."

A crinkle formed between Miram's pale eyebrows. "If they see your shoes, they'll know something's wrong. I don't think I've ever seen anyone in boots quite as awful as yours. You can't risk the future of your child on ugly footwear."

Maggie spread out her toes in her boots. Her precious boots. The one thing from the Academy she still had, her sturdy boots that had slogged through blood and battles and brought her out on the other side.

"I can't run through the valley in silk shoes," Maggie said. "I wouldn't be able to keep up with Bertrand."

Miram scowled, tapping her own silk-clad toes.

"I have one pair that might do." Miram opened a door on the side of the enormous wardrobe, revealing shelves upon shelves of shoes. "I wore them for a costume party. Leather, sturdy, but exquisitely made."

She pulled out a pair of heather-gray boots. Made of supple leather and lacing up to the knee in a glorious combination of comfort and beauty.

"They won't slip off"—Miram guided Maggie to a chair—"the leather should do in poor weather as well, and no one seeing those shoes would dare think you were too poor to afford privileges outside the city."

Maggie unlaced her trusty old shoes, carefully keeping the small dagger on her ankle hidden as she pulled on the new boots.

They fit like they'd been made for her, the leather flexing easily as she bounced on her toes.

"You're fit for a ball now." Miram clasped Maggie's hands. "I truly wish that was where you were going. But as one girl who's loved an impi to another, be careful, wherever your love leads you. And if it goes badly, don't bother with regret. There are a dozen people who would do anything for an ounce of love, and you're living a life full of it."

Maggie smiled, unable to speak and lie.

"Let's go impress that husband of yours." Miram tossed open the door to her grand sitting room.

Maggie gave one last look to her old boots.

Freedom for magic for a pair of shoes. Don't argue the price, Maggie.

Squaring her shoulders, Maggie followed Miram.

Three chandeliers drenched the sitting room in light. Alden and Bertrand stood all the way to the side of the room, examining a display on the mantle of the giant golden fireplace.

"Gentlemen." Miram swept toward them. "Histem has a new beauty."

Maggie followed behind, keeping her chin held high even as the feeling of being an imposter in her own skin burned her cheeks.

Alden and Bertrand spun to look at her.

Alden's eyes crinkled in the corners. "Maggie, you look absolutely breathtaking."

"Thanks," Maggie said.

"Careful, Alden." Miram swatted him playfully on the arm. "You'll make her husband jealous."

Bertrand walked slowly toward Maggie, examining her from her soft new boots, to the lace covering her chest, all the way up to the ringlets in her hair.

"Excellent, Miram," Bertrand said. "I can't thank you enough for your work."

An ember of anger burned at the center of Maggie's chest.

"My pleasure." Miram beamed at Maggie.

"We really should be going." Bertrand turned away from Maggie. "But before we go, I'd love for my wife to see your charming display."

"Oh that?" Miram blushed with pride greater than what she'd worn while pinching and prodding Maggie to perfection. "It's a miniature intet. The only one of its kind in Histem."

Maggie joined the others by the fireplace, steering determinedly past Bertrand to stand next to Alden.

Wonder stole her anger away. A miniature of the walls of Histem curved around the mantel. Built of thin metal with angles sharper than her daggers, every detail had been made to scale.

Miram reached forward and pushed a lever hidden in the side of the wall. With a *whirr*, tiny gears surrounding the gate spun to life. Slowly, the gate dropped down, receding into the mantel itself. Hollows appeared in the walls beside the miniaturized entrance to the city, three on each side that disappeared into darkness. A section of wall slid to cover each hollow as soon as the gate sank past. By the time the gate had fully opened, the walls on either side appeared to be solid and impenetrable metal.

"Amazing," Maggie breathed.

"It's a fully accurate replica." Miram pressed the lever again and the wall rose back into place. "My great-great-grandfather designed the gates. He made this to show the Regent of the time how everything would work. It's been my family's prized possession for years."

"The gate is quite a legacy," Bertrand said.

"I have books filled with his sketches as well," Miram said. "He really was a genius."

"We should go." Alden backed toward the door. "If we want to make it through your great-great-grandfather's gate and to a safe distance before the sniffers come, we have to move quickly."

"Of course." Miram's smile faded. "I wish you all weren't going out there. Hiding from the sniffers? Will you even make it through the night?"

"We have to try," Alden said. "For Maggie's baby."

"Of course." Miram looked to Maggie, her eyes glistening. "Well, best of luck to you all. Even you, Alden. You might have been an awful beast to me, but this world needs people like you. Even if I don't."

"Thank you, Miram." Alden bowed. "Be well."

He headed out the red door.

"Thank you, for everything," Maggie said.

Miram took her hand. "If your baby isn't born an impi, and you do come back to the city, come find me."

Maggie nodded and half-ran for the hall, her stomach churning at the tears running down Miram's cheeks.

Bertrand was out a moment later, shutting the door firmly behind them.

"Why the hell would you tell her I was pregnant?" Maggie whispered to Alden as they climbed onto the downward twisting stairs. "And where does she think we'd be running to anyway? You said there's nowhere to go but the Mira and a few mythical colonies no one's ever actually been to."

"Miram likes to believe there is hope for magicians without overthrowing the purra," Alden said. "That there are havens for those who wish to leave the city rather than death in the pacel or by the rammoc's claws. I told her you were pregnant because that was always her greatest worry when we were together and why she kept our relationship secret. Carrying a half-breed child would have ruined her standing in society. We needed help, and I gave her the story I knew would work."

"That's cold." Maggie shook her head, a knot of something between disgust and dread settling into her stomach.

"Her people enslaved my people," Alden said. "We left her with the memory of doing something kind and one set of finery fewer. Have we really done her a horrible wrong?"

Maggie looked away from Alden, watching the swirling walls pass by until her eyes blurred.

"It could have been worse," Maggie said when the ground floor came into view. "We could have hurt her or stolen from her. But I don't think I can take meeting anymore of your exes."

"There are none left to meet," Alden said. "Not alive at least."

Maggie opened her mouth to say, she didn't know what, but Bertrand spoke first.

"It's a pity you never formed an attachment to a soldier. It might have given us a shorter day's work."

"I might be able to see beyond purra and magician to the heart of people," Alden said, "but I would never be able to care for a person who had accepted it as their duty to torture and kill my kind."

Bertrand gave a nod, his gaze flicking to Maggie for a moment.

"And male or female, that doesn't matter to you either?" Maggie's cheeks burned as the people in the atrium stared at her.

"Of course not," Alden said. "I'm a student of medicine. Beneath the skin, everything is almost identical. And when falling in love, I prefer spirit, mind, and heart above all else. Should I choose not to love a person based on a few portions of flesh?"

Alden blinked at Maggie.

"Of course not." Maggie looped her arm through his. "It's just not the way everybody thinks where we come from."

"Hmm." Alden furrowed his brow. "Nor here, either. Lara had a fit about it."

Maggie bit her lips together and glanced at Bertrand.

"Don't pinch your mouth, Miss Trent," Bertrand said. "It ruins the illusion of grandeur. I would hate for you not to look your best when the time comes for you to repay our wager."

Maggie glared daggers at Bertrand as they emerged onto the street.

Studiously ignoring Bertrand, Maggie kept her arm looped through Alden's as they walked toward the center of the city, finally turning onto the second ring out from the library and the pacel.

A man trundled past on a four-wheeled intet. Cogs clicked together in the center of the wheels where hubcaps should have been. Handles like a bicycle took the place of a steering wheel for the driver who sat in a finely upholstered chair complete with tassels surrounding his perch.

"Glorious."

Maggie heard Bertrand, but didn't look at him. She didn't want to see his eyes wide with barely concealed wonder. Didn't want to know how brilliant he thought the intets were.

"Are you all right, Maggie?" Alden asked.

"What?" Maggie checked her bandage for signs blood.

"You're squeezing my arm rather hard," Alden said apologetically.

"Right, sorry." Maggie loosened her grip, concentrating on breathing slowly and ridding herself of the urge to punch Bertrand Wayland in his smug little face.

They rounded into the northwest quadrant of the city.

The people in this area were dressed so finely, Maggie's silk gown fit in perfectly.

Chatter and music poured out of the restaurants lining the streets. Young girls carrying fresh flowers moved from table to table, selling their blooms.

What would it be like to truly live in this world? All the money and comfort you could want.

Maggie breathed in the fresh air, her mouth watering at the warm scent of fresh baked pastries.

Rougher voices carried from around the bend. Men laughing, not caring as the noise bounced off the buildings, ruining the calm of the street.

Four men came into view, trailed by four shining nics. Each man wore a black leather suit. Thick belts held a sword and knife at their hips, but what Maggie couldn't look away from were the thick cuffs on their right arms, stretching from wrist to elbow—a golden box that took up their entire forearm with a menacing golden needle that trembled and spun like some kind of demented compass.

Alden dropped Maggie's arm, moving to walk just behind her shoulder. "Keep walking," he said in a low voice. "I'm your servant here to carry your packages home."

Bertrand stepped forward, draping Maggie's hurt hand over his elbow.

"Sniff, sniff here. Sniff, sniff there"—the man at the center of the pack let his voice ring off the buildings—"we give the impi pause."

The girls who had been selling flowers all scattered as though the man's words had been a siren.

Dropping her basket, the littlest girl ran, looking over her shoulder at the men and colliding with Maggie's side.

The girl fell onto the cobblestone street, her face twisting with fear as she looked up at Maggie.

"I'm sorry," the girl mouthed, her words not making any sound.

"You!" The men ran toward the child.

Maggie hauled the little girl to her feet, stepping between her and the men.

"There is no begging on this street," the man in the center spat.

"I'm sorry," the faint whimper came from behind Maggie's back.

The nics rolled forward, surrounding Maggie.

"*Sorry* doesn't change the law." An awful smile twisted the man's face. "I'm sorry the vermin collided with you, Miss." He bowed to Maggie. "We take our duties in this quadrant very seriously."

"I'm fine." Maggie's voice echoed through the silence that had taken over the street. "Really, no harm done."

"We'll be the ones to judge the harm." The man nodded to the nics. The one nearest her reached behind, grabbing the girl and lifting her high over its head. "It's what we're here for. No need for you to worry, just walk along your way."

The nic dropped the girl at Maggie's feet.

The man pointed the box on his wrist at the girl.

Maggie held her breath, frantically trying to think of a way to stop the man from hurting the child, sure the girl would start screaming in pain at any moment.

But the little girl didn't scream. She watched wide-eyed and trembling as the needle in the golden box quivered, pointing directly at her nose like a divining rod.

"Check her tags."

The two side men grabbed the girl's wrists, roughly pushing up her sleeves. Gold mottled her skin.

"Too bad," one of the men grumbled. "Been so long since we found an untagged one this old."

Tears streamed down the little girl's face.

"She's tagged," Maggie said, "and I'm fine. Surely you can just—"

"Impi begging is against the law," the center man said. Two of the nics grabbed the girl, twisting her arms behind her.

"Ouch!" the girl squealed.

"She was selling flowers," Bertrand said. "That really doesn't constitute as begging."

"The Regent's Justice can decide what to do with the girl."

The men bound the child's arms behind her back, leaving a long lead like a leash for them to hold her by.

"You seem like nice folks." The center man gave another twisted smile. "Go about your day and forget anything unpleasant happened. It's the will of the Regent, and her will rules us all."

Alden bowed, his head moving into Maggie's sight. Maggie sank into a curtsy, her fingers itching for her knife.

"The Regent's will will be done." Bertrand bowed.

The man kicked the girl to move. Maggie closed her eyes against the child's tears, wishing she could plug her ears to block out the soft sound of her crying.

"Come, Miss Trent." Bertrand placed Maggie's hand back on his arm, drawing her out of her curtsy.

"We let them take her." The words barely made it past the throbbing pain in Maggie's throat. "The woman at the gate and now a child. We let it happen."

"If we'd tried to fight them, we'd never have made it to the dress shop." Alden waved them down the street. "This is how it is every day. The sniffers get bored waiting to go out in the evening."

"And no one does anything?" Maggie's gaze darted around the street. She hated the woman sipping her tea, and the man eating his cake. They'd done nothing. A child had been tied up, and they'd done nothing.

You did nothing.

Maggie's knees buckled as the horror of inaction threatened to swallow her whole.

Bertrand wrapped an arm around her waist, half-carrying her down the street. "We are going to save them both, Miss Trent, and thousands of others besides. You must only be strong enough to keep moving forward. The time to fight will soon be upon us, and think how glorious the battle will feel."

Maggie took a breath, steadying her legs, reveling in the feel of the daggers hidden beneath her skirt. Sharp blades thirsting for blood. Ready to stop those men from dragging another child away.

Soon, Maggie. Soon.

A fine shop with wide windows cut through the images of golden needles and daggers racing through her mind. Maggie shook her head, willing herself into the present. Behind the store's glass, a display of dresses more exquisite than anything Maggie had ever imagined came into view.

Bodices with jewels woven into the cloth twinkled brightly. A gown with an intricately stitched design depicting the hills around the valley in sparkling thread stood next to a gown with a lace train fifteen feet long.

"I have no idea where in there the entrance might be." A frown tipped Alden's mouth. "Or if there even is an entrance. Or if we can get into it. Or—"

"Let's just go check it out." Maggie puffed up her chest and opened the shop door.

The scent of pale flowers wafted toward them. A woman sat in the corner, plucking the strings of a tall instrument, and another sat behind a long glass case. Even the warm glow of the lights gave the place an otherworldly feel, as though nothing could be, or had ever been, amiss in the world. There was nothing to any existence but peace and beauty.

"Wow," Maggie breathed.

A gorgeous woman in a lavender dress beamed as she walked

toward Maggie. "Good afternoon." The woman bowed. "I'm Angleca. How may I help you?"

Maggie glanced at Alden out of the corner of her eye.

"Maggie is about to be married." Alden bowed Maggie forward. "She's in need of a new wardrobe."

Angleca smiled sweetly as she circled Maggie, her eyes twinkling as she stopped in front of Bertrand. "Is this your betrothed?"

"No." Maggie shot a glare at Bertrand. "He's my brother."

Angleca's smile broadened. "Perfect. It would have been a pity to bring your betrothed to Gitchem's with you. You have to leave a few surprises for your husband." She spoke without looking away from Bertrand.

"Surprises are a most wonderful form of entertainment." Bertrand bowed.

"You'll be staying while Maggie shops…" Angleca's voice trailed away.

"Bertrand." He bowed deeply.

Maggie bit the insides of her cheeks to keep her face in check.

"What interesting names your parents came up with. I'd love to hear the story behind them." Angleca turned back to Maggie. "Is there anything in particular you're looking for?"

An entrance to the tunnels where the purra torture and kill magicians.

"Some gloves perhaps?" Angleca's gaze fixed on Maggie's bandaged hand.

"A bit of everything, I suppose." Maggie forced out a giggle. "Perhaps if we just stroll through, I'll have a bit more of an idea of what I'd like."

"Of course." Angleca swept an arm around the shop. "Take a moment and see what your heart desires."

Maggie gave a regal nod and stepped past Angleca, happy the shopkeeper didn't follow.

The store was small. That was something to be grateful for.

Dresses lined the sides of the space, each unique and breathtaking. Tables were scattered around the center of the shop, displaying fancy stockings, gloves, and hats. Jewels sparkled dazzlingly from a low case on the opposite side of the room.

"Take a breath, Maggie." Alden whispered as they looped around the back of the shop.

"The money for one of these dresses could feed those kids selling flowers for a year." Maggie scanned the floor and walls, searching for any sign of a hidden door.

"A cesspit of wealth." Alden paused, glowering at a mirror that hung behind two dresses with jewels dripping from the shoulders. "A disgusting display of beauty and the terrible side effect of a society where the rich care only for themselves."

Maggie stepped between the two dresses, studying her reflection.

Up close, it was easy to see the mirror wasn't set into the wall itself, but hung a fraction of an inch in front of it.

Too hard to move regularly.

Maggie kicked the base of the wall with her toe. A solid *thump* answered.

"How many dresses am I supposed to be getting?" Maggie asked, continuing her circle around the space.

A carved door nestled into one corner. A tiny lock sat right above the handle.

"A room for the shopkeepers?" Bertrand spoke right behind Maggie's shoulder.

Her heart jumped into her throat. "Don't do that."

"It might be the design room," Alden said. "Where Gitchem himself works. I've heard of people waiting on the street for hours to catch a glimpse of him."

"That would be the best place to hide an entrance," Maggie said. "What are the chances of us getting in there?"

"Zero," Alden whispered at the same moment Bertrand said, "Fairly good."

They reached the far side of the room. A golden curtain had been tied back, displaying an area with a raised pedestal and mirrors on three sides.

"Is there anything you'd like to try on?" Angleca pushed over a tray laden with deep red wine and the same leafy brew Maggie had suffered through that morning. "Everything is custom fit, of course."

"I wouldn't accept anything less," Bertrand said.

Angleca raised her eyebrow expectantly.

"Isn't there anything else you have? Something in the back room perhaps?" Bertrand poured himself a glass wine. "Her betrothed is very particular. He likes a woman with a tiny waist, and…" He furrowed his brow.

Angleca examined Maggie's waist.

Pain shot through Maggie's jaw as she bit back the string of insults she longed to throw at Bertrand.

"Fashion can do wonderful things," Angleca said. "A fuller skirt would fool the eye, but once the skirt is off, there's nothing to be done."

"She has to look right for the parties he'll be dragging her to." Bertrand's eyes twinkled. "As a personal favor to me?"

A hint of pink crept up Angleca's neck.

"If Gitchem were in today, I'd never dare it, but there are a few things in the back. I could show you if you'd like." She lifted the wine from Bertrand's hand. "No wine allowed." She glanced at Maggie and Alden. "And no crowds."

"Perfect." Bertrand winked.

She's practically purring.

Maggie let her smile slip as Angleca unlocked the door, closing it decisively behind her and Bertrand.

"Impressive," Alden said.

The woman with the harp still played blissfully, and the other waited behind the case of jewels, her eyes lit with longing as she stared at the backroom door.

"How is he going to search with Angleca clinging to him?" Maggie whispered. "This was a terrible idea. We should have just broken in like normal people."

"Potentially," Alden said, "but we might as well try and find something while we're here."

"Check the center." Maggie gave Alden a shove toward the table of gloves when he looked at her with terror in his eyes.

"Excuse me." Maggie smiled at the woman behind the glass counter. She was barely older than Maggie, but her hair had been pulled back so tightly, she had the severe look of someone twice her age.

"Yes, Miss?" The woman's face flipped into a practiced smile.

"I'm so sorry to bother you, but I have a rather odd question. See, I'm to be married soon"—Maggie blushed—"and I'd love to find a gift for my betrothed while I'm here. I know it's a ladies shop, but I have heard of men coming in here before. Is there anything special I might find for him?"

The woman glanced at Alden who had moved on to the far side of the shop, seeming to be carefully examining the hem on each of the gowns.

"We don't put them out." The woman beckoned Maggie to follow her to the dressing room. "We would hate to be thought of as that type of establishment, but…"

The woman pulled on the side of the leftmost mirror in the dressing room.

Maggie's heart flipped in her chest as the mirror moved with a click. The woman winked and swung the glass aside.

Lacy underthings hung in a lavish display. A corset with cutouts in all the wrong places took center stage, and none of the other garments were any more covering.

"Oh." Maggie searched for words as her face burned. "I don't know if that might be too much."

"We've found something perfect." Angleca appeared, holding a pale pink dress with a fluffy skirt, her hair the tiniest bit out of place and her lips far redder than when she'd entered the back room. Her gaze traveled from Maggie's red face to the open mirror. "I would suggest the corset if you wish to please your betrothed."

Bertrand stepped up behind Angleca, raising an eyebrow at Maggie.

"Maybe I should come back another day." Maggie stepped away from the wall of lace. "Really, I should think more about what I need."

"That's our job." Angleca pressed Maggie farther into the dressing room. "We'll see how much you adore this gown, then build you an entirely new wardrobe for your wedded life from there."

"Best to see how you like that gown," Bertrand said as the curtain slid closed. "I found nothing else of interest in the back room."

Angleca gave something between a snort and a laugh. "You can go." She waved the other shopkeeper out of the changing room.

Maggie shut the mirror of underthings. "I won't be needing any of that."

"You may change your mind soon enough," Angleca said. "Let me help you out of—"

"I can do it myself," Maggie said, the knives burning under her skirt. "Really, let me slip out of this, and I'll let you know when I'm ready to get into the other."

"As you please." Angleca hung the dress, primping it to perfection before slipping through the curtain.

Maggie undid the buttons under her arm, scanning the walls all the while. She dropped her blue silk dress to the floor and ran her fingers around the edges of the other two mirrors. There were no levers or hinges she could find.

Kneeling, she knocked gently on the wall under the mirror. A thick *thud* carried back. She sat on the floor, burying her face in her hands. They needed to leave. They needed to walk out of the store and come up with another idea. She'd tell simpering Angleca she hated all the dresses and Gitchem himself and storm out in a huff. They'd go back to the Asty and come up with a reasonable plan.

Maggie opened her eyes and reached for her silk dress, hating that she'd given up her boots for nothing. The dress had fallen on the pedestal in the center of the fitting room. Someone had taken the time to carve a flower pattern all around the metal base. The blooms looked almost like those of a rose, but the edges of the petals were different. Harsher in their angles. One flower's edges had been tarnished, giving the bloom a softer look. Like a thousand sets of fingers had run over the petals, wearing them down with time.

Maggie reached forward without thinking and pressed hard on the worn bloom. The tiniest *click* sounded before the pedestal rotated, swiveling away from a set of steep steps leading into the ground.

CHAPTER 17

*M*aggie leaned over the stairs. No light came from below to give her a hint of how far down the steps might lead. Her fingers itched to create a flame, anything to see exactly how magnificent her find was.

One bit of misplaced magic and it's done.

Maggie pressed the worn flower again. The pedestal didn't slide closed.

"Shit." Maggie knelt, pushing the metal platform with all her might.

"Are you adoring it?" Angleca cooed through the curtain.

"Just another minute." Planting her feet against the wall, her arms shaking, she inched the pedestal back into place. She leapt to her feet, yanking the pink dress off the wall, and shimmying into the layers of fluff.

"Would you mind fastening me?" Maggie called sweetly.

Angleca slipped through the curtain. "Oh, you look absolutely divine."

"Thank you." Maggie smiled, her heart racing out of her chest as Angleca started on the unending set of buttons. "It really is lovely."

"It wasn't even meant to be placed in the shop until next week. And"—Angleca finished the buttons—"look at that tiny little waist."

"Oh, thank you." Maggie's voice wavered. "It's just so beautiful. Like a dream." She sniffed loudly. "Could you send my brother in? I'd love for him to see it."

"Bertrand, come and see your lovely sister," Angleca called.

Bertrand stepped through the gold curtain.

If Maggie hadn't known him, she might have missed the humor that drifted through his eyes. "You look lovely, Maggie. I don't think I've ever seen you in something so fetching."

Maggie looked at herself in the mirror. Her waist did appear tiny, but only because the puffed pink skirt took up half the room, easily hanging over the edge of the pedestal.

I look like a fluffy idiot.

"I'm just so happy." Maggie covered her face with her hands. "I never thought I could ever be so beautiful."

"Gitchem's work is the only magic worth having," Angleca said.

"I'm so sorry." Maggie sniffed. "Could I have a moment alone with my brother? It's just like a dream come true."

"Of course." Angleca gave Maggie's shoulder a quick pat. "I'll pull some of the new sketches to see what you like."

Maggie peered between her fingers, waiting for Angleca to pull the curtain shut.

"I found it," Maggie whispered as the gold fluttered into place. "It's here right under the pedestal."

"Excellent work, Miss Trent," Bertrand whispered, all hint of humor gone.

Maggie stepped off the pedestal. She tried to kneel to show Bertrand the flower, but the layers of fluff surrounding her blocked the carving from sight. "We need to get Alden in here so we can slip out."

"I don't know if that will be possible," Bertrand said. "There's no one in the shop but us, and I doubt Angleca is likely to leave us alone."

"Leave *you* alone more like."

"If we all disappear, they'll know where we've gone. We'll have soldiers chasing us before can find our way to the pacel."

"Then we leave Alden behind. Have him make a scene—make it look like we've run out—and you and I go into the tunnels."

Bertrand considered for a moment, his face freezing in thought. "I don't think so. We don't know enough about the pacel to try and destroy it alone."

"And you think he knows anything at all?"

"We stay together, Miss Trent. We can't afford to separate, not yet."

"Then I guess we just forget the trapdoor I so wonderfully found." Maggie stood, smoothing out the many layers of the pink dress.

"There might be a time we can use this entrance. We need only be patient."

"Patient? We just watched a kid get arrested and did nothing. I'm going into the tunnels today."

"And how do you suggest we do that without arousing suspicion?"

"Do you trust me?"

"I travel with you, Miss Trent," Bertrand said. "I know no greater trust."

"Then it's time to get detention." Maggie took a deep breath. "How dare you!" she screamed as loudly as she could. "You promised I could have a whole new wardrobe, and now you won't pay?"

Bertrand cocked his head to the side, skepticism shaping his brow.

"This marriage was your idea." Maggie stormed through the curtain.

Alden waited on the other side, his eyes wide, his fingers picking desperately at the sleeve of his coat.

"You promised a whole new wardrobe," Maggie said. "You swore it would all be mine, and now you're being awful."

"Is everything all right?" Angleca asked, all trace of flirting gone as she eyed Bertrand.

"Nothing's going to be all right. Never, never again. I finally felt pretty." Maggie kicked Bertrand in the shin, grateful the absurd skirt was at least useful for covering her feet.

"You'll never be pretty enough to make me proud." Bertrand sneered. "You're nothing but a stain on the family. If your betrothed wishes to accept you, all the better. I'm only glad we found someone half-blind willing to take a disappointment for a wife."

"A disappointment?" Maggie shoved Bertrand, knocking him into a table of gloves. "A disappointment!"

The music stopped as the player dodged out the door and onto the street.

"You swore you'd set me up well in marriage," Maggie spat. "That was your promise, wasn't it, Alden."

"Well…I…" Alden shook his head, terror filling his eyes.

Maggie pushed him hard.

Alden stumbled toward Bertrand, knocking into the table laden with gloves.

With a sharp *crack*, the table collapsed, sending expensive silk fluttering to the ground.

"Oh no." Angleca crawled across the floor, saving the precious merchandise. "Please stop, all of you. Tell her how lovely she looks, Bertrand."

"I can't stomach such a lie," Bertrand said.

"A lie!" Maggie shrieked, grabbing the carafe of red wine. "You hateful monster."

Maggie tossed the scarlet liquid at Bertrand, letting the remnants drip on her skirt.

Angleca whimpered.

"I will not be paying for that," Bertrand growled. "You ungrateful, hateful beast. I'll not pay a cent for anything you've ruined."

"Well, you've never given me a cent to my name, brother," Maggie said, "so I suppose no one will be paying for anything today."

Angleca burst into tears.

The door to the street slammed open. The girl behind the jewel case fell to the floor with a squeak as Angleca curled up in a ball on the floor sobbing and five soldiers ran into the shop.

"This is all your fault." Giant tears streamed down Maggie's face. "And this was meant to be such a happy day."

The soldier at the front of the line stopped short, his gaze darting between the hysterical Maggie, the wine drenched Bertrand, and the terrified Alden. "What seems to be the problem?"

"He was supposed to pay—" Maggie wailed over Bertrand's "That ungrateful little—" while Alden shook his head in terror, squeaking, "I'm so horribly sorry."

The soldier held a hand in the air. "Quiet. Quiet!"

All three fell silent.

"All of you are coming into custody."

"They've done so much damage." Angleca pushed herself shakily to her feet.

"Send a tally to the prison," the soldier said. "I think all three will do well with a little time to calm down."

A soldier took Maggie's shoulders so gently she almost laughed.

"If you please, sir." The first soldier pointed Bertrand toward the door.

"This one's an impi." A reedy looking soldier pointed to a hint of gold glimmering from Alden's wrist where he'd torn the sleeve of his long coat.

"He's a servant," Maggie said. "Meant to carry my new wardrobe home. At least that's what I had in mind when we brought him here, before my wretch of a brother ruined everything!" Maggie wailed loudly, forcing fat tears to slide down her cheeks.

But tears didn't stop the soldiers from looping rope around Alden's wrists or from kicking him behind the knees when he failed to walk as the soldier holding his leash headed toward the street.

"They have to pay!" Angleca wailed. "If they don't, I'll be ruined!"

"Send the papers to the prison," the first soldier said. "There's nothing else I can do for you."

Maggie kept her eyes on Alden as she let the soldiers lead her out of the shop.

The knife in her boot could cut through the ropes binding Alden. The one on her thigh could stop the soldier who held her shoulder from smirking.

Not yet, Maggie. Not yet.

"Keep it nice and calm, Miss," the soldier steering her said. "I'm sure we can work this out just fine."

"Please don't punish poor Alden." Tears slid down Maggie's face, dripping black from her eyes onto her dress. "It's my brother who should be whipped. Alden would never have been so horrible to me. My brother is the real beast."

"The Regent's Justice will decide who's to be blamed for what," the first soldier said. "But you"—he jabbed Bertrand in the arm—"had better be prepared to pay well for the damages done at Gitchem's. The Justice can be very forgiving as long as one is willing to pay for their transgressions."

And was born a purra.

"I am more than willing to pay for my sister's indiscretions to save myself from humiliation," Bertrand said, "as long as she understands that generosity will not be extended again."

Their party reached the library. Maggie held her breath, hoping against reason the soldiers would swing the doors wide and usher them in for punishment. But the men guided them east toward a shining silver building.

Maggie blinked at the glittering structure, convinced her eyes had somehow forgotten how to see. Surely the palace didn't begin six feet off the ground. She blinked several more times, forcing her mind to come to a more logical conclusion.

The palace had been raised above the ground by a thick wall of stones that blended perfectly with the cobblestone streets. The silver of the walls seemed to grow from the stones themselves, as though the palace actually extended down into the ground and far out of sight.

A wall four stories tall blocked the palace proper from view, but four turrets with conical roofs peered over the barricade.

I'm Cinderella. Dressed to go to the ball and standing at Prince Charming's gate.

But as the road swept up toward the gate, the soldiers veered them aside, cutting south along the cobblestone portion of the wall.

"Please," Alden whimpered. "Please. I'm so sorry." His face had turned an awful mottled red, and his hands trembled so badly his leash shook.

"I've no time for the apologies of impi." A soldier shoved Alden toward the wall.

Maggie flinched, expecting Alden's face to meet stone. But the shadows swallowed him whole.

Maggie opened her mouth to scream, but the soldier behind her lifted her by the elbows, ushering her into the darkness.

"What are you doing?" Her pulsed raced. She blinked, her mind working frantically to make sense of the darkness around her.

"No, please!" Alden's wail carried from the left as Bertrand's, "Easy now. I'll not fight you," carried from the right.

"Just this way, Miss."

The ground under Maggie's feet was smooth and firm, like well-carved marble. The scent of damp minerals flooded the air. Her eyes adjusted to the black. A dull gleam of light carried from a recess in the ceiling, just bright enough to make out the gray stone walls, but not enough to see more than a few feet ahead.

Bertrand's lace collar floated in front of her like a faint beacon in the distance.

"Stay calm and quiet and you'll be out in a few hours." The soldier steered her down a side passage away from Bertrand. "Bringing in upstanding citizens like you is the worst part of our job. Please, make it easy on yourself. Be sorry and polite and you'll sleep in your own soft bed tonight."

Murmurs of voices carried from the shadows. Doors hid in the gray of the walls, nothing more than vague shapes looming in the darkness.

A *creak* reached Maggie before the door came into view. A slab of stone made mobile with metal bars crisscrossing a window at the top.

"Someone will be here soon."

Maggie didn't have time to think to ask how soon *soon* might be before hands pushed her through the opening and the door swung shut behind her.

She blinked in the darkness. The one weak light overhead barely illuminated four plain walls and a straw-covered cot tucked into the corner. She pressed her face to the bars, searching the darkness as footsteps clomped away, leaving Maggie alone in the tunnels.

CHAPTER 18

"Things could be worse." Maggie slipped the knife out of her boot. "I've got a semi-reasonable grasp on how magic works here even if I'm not supposed to use it." She dug the tip of the knife into the crack of the door, running the blade along the seam. "I've got two knives." Her blade hit the lock. She moved the knife beneath, testing the thickness of the bolt. "Sure, there's a two-inch piece of metal keeping me trapped behind a stone door and I'm dressed like a fairy princess, but let's look at the positive."

Maggie stared at the door. If she were on Earth, she could flip the lock with a simple spell. If she were in the Siren's Realm, she could wish the lock open.

"How is magic that likes to electrocute giant birds going to get you out of this one, Maggie? Don't bother trying to figure it out, because you can't risk it anyway."

Low voices carried from far down the hall. If she were Bertrand, she would lure them over and convince them they just had to let her out for some farfetched reason only Bertrand Wayland would be able to think up.

"Well, you're not Bertrand." Maggie paced the length of her cell. The dim light was maddening, glowing like a light bulb desperate to give up its fight against the darkness.

"Damn." Maggie reached under her skirt. "Damn, damn, damn." She cut away the bottom most layer of fluff. The oddly light material felt like nothing in her hand. A flammable puffball, meant to help her look beautiful.

"You're going to get yourself killed, Miss Trent." Maggie articulated each word in her best Bertrand impression. "You've never looked so well as you do, looking nothing like yourself, Miss Trent."

Maggie grabbed the straw-covered cot and dragged it toward the center of the room, directly under the light. She loosened her boot enough to shimmy the leather sheath free and wrapped the layers of fluff around the end.

"This is the second worst idea you've ever had." She climbed onto the cot, aimed the end of the sheath at the light, turned her head aside, and stabbed.

A *crack* and a *hiss* sounded as shards of hot glass struck Maggie's arm. Holding her breath, she looked to the sheath. Flames licked the fluff, and heat washed over her hand.

Maggie jumped off the bed and tossed the fire onto the straw mattress.

"Help!" She tore off another chunk of her dress and wrapped the blade in silk. "Fire! There's a fire! Please someone help me!"

She shoved the knife back into her boot as heavy footfalls charged toward her cell.

Maggie ran to the bars, clinging to the metal. "Please someone help me! There's a fire."

"What happened?" A soldier barked, peering past Maggie to the ever-growing flames.

"There was a funny sound coming from the light," Maggie coughed. "I pushed the bed under it to see what was wrong, and the whole thing exploded." Maggie held up her bleeding hand. "Please. I need help."

The soldier fumbled with the keys on his belt before wrenching the door open. He grabbed Maggie by the arm, yanking her into the hall as two more soldiers charged into the cell. Both men stared at the flaming cot in wonder.

"Don't just stand there," the first soldier shouted. "Get some water."

Maggie swayed on the spot, waiting for the two soldiers to reach her, before swooning and tumbling onto them both.

"Is she ill?"

Maggie kept her eyes lightly shut, willing her limbs to stay limp as they laid her out on the floor.

"You go get water, and you get a doctor."

"Does she need a doctor? Maybe we should just put her in another cell."

"Put her in another cell? Do you see how well dressed she is? It'll be all our hides if we let anything happen to her."

Maggie breathed slowly, keeping herself from smiling.

The stinging scent of smoke drifted into the hall.

"Well, we can't leave her here. I'll carry her down to the heldie and make sure she keeps breathing."

Arms looped under Maggie, lifting her easily into the air. Maggie let her arms hang behind her, careful to let her head flop away from the soldier, opening her eyes just enough to watch their path as he carried her down the hall.

"Is she hurt?" Bertrand shouted from his cell. "Is there something wrong with my sister?"

Maggie wanted to wink, or nod, or do anything to tell Bertrand she was all right and he could stop screaming, but she couldn't move enough to send a signal without risking the soldier's notice.

Voices echoed down the hall, carrying from her former cell,

but the soldier walked on toward a light slicing through the darkness up ahead.

Lights far brighter than the one Maggie had demolished peered out of an open door.

"What's going on?" a gruff voice said as the soldier carried Maggie into the room.

"A fire. You'd know that if you were sober enough to care. Get down the hall and help, would you?"

The *thud* of stomping feet faded down the hall as the soldier laid Maggie down on something hard that smelled horribly of bitter alcohol.

Two options: lay here and hope he leaves, or pretend to wake up and flirt with him so he'll take you on a walking tour of the tunnels.

The sound of water splashing came from the corner of the room.

You've never been good at flirting. It wasn't necessary at the Academy. Working with a captive audience doesn't require much effort.

He laid a cool cloth on Maggie's head.

He seems nice and fairly determined to make sure you're not dying, which means he'll probably stay with you until you wake up, so there's no point in lying here pretending to be Sleeping Beauty.

A hand trailed up Maggie's ribs. Fingers draped over her breast.

Option three.

Maggie kicked as high as she could, catching the soldier in the face. Her eyes sprang open as he grunted. Not caring about the inevitable pain, she punched him hard in the nose.

The soldier stumbled back. "What in—"

Maggie swung again, feeling her stitches tear as she hit his face.

"You evil little monster." The soldier held his hand up to his nose. "I don't care how much money your family has, you'll pay for this." He charged forward, grabbing Maggie around the middle and knocking her back onto the table. A glass bottle fell sideways with a *thud*, rolling toward Maggie's head.

Maggie grabbed the bottle, bringing it down over the man's skull with a satisfying *crash*. Foul smelling liquor and glass rained over her as the man slid off her and onto the ground.

She leaned against the table, panting, waiting for the soldier to get back up, or worse, for some of his friends to come charging in.

Her heart rate slowed as the seconds passed.

"Keys." Maggie kicked the soldier over, kneeling on his chest as she searched him. A leather pouch hid a thick ring of shining keys, at least twenty with no distinguishing feature to assign them to cells. "Just great. And what am I supposed to do with you?"

Maggie contemplated the unconscious soldier. There was no giant wardrobe as there had been in Miram's room. Only the wide table at the center of the chamber, chairs scattered about, and a smaller table in the corner strewn with food that looked beyond the point of edibility, bottles of liquor like the one Maggie had smashed, and a pitcher of water.

"I really hope you're a drinker." Maggie hoisted her skirt up, balling it around her waist. Blood trickled from the soldier's head and nose. "And maybe a guy who likes to get into fights, too."

She grabbed him under the arms, dragging him to the back of the room and leaning him against the stone wall. Snatching a random bottle from the smaller table, she wrenched the cork out with her teeth, dribbling half the bottle down the soldier's chest before setting the rest by his hand.

"I really hope you get court-martialed for this."

She brushed out her skirt and palmed the keys as best she could. The soldier had left the door to the hall open wide enough for Maggie to peer through the crack. There was no one in sight, only the ruckus still going on down the hall.

I wish I had a soldier's uniform.

She eyed the passed out groper slumped against the wall. They would know something was wrong if they found him without pants.

"Next time I get shoved in a gown, it'd better be black."

Maggie inched out into the corridor, waiting for someone to yell or tackle her. She made it five feet from the door, then ten, creeping back in the direction of Bertrand's cell.

Get Bertrand out, then figure out how to save Alden. And the little girl. And the rest of the magicians.

A figure moved in the darkness up ahead.

Maggie froze, too far from the door to run back to the room, too pink and fluffy to hide in the shadows.

She yanked the knife from her boot as the figure ran toward her. "Don't you even try and touch me."

"Miss Trent?"

"Bertrand?" Maggie stepped toward the voice, her knife gripped tightly in her hand.

"Miss Trent, are you all right?" Bertrand's features emerged from the darkness as he stepped forward to meet her, paying no attention to the blade in her hand.

"I'm fine," Maggie said. "I was coming to save you."

"But I saw a soldier carry you past my cell." Bertrand's brows pinched together. "You were unconscious."

"I was faking it." Maggie shook her head. "I lit my cell on fire so they'd let me out and pretended to faint so they'd help the damsel in distress."

"You couldn't have just batted your eyelashes at them and begged to be taken someplace more humane? It would have saved me a few moments of extreme anxiety."

"Sorry, I've never been one for flirting. I don't think I've ever batted my eyelashes at anyone, and, as you made so utterly clear, it's not like I look pretty enough in this mess of a dress for anyone to want to flirt with me anyway. Let's just go save Alden, okay?"

"Absolutely." Bertrand bowed Maggie down the hall.

They crept forward, Maggie's hand sweating as she gripped her knife.

"For the record, Miss Trent," Bertrand whispered. "You do look abominable in that dress, and the blue silk wasn't much better. You look your best in your clothes from the Siren's Realm. You belong with your hair wild and your arms bare while running off on an adventure. You're not the type to be primped for beauty. Rather, beauty chases your wildness and hopes to attain its match."

"Thanks." Maggie took a shuddering breath.

"And you really should have tried flirting before fire. You've caused an awful commotion."

"I was trying to get to you and Alden. And I do have the cell keys, you know." Maggie held up the ring of keys.

Bertrand gave a *hmm*.

"And how did you get out anyway?" Maggie slowed as they neared her former cell. Flames no longer flickered up ahead, but the stench of smoke burned her nose.

"I used magic to open the lock."

"I thought we weren't supposed to use magic until we reached the pacel?"

"I was under the impression you were dying, Miss Trent. It seemed time to make an exception."

"Thank you."

A *rumble* of voices carried from up ahead.

"I don't know how the damn light went bad. I'm a soldier, not a light maker."

"Well, if this one sparked a blaze, is the whole place going to light up?"

"We should report to the captain," a third voice spoke. "These prisoners aren't to be harmed. We can't risk anyone burning to death."

"I'm not going to be the one to tell that bastard anything," a fourth voice chimed in.

Maggie tiptoed forward, wincing at the swishing of her skirt.

The soldiers were all in her cell. They hadn't left anyone in the hall while they dithered on about what to do with a broken light.

Maggie clutched the ring of keys. Either she'd be very right, or very very wrong.

She leaned into Bertrand's ear. "You slam, I'll try and lock."

Bertrand shook his head. "Other way around."

Without waiting for Maggie to ask how he was going to secure the door. Bertrand ran forward.

"Shit." Maggie lifted her skirt, tearing after him.

A dim light crackled from his hands, pulsing with every foot-fall. He dodged to the near side of the door, keeping out of Maggie's way as she slammed it shut.

"Move!" Bertrand shouted, laying his palms on the door.

Maggie leapt back, plastering herself to the wall, as magic shot from Bertrand's hands.

The metal of the lock melted, stretching through the stone, flowing into the wall to form a solid molten river.

Shouts echoed inside the cell as bodies battered the door.

Bertrand let go of the magic, and the metal faded instantly from orange to black. He raised his hand to the bars that blocked the window. The furious face of a soldier peered out at them, but the bars morphed, forming a solid sheet of metal that blocked the man's face from view.

Bertrand stepped back, his shoulders heaving as he panted.

"That was a lot of magic." Maggie watched the last of the heat fade from the metal.

"It was." Bertrand fluffed his collar. "Despite the ineptitude of these men, we can only assume more soldiers will be along shortly."

"Then let's find Alden and figure out how to get to the pacel."

Maggie took two steps down the hall to where Alden had disappeared before stopping. "Unless you think it's time to split ways?"

"I don't think either of us would ever be able to forgive ourselves if we left Alden in the hands of these murderers."

"Right." Maggie lifted her skirt and jogged down the hall. "Alden first, then the rest of the magicians."

CHAPTER 19

The sweetness of fresh air wafted over them as they crept past the opening to the outside. The door was smaller than normal and set two feet off the ground as though the people entering and leaving the tunnels hadn't been a consideration in their construction. Shadows of soldiers blocked their view of the street beyond, swords drawing long lines at their sides. Maggie held her breath and tiptoed until the light faded from view.

Bertrand stayed in front of her, moving silently through the darkness. He glared back at Maggie as her dress swished with every step.

"I don't know what you want me to do," she whispered. "You're the one who picked this monstrosity."

"Fair enough."

The tunnel swept downhill. The air gained moisture as the corridor became narrower and any pretense of lighting the hall disappeared.

"We can't search for Alden in the dark." Maggie trailed her hands along the walls, searching for breaks in the stone.

"There isn't anywhere to search yet," Bertrand said. "Wait until we need to see."

Need to see. Is there ever a time you don't need to see?

Goosebumps coated Maggie's bare shoulders. A hundred sets of eyes could be watching her and she'd never know.

A minute ticked by, then another.

"Shouldn't we have met some soldiers by now?" Maggie asked.

"Don't question good fortune."

"But where is everyone?"

"I'm sure we'll find out when things go horribly wrong." Bertrand stopped short.

The knife slipped from Maggie's hand as she ran into his back, tripping on her skirt and landing on her butt in a sea of fluff.

"The tunnel branches off here," Bertrand said.

Maggie felt around on the ground, searching for her knife. "Which way do we go?"

"Quiet for a moment, if you please."

Maggie froze, her fingers wrapped around the hilt of her knife.

Soft footfalls carried away from her, first in one direction then in another.

"This way." Bertrand's hand found Maggie's good wrist, and he helped her to her feet. He didn't let go as they turned off their path and down the passageway to the side.

Maggie slowed her breathing, ignoring the dull stink that tainted the air, and tasted the world around her for magic, willing the energy that flowed through every inch of her to find its like in the darkness. She felt nothing but Bertrand. "How do you know this is the right tunnel?"

"It smells worse down this way," Bertrand said. "People tormented and left to rot until their magic is drained by the pacel—it's bound to leave a stink in the air."

Maggie shivered, hating herself for betraying her fear as

Bertrand whispered, "Don't let the darkness frighten you, Miss Trent. You need only remember you are the light."

Maggie's heart seized as a person spoke up ahead.

"Please, kill me. If you're going to do it, let it be done."

Not Alden. That isn't Alden.

A thick queasiness swept through Maggie's stomach, washing away her moment of gratitude. Someone in the darkness was begging to die.

Bertrand started forward again. A hint of light played on a curve in the tunnel ahead, casting shadows that grew clearer with every step.

A big man holding something large in his hand. Bertrand hugged the wall. His features drifted back into being as they neared the light.

"Your turn for the pacel hasn't come yet," a rasping voice said. "You need to keep your strength up. It's your place to serve the Regent, and you've got to be strong to do it."

"No, please."

A whimper followed the *splash* of water striking stone.

"Lick it off the ground."

Bertrand leaned close to Maggie's ear. "We need that uniform. Unharmed."

"Wait here, and be ready to stop him."

Maggie stepped past Bertrand and rounded the corner, not waiting for him to argue.

A man stood in front of a door made entirely of bars.

He was as tall as Bertrand but fatter around the middle, like he'd enjoyed far too many drinks in his abominable life. The soldier held a bucket in one hand and a torch-like light in the other.

"Excuse me," Maggie said sweetly.

The man turned to face her, his eyes moving from disbelief to amusement in a moment.

"I'm so terribly sorry, but I'm lost." Maggie stepped forward, studying the torch in the man's hand. A bright sphere balanced on the end of a thick stick, but the light wasn't made of flames. It simply glowed like a magic wand.

I've found my fairy godmother.

A laugh slipped from Maggie's lips.

"What are you doing down here?" The soldier tipped his head to the side, leering at Maggie from beneath crusted eyebrows.

"I guess you haven't heard," Maggie said. "There was a fire up above where my cell was. They let me out and told me to run from the flames. But I think I went the wrong way. I've no idea where I am, and I'm sure they'll be looking for me soon. I don't want to get in trouble for being in the wrong place. I was only meant to be held for a few hours. It was a simple misunderstanding with my beastly brother."

"You shouldn't be down here." The soldier stepped forward.

"I know that, sir." Maggie took a step back. "I'm only trying to find my way back above."

"They're going to flay whoever let you wander this far." The soldier tossed his bucket aside. The *clatter* of wood against stone filled the tunnel as it rolled down the hall.

"The soldier who told me to run, he said he was going someplace called the heldie, I believe, and he just left me." Maggie let the corners of her mouth quiver. "Oh please help me, sir. I'm just so afraid."

"I'll take you up to the captain myself." The soldier smiled. It wasn't a pleasant expression. "I'm sure he'll be thrilled I returned a high ranking prisoner. Someone else will be taking impi duty for a while. This way, Miss."

The soldier bowed and stepped around Maggie. Shadows danced on the wall as she rounded the corner. Maggie barely glimpsed the black of Bertrand's sleeve and the glisten of his dagger as he knocked the soldier on the head with the hilt of his blade.

As the soldier crumpled to the ground, Maggie leapt forward, grabbing the torch from his hand.

"Nice." Maggie held the torch low, examining the man's head. A faint trickle of blood spilled from him temple.

"See to the door, if you please." Bertrand tossed Maggie the key ring.

Maggie had noticed the shortness of the barred door to the cell—she hadn't realized the cell ceiling was far too low for a person to be able to stand. The three-foot cube looked more like a kennel for a medium sized dog than anyplace a human should be.

"Please don't hurt me," a man whimpered from the back of his cage.

Maggie had to blink several times to make out the man's face. His beard and hair had grown into one giant, matted mass. A thick layer of dirt covered his face, tainting his skin with the same filth that covered his clothes.

The purra are monsters.

"It's all right." Maggie leaned the torch against the wall next to the cell and knelt, fitting the first of the keys into the lock. "We aren't here to hurt you. We're going to let you out."

"Out?" The man cowered at the back of his cage.

"Yes, we're going to let you out so you can run away from here." Maggie tried the fourth key on the ring.

"To go to the pacel." The man nodded.

"No, not to the pacel," Maggie said, trying the tenth key. "No one is going to make you go to the pacel."

"The pacel is the only way out."

"Not today." Maggie tried the thirteenth key.

"Those keys won't open the door to take me away." The man crawled forward an inch. "The key to open my door is black and heavy. You can't feed me to the pacel without that key."

Maggie finished trying the last key on the ring. "Do you know who has the black key?"

The man shook his head. "They showed it to me when they locked me in. Said when the time came for mercy the black key would bring me to the pacel."

"No luck?" Bertrand dragged the half-naked soldier around the corner. He'd already pulled on the bulky uniform, his heavy coat beneath filling out the baggy spots.

"These keys don't work down here," Maggie said.

"Pity." Bertrand dropped the soldier and placed his hands on the lock.

His eyebrows curved in concentration for a moment before the lock turned.

"How did you do that?" Maggie swung the door open, letting Bertrand shove the soldier through.

"Magic here works excellently on metal," Bertrand said. "How do you think this city was formed?"

"You're magicians?" The prisoner gasped.

"We most certainly are," Bertrand said. "Head up this tunnel and turn right at the dead end, that will lead you to the street. There are two soldiers standing guard, but I don't know of any other exit. Do be careful. I doubt our antics will go unnoticed much longer."

The man stared at them, his gray teeth poking from his open mouth.

"Move quickly please, if you don't mind. Your cell has a new resident."

The man crawled toward the door, his eyes darting between Maggie and Bertrand as though waiting for them to attack.

Maggie reached for his hand as he inched through the door. The man flinched as though she'd hit him.

"Are there more magicians down this way?" Maggie dropped her hand to her side.

The man pushed himself to his feet, his legs shaking. He tried to straighten up but only managed to rise as high as a half-bow.

"I don't know how far they take them, but they come past here."

The man leaned on the wall, watching as Bertrand closed the cage and tripped the lock back into place.

"Was a man brought by a little while ago?" Maggie asked. "A man in a long black coat with wild looking hair."

The man shoved himself away from the wall, wobbling as he moved up the tunnel. "They dragged him past. He was screaming dreadfully, kicked a soldier in the knee. Should have known better than to do that. They'll take him straight to the pacel. He'll be dead before the bruise blossoms on the soldier's leg."

Maggie grabbed the torch.

"Allow me." Bertrand took the torch from Maggie, grabbing her arm with his free hand.

"What are you—"

"I doubt we will go unnoticed for much longer, Miss Trent." Bertrand led her down the hall, keeping half a step ahead of her as though he were dragging her. "If anyone sees us, the best story is that I am a soldier and you are my impi prisoner."

"An untagged impi?"

"We can only hope they don't look too closely."

"At least I'm not supposed to be a damsel in distress who's pregnant or getting married this time."

"Despite your loathing of the role, your helpless beauty has proven quite helpful today."

Maggie opened her mouth to say *thank you,* but the words faded away.

Another short door had been cut into the wall. Maggie coughed at the wave of stink wafting through the bars.

Please don't let there be a person in there.

Bertrand walked forward, actually dragging Maggie behind him.

"We have to see if someone's in there." Maggie tried to yank her arm free.

"There was."

"Then we have to go back."

"It wasn't Alden." Bertrand didn't slow his pace.

"It doesn't matter, it was still a person."

Another cell came into view.

"We can't open each of these cells, Miss Trent. It would slow us down and draw too much attention to our position besides."

"What if they decide to take out our destroying the pacel on the magicians stuck in here?"

Bertrand gave the inside of the cell a glance before dragging Maggie forward. Maggie peered into the shadows that filled the cage, trying to burn the dark eyes that gazed back at her into her memory.

"We cannot allow the freedom of a few individuals to distract us from destroying the pacel. Not when there are generations at stake."

A faint murmur of voices carried from up ahead as another cell came into view. This barred door faced another on the wall opposite. As the torchlight spread down the corridor, more cages came into view, stretching out of reach of their light.

"How many people are down here?" Maggie asked.

"Far too many tortured souls to allow a decent society's conscience peace."

The murmured conversation between cells stopped as Bertrand and Maggie passed, peering through each barred door.

Men and women huddled in the cells.

"Forgive me," a woman murmured as Bertrand glanced into her cage. "Forgive me. I did not mean to offend."

Sour flooded Maggie's mouth as they moved past each cell, searching for Alden.

"What if he isn't here?" Maggie asked. "What if they did take him straight to the pacel?"

"Then we find the pacel."

They reached the end of the row. The walls on either side were solid rock once more.

A clicking sounded, and metal tinging against metal bounced off the walls. Murmurs followed the strange noises.

Maggie tucked her knife hand into the folds of her skirt, hiding her blade.

"I'm sure you can manage it if you only keep trying," a voice whispered. "Don't give up."

Bertrand slowed his pace, holding the torch high overhead.

"I know I never trained you for this sort of thing, but I never really saw the need."

The torchlight glinted off dull metal. A teardrop-shaped body and head with a dozen metal prongs poking at a thick lock came into view.

The nic's head swiveled, its one bright eye finding Bertrand and Maggie. The nic whirred, retracting all its arms. If an intet could look guilty, this one did.

"Who's there?" a voice whispered.

Maggie stepped past Bertrand toward the undersized, well-worn nic.

"Nic?"

"Maggie?" Alden's face appeared between the metal bars.

"Alden." A weight she hadn't realized was there lifted from Maggie's chest.

Alden's face was bloody and bruised, but he was very much alive.

"How did you find me?" Alden asked.

"I followed the rancid stink of captivity. Move your hands, if you please." Bertrand placed his palms on the lock.

"How did Nic find you?" Maggie patted the intet on the head.

"I told you, he's attached to my tags," Alden said. "He rolled up about ten minutes after they tossed me in here. I thought maybe he could get me out—those arms of his should work well as lock picks—but neither of us has any experience."

The lock clinked.

"Lucky for you, Bertrand is a quick study." Maggie yanked the door open.

"Thank you, Miss Trent." Bertrand turned to Nic. "Do you know where the pacel is?"

Nic tapped his chest.

"That usually means yes," Alden said, "though it's not always consistent."

"Can you lead us to it?" Bertrand asked.

Nic purred and trundled down the hall.

Alden scrambled out of his cage and to his feet.

Bertrand ran down the hall after Nic.

"Come on," Maggie said.

"I thought you would leave me here to rot." Alden stared at the point where Bertrand had disappeared into the dark. "You could have. I wouldn't have blamed you."

"We're here to help people. You're people. Now let's go."

Alden nodded and loped into the darkness.

CHAPTER 20

*T*ink. *Tink.*

"I don't think he really understood what we were asking for." Maggie leaned against the wall, catching her breath after the long sprint through the darkness.

Tink.

"He does seem to know where he wants to go." Bertrand frowned, watching Nic bounce off the stone wall again and again. "It's the getting there the fellow seems to be having trouble with."

"Why is there even a tunnel here?" Maggie asked. "We ran for what, ten minutes? I'm in a big dress, but even with that slow down, we've still gone nearly a mile."

"If we were heading straight for the library, we would have found it by now." Alden dabbed at the blood on his face with his sleeve.

Nic whirred, his many arms coming to life to scrape against the stone.

"Okay." Maggie pinched the bridge of her nose, wishing Nic would be quiet for even a few seconds. "Let's say this is the pacel, or the passage right below the pacel. Can we tunnel up?"

Bertrand held the torch close to the wall, running his fingers over the stone. "I could collapse the tunnel, and we could shelter ourselves with a shield spell."

"But?" Maggie said.

"I would have no way of keeping the cave-in from spreading, or of limiting the damage aboveground," Bertrand said.

"If we weren't stuck in a dark tunnel that smells like rotting rat, it would almost be nice to hear you say you can't do something." Maggie closed her eyes.

We're where we want to be but can't get where we need to go.

"Why would there be a tunnel here if it doesn't lead to the pacel?" Maggie said.

"The tunnels were built beneath the city long before the purra took control," Alden said. "Some say as a prison for purra, but we've already seen the tunnels are too lengthy to be properly guarded and the cells ill spaced to have been built for prison purposes only."

"Those who don't agree with the tunnels being built as a prison," Bertrand said. "What do they believe was their original purpose?"

"An insurance policy of sorts," Alden said. "An escape route in case of purra attack. A spider web of tunnels, if you will, leading from all the places of Convocation power to points outside the city."

"Bertrand, do you have the map?" Maggie asked.

"The tunnel has been curving, Miss Trent." Bertrand unfastened his black soldier's coat to reach his pockets beneath. "There's no way to know which direction we've been going. Nic might be directing himself to the pacel a quarter mile away."

"But the tunnel has been used." Alden peered up at the ceiling. "And often, too. There aren't webs hanging down past head height. Someone's kept the spiders from spreading."

"We can't go back the way we came." Maggie dug the heels of

her hands into her eyes. "It's a miracle we haven't been stopped by anyone yet."

"You've ripped your stitches." Alden fumbled in the pockets of his coat.

"I'll be fine." Maggie didn't fight as Alden began unwrapping her hand. "We have to keep going."

"I agree." Bertrand squinted at the map. "Though it is worrying."

"What is?" Maggie asked.

Alden spread goo on her hand. "I should redo the stitches."

"I'd just rip them again," Maggie said. "Bertrand, why is it worrying?"

"What could be down this way that is worth traveling to if not the pacel?" Bertrand asked.

"The bank, the Academy," Alden said.

Maggie's stomach knocked into her heart.

Wrong Academy, Maggie. Wrong Academy.

Alden wrapped Maggie's hand in a fresh, pale blue bandage. "There aren't many buildings left in Histem from the Convocation's original construction of the city. Only the grandest and most important buildings survived."

Nic stopped banging on the wall. His body rotated so he could stare down the corridor instead.

"I have a really terrible feeling about this," Maggie said.

Alden held carefully onto her fingers.

"What do you mean, Miss Trent?" Bertrand asked.

"If this tunnel isn't going to magically spiral us up into the library, then it's going somewhere else," Maggie said.

"That would appear obvious," Bertrand said.

"And they bring prisoners down this way," Maggie said. "There's no other reason this tunnel should be so well traveled."

"That's true," Alden said. "I called to the others up the way from me. They said no one but soldiers and magicians ever came through."

"Where would they be taking them if not to the pacel? Why else would you risk moving prisoners?" Maggie's question hung in the air.

Even Nic turned his eye to stare at her.

"I believe we've tarried here long enough." Bertrand started down the tunnel.

Nic looked to Alden.

"We have to keep going," Alden said. "There's no other path to follow."

Nic tapped the wall again before trundling after Bertrand.

"How wide is the city?" Tension crept into Maggie's shoulders as they walked away from Nic's wall.

"Approximately three-and-a-half miles," Alden said.

"So little space to hold so many people," Maggie said.

"And so much hidden beneath it," Alden said.

They walked on in silence for a while. The tunnel sloped downward, carrying them deeper into the ground.

Maggie quickened her steps, walking closer to Bertrand's heels.

"I'm sorry," Alden said.

"Sorry for what?" Maggie asked.

"That you came to our world. That you found me. That you're wandering blindly through tunnels."

"It's what we do."

A sound echoed through the tunnel in front of them.

Before Maggie could tell Bertrand she'd heard something, he stopped walking and reached down to block Nic's path.

Maggie leaned in close to Alden's ear. "What is that?"

"I don't know." Alden's lips brushed against her ear.

The sound rumbled through the floor—a constant *hum* of churning just ahead of them.

Bertrand raised a hand, beckoning them all slowly forward.

Maggie tapped the sword hidden at Alden's hip.

His eyes widened, but he reached under his coat, pulling the blade free.

Bertrand stopped, reaching behind to give Alden the torch and taking the sword from him.

Alden's shoulders relaxed the moment the weapon left his hand.

Maggie inched in front of him, digging through layers of fluff to free her second dagger. The grinding stopped. Maggie froze, the sound of her rustling skirt suddenly loud beyond belief.

Gritting her teeth, she let her skirt fall slowly to the floor.

With a scowl, Bertrand started forward again.

Voices carried from up ahead. An angry man speaking to someone, and a frightened voice replying.

Maggie tapped on Bertrand's shoulder, pointing to herself and then holding up one finger. Bertrand shook his head, laying his hand on his uniform.

Maggie nodded, keeping tight to Bertrand's shoulder as they moved closer to the voices.

"If you are incapable of success, the Regent will find someone else to do her work." A man growled.

Maggie could picture the sneer on his face. He sounded close enough she should be able to see him, but there was no light coming from up ahead.

"I've been trying," a terrified man answered. "You need to give me more time. Why would you expect me to be able to do in a year what others failed to accomplish in a decade?"

A door came into view, ending the tunnel.

A long and ancient handle waited for them on the worn, wooden door.

Bertrand gripped the handle as Maggie pressed herself against the narrow piece of wall beside it, squishing her skirt up behind her.

Alden stood in the center of the hall, torch held high, sweat dripping from his brow.

With a nod, Bertrand wrenched the door open.

Bright light burst into the tunnel.

"I'm so sorry to interrupt the two of you," Bertrand said, "but I'm afraid it's rather urgent."

"Urgent?" the frightened voice asked.

"Who in blazes do you think you are?" the angry man growled.

"There's been a breakout in the impi cells." Bertrand strode into the room and out of sight. "I need to secure this space, and both of you, of course."

"A break out?" the frightened man said.

"Indeed," Bertrand said. "We feel it would be best to keep you both in here until we hear from the prison. Is this door secure?"

"Well, yes, but—"

"Wonderful," Bertrand said. "Then the rest of the party can join us."

Maggie stepped through the door, a knife gripped in each hand. Nic bounced off her calves as she froze in the doorway.

Whatever she had thought they might find, this wasn't it.

The room was twelve feet tall and four times as wide. The walls were lined with books, charts, and jars with things floating in them that looked horribly like human organs. A table with metal loops and leather straps running along the sides, as though to bind victims down, took up the center of the space, with a smaller table filled with saws, scalpels, and knives close by.

I've walked into Frankenstein's laboratory.

"Miss Trent, would you mind seeing to the tunnel door?" Bertrand stood next to two men. One in a long black coat, and one dressed in fine, colorful silks. The tip of Bertrand's sword kissed the neck of the larger, silk-clad man.

"Sure thing." Maggie stepped into the laboratory, letting Nic and Alden follow her in before slamming the door shut.

Alden swayed on the spot, his face paling to gray.

"Just breathe," Maggie whispered.

She turned to the door. A simple, if heavy, slide lock was the only thing to bar the exit. Maggie slid the lock into place and laid her palm on the bolt.

The metal held a slight hum in it. Almost like what she would expect a flower or a tree back home to possess. Carefully, she pushed a bit of her own energy into the metal. Heating it. Willing it to stretch across the door and block any soldiers from breaking through. The metal glowed, lengthening across the wood to form a solid bar.

"That's impossible," the black-coated man whimpered.

"If you believe that to be impossible, this is going to be a very trying evening for you," Bertrand said. "Well done, Miss Trent."

"Not too hard." Maggie shrugged.

"Who are you, and why do you dare to barge in on the Regent's business?" the big man demanded.

"I believe the more important question to be, what is this place?" Bertrand said.

The big man didn't answer.

"You." Maggie stepped up to the man in the black coat, aiming one dagger at his face and the other below his waist. "I think you should answer."

"I-it's a laboratory," the man stuttered.

"What do you use the laboratory for?" Maggie asked.

"Performing postmortem studies," the man said.

Alden whimpered.

"Postmortem studies on who?" Maggie asked.

The big man laughed. "If you don't know where you are, why bother to be here?"

"I wouldn't laugh when Bertrand's got a sword to your throat," Maggie said. "He might sound calm, but just below the surface is a hell of a temper."

Bertrand pressed the point of his sword to the man's throat. A drop of blood slid down the man's neck, staining his silk collar. The man didn't flinch.

"Who are you doing autopsies on?" Maggie asked the black-coated man again. She stepped closer to him, feeling his ragged breath on her face.

"The impi from the pacel," the man said. "It's all in the name of science."

"Science?" Alden spat, grabbing a scalpel and charging toward the man. "You torture magicians. You use them to power your pointless intets and then chop them up. Why?" The scalpel trembled in Alden's hand, its point an inch from the man's eye.

"T-to learn."

"Specifics," Maggie said.

"The effects of the pacel on different specimens." The man closed his eyes against Alden's blade.

"Don't call my people *specimens.*"

"I'm trying to help them." The man quivered.

"Help them by cutting them up and putting them in jars?" A hateful bitterness flooded Maggie's mouth.

"I only work on those who have already been ended by the pacel."

"*Ended,*" Bertrand said. "How funny the phrases we use to avoid the true words for death. You cut up the dead, killed by the pacel."

"Yes." The man dared to open his eyes, looking toward Bertrand. "I study the dead."

"Why?" Maggie said. "You know how they died. You killed them."

The big man laughed.

"Don't you dare." In two steps, Maggie was by his side, running her blade along his cheek. A line of blood blossomed across his flesh, and the man finally flinched. "Make a sound without our asking you, and I'll give you a matching scar on the other side." She turned back to the man in the black coat. "Why are you studying the dead?"

"To…" he glanced around the room as though hoping for a sudden savior. "To learn how we can prolong their service to the pacel."

CHAPTER 21

Maggie swallowed the bile that soared into her throat. "Prolong their service to the pacel?"

"Explain," Bertrand said. "Succinctly."

"T-the pacel has different effects on different cun—"—the black-coated man glanced desperately around the room—"magicians. Some magicians can only survive one service."

"Don't you dare," Alden said.

"They can only survive being connected to the pacel once," the man said. "Others can survive for weeks. The longest recorded is thirty-four days."

"Thirty-four days of torture," Alden said.

"And you're doing autopsies to figure out why some can last longer?" Maggie's hands throbbed as she gripped her daggers. "You want to have more time to hurt them?"

"No!" The man shook his head, freezing in place as Alden's scalpel neared his eye. "The legends of old seem to imply magicians had an infinite supply of magic. Which should mean they could send that energy into the pacel everyday with no effect on their lifespan. It's not the draining of the magic—it's the process that's killing them. I'm studying the dead in hopes of creating a non-lethal method of feeding the pacel."

"So you can trap people for years at a time," Maggie said. "Make them spend their whole lives locked up serving you. That doesn't sound like mercy."

"The people used for the pacel are criminals," the man said.

"Every magician is a criminal when the crime is being born." Alden's quiet words stilled the room.

"Impi become criminals when they go against the will of the Regent," the big man growled.

"Alden was present while Miss Trent and I made a fuss in a shop," Bertrand said. "They left him in a cage. Would he have been sent to die in the pacel?"

"If the soldiers deemed him guilty of contributing to a disturbance, then yes," the big man said.

"Then we are not speaking of punishment for crimes. We are speaking of genocide," Bertrand said.

"I have no place in any of that." Fearful tears slid down the doctor's face. "I do only as I am ordered, and I work only on the dead."

"Then why are there straps on the table?" Maggie pointed to the metal and leather straps with the tip of her dagger. "Why tie down corpses?"

"I—" the man's gaze darted around the room. Sweat joined the tears on his face. "I-I'm not the only doctor to use this laboratory. My r-research has led me to believe the method of tagging is at least partially to blame for the destruction of the subjects."

"For the murder of magicians," Maggie said.

"Yes, that," the doctor said. "The placement and scarcity of the tags seem to be the deciding factor. The other doctors have been working on finding different ways to tag to cause less damage."

"That's why the tunnel has been used." Numb anger replaced Maggie's burning rage. "They bring them here to be experimented on before shipping them to the pacel. And you don't see how evil all of this is?"

"And your people did nothing to ours?" the big man laughed. "Generations of impi lounging in comfort, watching us die. Doing nothing to save a starving child. Sitting in their palaces as rammocs ravaged whole villages. Is murder by complacency so much better than murder by design?"

Maggie opened her mouth but couldn't find the words.

"We aren't here to right centuries-old wrongs," Bertrand said. "We are here to save magicians from extinction. How do you transport the newly tagged magicians from here?"

"Do not assist the enemy," the big man said.

"I-I—" the doctor began.

"I'm really sick of your stuttering," Maggie said, "and I can't take another excuse for why you think killing innocent people is okay. I don't think you're blameless, and I have no problem cutting off your fingers or just plain gutting you. So who are you going to listen to—the girl with the knife or the guy she already used it on?"

"The cart tunnel," the doctor said. "It's through the door and past the bank vaults. We put the impi in the cart and bring them to the pacel. Once the tags are placed, they tend to be unwilling or unable to move of their own accord."

"What do the tags look like?" Alden asked.

"There are diagrams." The doctor pointed to a stack of papers on the bookshelf.

"Bertrand," Alden said, "would you mind doing something with the bleeding one. We won't need to take him with us."

"Of course." Bertrand bowed.

Alden hurried to the bookcase. "Where is the metal kept?"

"I don't know what you think—"

"Tell me where the metal is or Maggie will cut off your right thumb." Alden grabbed the stack of papers.

"Press the bottom corner of the bookcase." The doctor tucked his hands behind his back.

The big man hit the ground with a *thud*.

"Have you killed him?" The doctor trembled.

"No," Bertrand said. "I don't believe in murder."

Alden pressed the bottom of the bookcase. A drawer slid free.

If Maggie hadn't recognized the sparkling metal as a tool of oppression and murder, it might have seemed like a treasure chest, casting its twinkling light across the room.

"Maggie"—Alden chose a few pieces of metal—"I need you to trust me."

"Trust you with what?" Maggie kept both her daggers pointed at the doctor.

"I'm going to stick some of the metal to you so you look newly tagged," Alden said.

"You're not blocking my magic. How am I supposed to help you without it?"

"I won't insert them into your skin," Alden said. "It might feel unpleasant, but it won't block your magic, and you'll be able to take them off."

"Why don't we put them on you?" Maggie asked. "You've already got tags."

"I'm dressed as a doctor. I can enter the tunnels." Alden patted the chest of his long black coat. "Bertrand is dressed as a soldier. You have to be the magician."

"Can't I steal his doctor coat?" Maggie jabbed her dagger at the doctor.

"We need him to guide us." Bertrand stretched the metal of the table to the floor, encapsulating the big man. "Besides, whoever is guarding the cart might recognize him."

"Oh they will, they will." The doctor nodded.

"I really don't like this," Maggie said.

Bertrand took Maggie's place, sword to the doctor's heart.

"It will only take a moment." Alden took Maggie's hand, leading her to the table.

Maggie lay on the metal. The surface still radiated the heat of Bertrand's magic but held firm beneath her.

"There's really no other way to do this?" Maggie said.

"This is for the best. We're too far in. The only path left is forward, whatever the cost." Alden fumbled the papers in his hands. "It can't be more than we've already paid."

Maggie stared at the ceiling, ignoring the clinking of metal on metal as Alden laid out the pieces of gold.

"If you need to take them off, just pull at the corners." Alden pressed a piece of metal to her chest right above her heart. "It will hurt, and it may take off a few layers of skin, but the metal will pry free. Pardon me." He reached down her dress, adding another piece to the bottom of her sternum and one over her left breast.

A prickling heat stung Maggie's skin under each piece of gold. Like a conduit pulling her magic to the surface, keeping the energy hovering on those bits of skin.

"*Inexuro.*" The flames formed in Maggie's hand as easily as ever, but the power of the magic buzzed beneath the gold.

"Miss Trent—"

"It's fine." Maggie gritted her teeth against the sting that cut down to her bones, and let the fire disappear. "I'll be fine."

"Don't forget her wrists," the doctor said. "I-I only mean she would have to be marked there as well."

Alden chewed his lips together.

"Just do it," Maggie said.

She waited patiently as Alden stuck tiny bits of gold to her wrists. A constant buzzing like nails on a chalkboard scratched under her skin.

Alden took a step back, squinting at her wrists.

"Do you feel your tags all the time?" she asked.

"I have no idea," Alden said. "I've had them since I was ten days old. I have no concept of being free of the tags."

Maggie sat up, the buzzing staying with her through the movement.

"Are you ready?" One tiny crinkle hovered between Bertrand's eyebrows.

"Let's go save some people," Maggie said.

"If you betray us in any way, we will be forced to kill you, and I will not consider it murder." Bertrand pressed the tip of his sword to the doctor's chest. "We will also have to kill everyone you inform of our disguises, and I make no guarantee your death will not be horribly painful. Do you understand?"

The doctor nodded.

"Miss Trent, your daggers." Bertrand guided the doctor to the door.

With a sigh, Maggie replaced the daggers under her skirt. "Why don't they search prisoners here anyway? Shouldn't they check for weapons?"

"It's the comfort of domination," Bertrand said. "The cat never checks the mouse for poison."

"Touché." Maggie fluffed her skirt.

"Might I suggest," the doctor said, "Miss Trent should not be moving of her own accord. The actual insertion of secondary tags leaves most too weak to walk."

"Don't call me *Miss Trent*. It sounds weird." Maggie scanned the room. "Is there a stretcher or something I should be riding?"

"They usually just drag them," the doctor said.

"Next time, I get to be the soldier." Maggie sat on the ground.

Alden tucked the torch in the sword sheath under his coat and grabbed Maggie's arms, dragging her toward the door. "Am I hurting you?"

"It's fine." Maggie half-closed her eyes as Bertrand swung the door open.

"Lead us directly to the cart tunnel." Bertrand's sword hung casually at his side.

Alden dragged Maggie out of the laboratory. Her skirt caught on the doorframe, tearing a tiny scrap loose.

Angleca would have a fit.

Nic shut the laboratory door and kept close to the toes of Maggie's gray boots, his one eye fixed on Alden's back.

At least the floor is smooth, Maggie thought as they entered the hall.

Bright lights had been recessed into the polished stone ceiling. Voices carried from up ahead. Steady, normal voices with no hint of anything outside routine conversation.

Shining metal bars took the place of the stone walls. Maggie let her head fall to the side and her eyes slide open. A gasp escaped her before her mind could think through what she was seeing.

The metal bars weren't trapping prisoners, but blocking thieves from the mounds of gold and jewels locked far behind. Numbered vaults, some as small as the cages that held the magicians, others as large as the laboratory, lined the hall, which seemed to go on forever.

One corridor holding the enormous wealth of Histem.

Shouldn't the doors be solid?

"Afternoon," the doctor said.

Maggie snapped her eyes shut as they passed men speaking in low tones.

Why are they standing in a tunnel of riches casually chatting?

Maggie filed the question away with a dozen others as they turned out of the vault corridor. Her feet hit the side of the doorway. She opened her eyes a slit.

Nic whirred disapprovingly at Alden.

"Sorry," Alden murmured.

The stone in this hall was as rough as the tunnel they'd already escaped, though well-lit and much wider.

"Good evening, Doctor Wilhelm," a man's bright voice spoke.

"Good evening." The doctor's voice wavered.

"Are you heading to the library?"

"Yes, actually."

A *clunk* and a *hiss* sounded. Maggie closed her eyes, willing herself not to twist her neck to search for what could be making the sounds.

"Haven't seen you accompany a live impi before," the bright voice said. "Have you switched your research?"

"I, um, want to see for myself how this pattern of tags works," the doctor said.

Alden dragged Maggie forward.

"I have a feeling this could be a very interesting night," the doctor said.

"We should be moving along, Doctor Wilhelm," Bertrand said.

The doctor murmured a response Maggie couldn't hear.

Arms shook as they lifted Maggie, carrying her a few steps before laying her down again. A hand cradled her head, guiding it to the ground.

"Why is this one dressed so fancy?" the bright voice laughed. "One of the big men get tired of his mistress?"

Energy crackled in Maggie's hands. She squeezed her fists to hide her magic.

"Something like that," Bertrand said. "Got herself bumped to the head of the line."

"No nics near the pacel, doctor," the bright voice said.

"Of course," Alden said. "I'm so excited about the tags, it slipped my mind. Wait here for me."

Nic whistled a low note.

The man laughed. "Well, best of luck with the new tags."

With a bump and a *squeak*, the floor under Maggie began to rumble. A grinding sound, loud enough to shake Maggie's teeth, began a moment later as the floor lurched forward.

"You're all right." Alden squeezed her shoulder.

Maggie opened her eyes.

They were in a cart with two benches. Bertrand and the

doctor sat up front while Maggie lay across the back with Alden perched by her head. The horrible grinding noise came from the gears of the cart, which drove the metal wheels along the track.

"Did you know about this?" Maggie lifted her head enough to peer over the edge of the cart.

"No," Alden said, his voice barely audible over the grinding gears and whipping wind as the cart picked up speed. "The magicians would never have made anything like this. The purra must have built it to carry materials for the pacel."

The lights had been placed far enough apart that darkness swallowed the cart before brightness flashed again, never allowing Maggie's eyes to adjust.

The lights flashed on.

The doctor held a lever in his hand as though controlling the speed.

Darkness covered them as Bertrand pressed a knife to the side of the doctor's neck.

The lights flashed on, and the cart began to slow, the doctor shrinking away from the blade.

Darkness swallowed them as Bertrand spoke. "Do not forget, I will gladly kill you if you betray us."

The lights flashed on.

Words had been carved into the wall.

The education of the masses is the greatest power under the sky.

Darkness came again, but a bright light shone up ahead.

"Get down." Alden pressed on her shoulder.

"Do not forget your role," Bertrand said.

The grinding dulled as the cart slowed to a shuddering stop.

"Doctor Wilhelm." Another man spoke as though they'd never left the vaults at all. "How are you this evening?"

"F-fine, just fine," the doctor said. "I'm eager to try this one in the pacel. I believe it might be the breakthrough I've been waiting for."

"Funny to see you in a cart with a live one," the man said.

Alden lifted Maggie, holding her close to his chest. The thudding of his racing heart pounded against her ear.

"A special occasion," the doctor said.

Maggie opened her eyes just enough to peer through her lashes as Alden carried her forward.

His breathing came in quick gasps.

Breathe, just breathe.

She wished she could whisper the words.

A high wooden door swung open in front of them. Bertrand and the doctor blocked the room ahead from view.

Bright light bathed the space, glittering off of shining metal walls.

A faint *hum* pulsed through the air like a heartbeat resonating through everything. The tags on Maggie's skin amplified the *hum* like a shock of electricity with each crescendo.

Men in black soldier's uniforms flanked the door, closing it as soon as they passed through. The thumping of heavy boots came from all corners of the space.

How many soldiers are there? Move, Bertrand.

As if he'd heard her thoughts, Bertrand stopped, blocking the doctor's path with his hand. Alden stepped up next to them, his whole body shaking.

Maggie couldn't think about bracing herself against a fall, or if her eyes had drifted too far open.

The towering machine in front of them blocked all other thoughts from her mind.

The pacel.

CHAPTER 22

*I*t's beautiful.

The absurdity of the thought frightened Maggie more than the thing itself.

They stood before a wall of gold so thin, the light pulsing behind it cut through the metal in a dazzling pattern. Like a sunrise bursting across a sky, or the dancing northern lights turned gold, or…

The magic of thousands of magicians sucked up into a machine.

Sour shot into Maggie's mouth.

"Doctor."

Maggie snapped her eyes shut as a man spoke.

"Have you brought some new food for the pacel?"

Alden stopped shaking. His arms clamped around Maggie like a vice.

"Well, I-I wouldn't say"—the doctor coughed—"I have a new pattern of tags I'm very eager to try."

"Good thing for you we've just had some slots open up," the man said. "Seems like a bad batch we've had lately. Rumors are going around that the pacel is starting to lose strength. All the bits that sit in her belly are breaking up after so much use."

Alden moved forward

Maggie opened her eyes a slit.

"I think they've got it all wrong." The man walked two steps in front of them as he spoke. His shoulders were broad, displaying a golden cog stitched on the back of his uniform. "It's not the pacel that's gone bad, it's the impi. Like breeding animals in darkness. Each generation will get smaller and weaker until the best of them is no larger than a runt."

"Indeed." The doctor glanced toward Bertrand.

Bertrand kept his eyes ahead, on the towering wall of gold.

"East lot today." The soldier cut to the right, past the golden wall.

As soon as they passed the pacel, the ceiling dropped down, cutting them off from the grandeur of the room. It was easy to imagine how the building had looked as a library.

The pacel would have been the grand entryway. There had probably been a painting or a tapestry hanging on the large wall—something to display the wealth and greatness of the magicians.

Where the soldier ushered them would have been a corridor leading to rows of bookshelves, where normal magicians could come and peruse the learning accumulated by generations.

There were no books left in the library now. Doors had been haphazardly cut into the polished wood. The few in front of them were dark, but farther down, the doors radiated the same bright pulsing light as the pacel.

"We can toss her in this pod if you like." The soldier grabbed the handle of a glass door, twisting it sideways before swinging it open. "It'll be easy to keep an eye on her."

"That would be—" the doctor began.

"We'd like to go farther down," Bertrand said. "You know how competitive the doctors can be. We wouldn't want someone else claiming credit for this."

"Fair enough." The soldier chuckled. "The Regent's bound to

reward whoever can figure out how to make the impi last longer."

They moved past the first few dark doors.

Maggie let both her eyes slide open as they reached the glowing pod. At first, it seemed like the wall of the pacel, the light within shining in a pattern that made no sense. But the darkness in the pod had shape—arms splayed out to the side, chained to the wall. A head of dark hair, covering the magician's face. Chains wrapped around the magician's chest, holding her up.

Maggie sank into Alden's arms.

Terror stole the heat from her limbs. She should be fighting, driving her knife through the soldier who laughed at the magicians in the pods. Chopping off the doctor's hands so he would never be able to cut an impi again.

Holding helplessly still, letting Alden carry her past more pods, was almost too much to bear.

An old man with veins so blue, it looked as though someone had traced them on with a marker.

A little girl who couldn't have been older than ten, her braids messy and crooked.

A man with broad shoulders and a bald head, his eyes darting behind lids.

"How's this?" The soldier stopped at a dark door.

"This will be fine." The doctor cut up questioningly at the end of his sentence.

"If you wish," Bertrand said.

"I can help you with her." The soldier reached for Maggie.

"We can do it on our own." Alden twisted away, keeping Maggie out of the soldier's grasp.

"We'll get her in," Bertrand said. "As you know, the Regent's reward will be great."

The soldier paused for a moment.

Maggie shut her eyes tight.

The soldier chuckled. "Too fair. Well, when you give up on doing it on your own, give a holler."

Heavy bootfalls thudded away.

"Lay her down," Bertrand murmured.

Hands cradled her head as Alden lowered her to the floor.

"We need to get rid of him," Alden whispered. "We won't be able to work with him hovering around."

"I quite agree," the doctor said. "I think it's high time for me to leave."

"You take one step, and I'll gut you." Maggie opened her eyes.

The doctor winced.

"You'll have to put her in the pod," the doctor said. "They can see us, and there would be no reason to delay."

"Tell us how the pacel runs." Bertrand leaned down, making a show of squinting at the bits of gold stuck to Maggie's wrists.

"That information cannot be divulged —"

"I don't think you appreciate your position," Bertrand said. "You will cooperate, or we will kill you."

"I could scream," the doctor said. "The library is filled with a dozen soldiers."

"Good," Maggie said. "I'll start with you, then kill all of them."

The doctor paled. "These are highly trained soldiers under the Regent's command."

"Then it'll be fun," Maggie said.

Bertrand glanced at Maggie for the barest moment.

"Tell us how the pacel works," Bertrand said, "or I will not stand in Miss Trent's way."

"I don't suppose it matters if I tell you, there's nothing anyone can do to harm the beast." The doctor worried his lips together. "It's a system of relics from when the impi were in control. They used to make objects that held magic within them. They built the things magic can be funneled into—they did that themselves. We only figured out how to use that stored magic as a power source for intets."

"And how to drain the magic out of people," Maggie said. "You kill people to power machines to make your life easier."

Maggie's heart raced as the *thrum* of the pacel vibrated in her chest.

Magic. Magic pulsing through every bit of her. The magic of uncountable dead.

"Where is the heart of it?" Bertrand said, stepping behind Maggie and out of her line of sight.

The urge to stand up or at least turn her head curled Maggie's toes.

"There is no heart," the doctor said. "It's all one. Every relic is as important as the others."

"Do you need help hooking that one up?" The pounding of boots thundered up behind them.

"Yes," the doctor said. "We need to get her in right away."

"We can manage on our own," Bertrand said.

"I won't hear of it," the doctor said.

"You're right." A smile sounded in Bertrand's tone. "You did promise to show me the pacel. I'm sure Alden can stay and be sure she's placed properly."

"W-well," the doctor said.

"Come along," Bertrand said. "We've all got promises to keep."

"I'll chuck her in." Hands grabbed Maggie's wrists.

"I can lift her," Alden said.

But the hands didn't let go.

Breathe, just breathe.

Maggie didn't know who her thoughts were trying so hard to calm. She let her head flop backward as they dragged her over the ledge and into the pod. Hands lifted her under the arms. Hot chains looped around her chest, binding her to the wall. Metal wrapped around her wrists, stretching her arms out to her sides.

"I think we should wait for Doctor Wilhelm to turn it on," Alden said. "It is his project, after all."

"If he wanted to see it, he would have stayed."

Pain whipped Maggie's cheek as a hand slapped her.

"Wake up." A pain shot through her other cheek.

Maggie fluttered her eyes open.

A balding man with bad teeth stood in front of her, his hand raised to strike again.

"I don't see how this helps power the pacel," Alden said.

"It's the best part." A smile curved the balding man's lips. "You have to see the look in their eyes when it starts."

The man backed away, reaching toward a golden switch near the door.

"You get to see them as they are. Caged animals. Do you want the honors?" His gaze flicked to Alden.

Alden's eyes darted from the man to the switch, then to Maggie. He reached for his waist where the torch lay hidden beneath his coat.

"Just do it." Maggie met Alden's gaze.

Alden kept his eyes locked on Maggie's as he fumbled for the switch.

The golden lever moved easily. No hesitation or effort to stop the pacel from working.

The balding man shut the door.

The metal around the pod began to glow. Starting at the bottom, like the promise of a beautiful sunrise. But the glowing didn't stop—it crept up the walls, the pulsing of the pacel growing every moment.

The balding man's mouth moved, but Maggie couldn't hear his words over the horrible *hum*.

The light reached her waist, climbing up toward the chains that bound her. The links vibrated with every pulse. Sparks leapt from the walls to the chains, lighting them with an invisible fire.

Heat seared Maggie's wrists and cut through her dress to her ribs as the chains began to glow. Maggie swallowed her scream. She would not give the man on the other side of the glass the joy of watching her pain.

She set her jaw as fire flooded her chest. Tunneling into her lungs, racing through her veins. The heat filled every inch of her, burning away every thought but the need to not scream.

But the fire didn't stop once it had filled her. It flowed back out of her chest and her wrists, doubling the heat of the chains and the brightness of the walls.

The man laughed and patted Alden on the shoulder.

Tears glistened in the corners of Alden's eyes.

Maggie shook her head.

Do not give in. We will not break.

The agony of someone tearing out her veins through the gold on her wrists and chest blurred her thoughts. Alden's face faded from view, leaving the other side of the glass blank. A void with nothing to track the seconds by but pain.

The heat of the chains had become insubstantial—a buzzing fly next to the magic dragging itself from her soul, lighting the wall, thrumming with the pulse of the pacel.

No.

Not the pulse of the pacel.

Her pulse.

The pulse of the others locked in the horrible machine. There were others still alive. Still suffering.

Maggie squinted into the light. Searching for a brightness she might recognize as her own magic, for a pattern that might be someone else's.

The darkness between the light took shape as she stared at the wall, the humming breaking through her thoughts with each pulse.

Something in the wall. Long and pointed.

A sword.

Wrapped around the tip. Wide and thin. The edges fluttering, buzzing with each beat. Fabric. A cloak.

Attached to a spear. Joined with a wheel. Bound to a shimmering rope. Strung through a ring. Melded to a crown.

The relics of an entire magical civilization, spun into a web. Feeding off the descendants whose ancestors had forged the treasures.

Maggie let her head drop. The bits of metal on her chest danced with light, stealing her magic. But this wasn't the Siren's Realm. Here, the well of her magic ran deep, and had no end.

She wrapped her hands around the chains that bound her wrists, not flinching as the heat of the metal burned her. Willing her magic past the tags, she fed it into the chains. Twisting the links, letting them drip from her hands like melted butter.

The light in the pod faltered. The humming faded enough to allow her mind more than one fractured thought at a time.

She grabbed the chains that bound her chest, shattering the gold like glass. She brushed the dust off her gown as the lights dimmed to nothing.

The blisters on her hands stung as she pulled the daggers out from under her skirt. The skin that bordered the chunks of gold stuck to her chest flaked away, leaving black sooty patches beneath.

Maggie held the tip of the dagger to the largest chunk, ready to pry it away. But magic crackled from her fingertips, unhindered by the worthless flecks of gold. Every heartbeat she wasted was an eternity to those still trapped in pods, feeding the purra's beast.

She reached toward the door, her fingers finding smooth glass where a handle should have been.

"Of course you don't want to let me out." Maggie's voice crackled. "Smart."

Pressing her palm to the glass, she trickled her magic through the door. The metal dripped to the floor in the hall beyond, forming a pool of gold.

The hatch released. Fresh cool air flooded her prison.

Hands shaking, she pressed the door open just enough to peer into the library.

There was no sign of Bertrand or Alden.

They left you to suffer.

Maggie shook her head, batting the thought away.

We're not here for me. A few minutes' pain is a worthy price to stop this.

Soldiers milled around by the great wall of the pacel, but her section of the library was empty.

Maggie slipped out the door, careful to step over the pool of liquid metal, and shut the pod behind her.

Carved niches and shelves where books should have lived filled the wall opposite the pods, forming a corridor that angled away from the center space and provided shadows to hide in.

Maggie gripped her daggers. The need to stop the soldiers from inflicting one more second of torment battled with the more reasonable want to destroy the pacel itself. Maggie darted across the hall and into the shadows, not looking behind until she'd pressed her back against the wall.

"Where are you, Bertrand?"

He'd led the doctor away. He wouldn't have done that unless he had a reason.

"Alden." Maggie squinted into the shadows. He'd left her as well. He wouldn't have gone without a reason either. She shut her eyes, thinking back through the pain to where Alden had disappeared.

He'd left with the bald man, gone farther down the hall.

Taking small steps to keep her skirts quiet, Maggie started down the corridor, stopping every few feet to listen.

The *hum* of the pacel, the *thump* of heavy boots, and the *rumble* casual voices came from behind.

Bertrand hasn't started the chaos yet.

The voices faded as she crept farther down the corridor. Pods were still cut into the walls, but the doors were dark. If all the pods were filled, there would have been nearly a hundred magicians being slowly killed in this hall alone.

Maggie swallowed her anger as sparks tingled her fingertips.

Were all the magicians in Histem this powerful once? Did magic course through their veins barely hidden by their flesh?

The purra are right to be afraid.

She stopped again, listening hard though the voices from behind had been swallowed by the pulse of the pacel. There was a new sound though. Like an animal sniffing.

A smaller hall intersected the corridor up ahead.

Maggie tiptoed forward, pressing herself against the wall.

The sniffing didn't stop. A faint whimpering joined the sound.

Holding her breath, Maggie peered around the corner.

A pool of blood stained the floor, blossoming around the head of the balding soldier. Alden knelt just outside the puddle, clutching his torch. The light from the sphere perched on top flickered feebly through the cracked and blood-stained glass.

"Alden." Maggie slipped around the corner. "Alden, are you okay?"

Alden looked slowly up at her, blinking as though confused as to what she, Maggie, might be.

"Alden, what happened?" Maggie reached for the torch.

Alden followed the motion of her hand, his eyes widening as they fell upon the bloody object in his grasp.

"He wanted to kill you," Alden whimpered. "He said he'd have fun taking you out of the pacel for the night if you lasted that long. I couldn't let him touch you."

"It's okay." Maggie lifted the torch from Alden's hands and laid it on the floor. "I'm okay. You're okay. Everything is going to be okay."

Alden shook his head. "No. We're not going to be okay. We're going to die." He touched Maggie's cheek with trembling fingers. "None of us will survive this. Destroying the pacel is suicide. That much magic will not fade gently. I've known that from the start. Everyone in the Mira knew. They sent us here to die, and I never told you.

"I led you all the way here knowing we would die. Willing to let you get yourself killed for a fight that has nothing to do with you. I'm a traitor, and now I'm a murderer." He looked back at the man on the floor. The pool of blood had spread, reaching his knees and the hem of Maggie's dress. "I killed him because I couldn't let him kill you. But I was willing to let you die. I'm no better than he is, than any of them are."

"Alden, we're not going to die." Maggie put a dagger in his hand and dragged him to his feet. "We're going to destroy the pacel and get out of here."

"It's impossible." Alden looked down at the dagger in his grip. "To stop the pacel forever the whole thing would have to be obliterated. No one would survive that. Everyone in this building will die. Us included."

"So says you." She took his chin in her hand. "You don't know me, and you don't know Bertrand. Don't tell me what we can't do."

"You'll die." A tear trickled down Alden's face. "We'll all die. I deserve it. I betrayed you, but I can't let you suffer for the sins of this world. You have to go, Maggie. Take Bertrand and go."

"Do you think I could walk out of here knowing the pain the pacel causes, knowing the evil of the purra, and just jump back into the Siren's Realm and pretend everything is great? Do you really think that's the sort of person I am?"

"You have to be," Alden said. "It's the only way you'll survive."

"Life isn't just about surviving. It's about making living worthwhile. And if that means you have to fight, or kill, or even die, so be it. Better to go out doing something that matters than live a long life of nothing."

Alden tightened his grip on Maggie's dagger. He stared at the blade for a long moment before nodding. "Better to mean something."

"Right." Maggie smiled and brushed the curls off Alden's forehead. "Now take a breath, and let's go beat the bad guys."

Alden took Maggie's hand, pressing his lips to her fingers.

"If the end should come, please know how very sorry I am to have led you here, and how utterly grateful I am to have met you."

"Me, too."

Maggie twined her fingers through his and inched out toward the pod corridor.

The *hum* of the pacel buzzing through the gold on her flesh kept her heartbeat on edge, but it was nothing to the racing of Alden's pulse as his hand shook in hers.

"We have to find Bertrand," Alden whispered, his shoulder pressing into Maggie as they crept along.

"He'll find us," Maggie said.

"How? He thinks you're still in the pod."

"Easy. I make a scene no one can ignore." Maggie smiled, her shoulders relaxed, and her grip on her dagger eased so she could feel her fingers. The time for action had finally come. No more waiting, no more plotting. Time to fight.

I can do this.

Letting go of Alden's hand, she allowed sparks to trickle down into her fingertips.

"Alden, I need you to trust me and do exactly as I say." She rubbed the sparks together, forming something of substance, crackling and glowing like lightning made miniature. "Go to the cart—"

"I won't leave you."

"You aren't leaving. You're my exit plan. I'm not giving up on all of us making it out of here, but we're going to need that cart. Get there, get it ready, and don't let anyone else take it."

"But I—"

"I'll make sure no one's watching the entrance to the tunnel. Bar the door if you have to." They reached the end of the hall. "Move quickly."

She threw the shard of lightning at the pacel. A ringing carried from the golden wall as though she'd struck a gong.

Circles of light scattered from the tiny black scorch mark left by the spell.

Every soldier turned toward the pacel.

"Run, now." Maggie stepped out into the open, another bolt of lightning forming in her hand.

Alden's footsteps pattered behind her.

She tossed the second bolt, hitting right above the soldiers' heads.

The man nearest screamed and staggered back.

Maggie laughed, reveling in the sound echoing over the throb of the pacel.

"Did I scare you?"

Everyone in the room turned to face Maggie. The man straight in front of her stepped aside, cowering behind his fellows, leaving Maggie a clear view of her reflection in the gold.

Her hair had fallen wildly around her shoulders. The dark liner Miram had so carefully placed had smudged, giving depth and danger to her eyes. Black singed the bodice of her gown and red trailed from her skirts. The skin around the gold Alden had pressed into her flesh had blackened.

I'm terrifying.

Maggie laughed again, refilling her hand with magic.

"Stop her!" a man in a black doctor's coat yelled as he snaked his way behind the soldiers.

"Please do." Maggie tossed the ball of molten magic at the nearest soldier, striking him in the face. He fell to the ground, shrieking with pain, but others ran past him, charging toward Maggie.

A man with red hair gave a guttural cry as he raised his sword. Maggie hit him in the chest with lightning. Another dodged around him, his blade slicing through the air.

A flutter of pain tickled Maggie's arm as his blade drew blood. She thrust her dagger under his ribs and punched him in the chin, letting her magic fly into his flesh.

"Primurgo." The shield shimmered around her before the next soldier could strike.

His sword struck the spell, shock waves of magic flew up his arms, and he fell to the ground screaming.

Another soldier stabbed the shield, his blade aimed to drive through Maggie's heart. Magic coursed through the metal, but he held on, screaming as he pushed into the spell.

Maggie stepped forward, bringing the shield closer to the man. He fell to the floor, writhing in pain.

Soldiers surrounded her, all of their weapons raised, none daring to get near her. She stepped forward—the men in front of her inched back. She stepped forward again.

"Keep her away from the wall!" a man bellowed from out of sight.

"Go on. Try." Maggie stepped forward, but the soldiers blocking her path didn't move. She reached her hand toward the shield, and five blades moved to pierce her palm. "Fine." Maggie took another step, the weight of her shield pressing her back as it fought against the mass of men.

Again, she moved forward. The men's boots squealed on the floor as the spell shoved them aside. Men ran around from behind her, joining the blockade between her and the pacel.

Maggie screamed, lurching forward step after step, pushing against her own shield as though trying to move an entire world. "Get—out—of—my—way."

Five feet from the pacel, her boots slipped on the shining floor, unable to match the weight of the men as she fought to gain ground. Maggie fell to her knees, and the shield shifted back a foot.

More men crammed themselves in front of her.

"Push her back!" Soldiers threw themselves at her spell, screaming in agony as the magic shot through their bodies.

A bolt of white molten light flew from the side, blasting the soldiers away from Maggie's shield.

She stood, stumbling forward, gaining two feet as another bolt struck, scattering the rest of the men. Maggie lunged, her shield bending as it reached the pacel.

"*Primurgo!*" Bertrand shouted. His shield blossomed to life, its edge touching Maggie's. "Miss Trent, you freed yourself more quickly than I expected."

"Yeah well, that pod thing really sucked." Maggie closed her eyes, focusing on the shape of her shield, willing the spell to rearrange itself.

"Indeed," Bertrand said. "I assume you know how to destroy the thing if you've come this far?"

"Yes." The shield drifted behind Maggie, encasing her as the pod had, leaving her free to touch the pacel. "You get the people out of the pods, I'll get rid of the pacel."

"I'll stay with you, Miss Trent."

Maggie tucked her dagger into her boot. "There won't be time after. Get them out now, Bertrand."

"There's no use, Miss Trent."

The pain in Bertrand's words pummeled her chest.

"I've already attempted it. The husk of a magician I pulled from the pod could not be saved."

Salt from Maggie's tears trickled into her mouth.

She blinked, shoving the horrible sadness into the void behind her magic. The dark place where forgotten horrors hid.

She pressed her palms to the golden wall, willing every ounce of burning hatred and rancid fear to pour out of her soul. The metal around her hands dripped away, flowing to the floor as if it were nothing.

And it was nothing. Nothing but a thin layer of gold. A façade to hide the real power of the pacel. The artifacts of the civilization the purra hated so much. The treasures they used to oppress generations of magicians.

The gap in the gold spread, dripping away until there was nothing between Maggie, Bertrand, and the pacel.

A spinning wheel, a dagger, a dented shield, and a wide swatch of delicately woven lace formed the center of the pacel.

Maggie trailed her fingers along the lace. The threads were beautiful, perfect. The lace hummed with magic.

"Are you quite sure about this, Miss Trent?"

"Yes." Maggie grabbed the lace with both hands, letting the veil funnel magic into her. She let the power flare within her, doubling its strength with her own, sending more magic flooding back into the pacel.

Fiery pain began in Maggie's toes as she pushed harder, forcing out more magic than she had ever used before.

The lace glowed, sparks running along its surface as it tried to devour Maggie's power.

A scream cut through the air. Maggie recognized the voice as her own, though her senses had nothing left to feel the wailing dragging itself from her throat.

"Miss Trent!"

Maggie pushed harder. Every inch of her skin blazed with magic. The pattern of the veil twisted, melting as sparks leapt from one thread to another.

"Miss Trent."

She turned her head just enough to see him. It was all the movement she could manage.

He pressed his fingers through his shield, reaching for her hands.

She let her shield fall. Bertrand was there in an instant, surrounding her with his own spell, pressing his hands on top of hers.

This is how we burn.

Flesh was not made to withstand such heat. But the flames that scorched her couldn't be seen, only felt as Bertrand funneled his magic through her skin.

Wild magic. Untamed. Unnamed. Tasting of a hundred

different worlds where different magic reigned. Beneath it all, something of Earth. Of the home she'd grown up in. Magic that could save a flower and devour you whole.

Maggie latched onto that taste, forcing it into the pacel. Flooding the beast with magic it had never met before.

Flames licked the corners of the lace as the gold pulsed wildly. With a surge of light and a terrible *screech*, the veil exploded with a *crack!*

Maggie moved her hands to grasp the dagger, not stopping to wonder that her fingers were still attached. The dagger had already begun pulsing wildly, the light spreading to the shield beside it. The dagger didn't fight her magic as the lace had, it devoured the power even as the metal sparked and flashed, dissolving into nothing. Maggie reached for the spinning wheel.

"Enough." Bertrand pulled her hands away. "We need to leave."

"We have to destroy it all." Maggie grasped the spinning wheel. Her knees buckled as the wheel exploded, taking the throne it leaned upon along with it.

"The fuse has been lit, Miss Trent." Bertrand seized her shoulders. "We cannot be here when the final flame ignites."

Maggie looked back at the pacel. The golden facade had melted entirely away. The cascade of sparks, explosions, and fire she'd begun spread slowly through the wall, each object contaminating its neighbor.

"Tell me you're sure," Maggie said.

"I'm sure."

"Then let's get the hell out of here."

Together, they rounded on the sea of soldiers.

"On three?" Bertrand asked.

"Sounds great." Maggie pulled the dagger from her boot as Bertrand raised his sword.

"One, two—"

The soldiers pressed in toward the shield, blocking the door to the cart from view.

A blazing ball of lightning formed in Maggie's hand.

"Three."

CHAPTER 24

Maggie tossed the lightning at the soldiers nearest them, spinning to drive her blade into the man waiting on the side.

"Down."

She obeyed Bertrand's command, ducking as his sword flew over her head. She didn't waste the moment, plunging her blade into a soldier's thigh as she sprang to her feet.

A wave of light burst from Bertrand, knocking the soldiers backward. Together, they ran forward, making it twenty feet before the soldiers regrouped, surrounding them.

Maggie pressed her back to Bertrand's. A soldier lunged forward. She parried his sword with her dagger and grabbed his wrist, shooting magic up his arm. He fell, knocking two down with him as he writhed on the ground.

A *screech* split the air as a spear burst out of being.

"We need to move faster!" Maggie said.

An arrow shot toward her head, missing her by inches.

"A lot faster."

A pair of soldiers charged, bellowing as they raised their blades.

Screaming, Maggie forced magic into her hand as she had done with the pacel. Golden light flared from her, striking the men, tossing them backward as though they were nothing more than dolls.

Bertrand shouted.

"Bertrand!" Maggie screamed, but she couldn't turn to look. A man was leveling his bow at her chest.

She dropped to the ground, pressing her palms to the shining floor.

The pacel screeched, shaking the whole library.

Maggie tasted the magic in the air as it disappeared. She shot her own magic into the floor, willing it to burn, leaving only a path between her and the door.

"Run!" Maggie seized Bertrand's sleeve as flames danced up from the ground and the soldiers around them shrieked in pain.

Sparks burned her skin and smoke filled her lungs, but she didn't dare slow down.

"Alden!" she screamed as they neared the door. "Alden!"

Let him have stayed. Let him be ready.

The doors swung open as they reached them.

Alden grabbed her hand, dragging her toward the cart. She leapt into the front with Alden as Bertrand perched in the back, his sword ready to defend them.

"Go!"

Alden didn't need the order. He had already pulled the lever all the way back.

A scream like the dying of a centuries-old beast rent the air as the cart gained speed.

Maggie looked back. They hadn't closed the door. The light of the pacel chased them as the throbbing grew. Maggie shielded her eyes as a light brighter than the sun burst from the library.

The tracks trembled as the walls behind them crumbled. Even as the light faded, flames took its place.

"Go faster!" Maggie shouted.

Rocks smashed behind them as the ground shook again.

"If I knew how this worked, I would be happy to try," Alden said.

The wind whipped passed them, but the scent of smoke didn't fade.

"We did it, right?" Maggie said. "We didn't just blow up the library, we destroyed the pacel."

Bertrand opened his mouth, but Alden spoke first. "Without the relics, the pacel can't be remade."

The end of the tunnel came into view. Nic stood in front of three soldiers. The four of them stared, not at the cart, but toward the inferno far beyond.

"What's happened?" A soldier shouted down the tracks.

Alden yanked on the lever. The wheels squeaked in protest, and the cart shook as it slowed.

"A fire," Bertrand said as the cart shimmied to a stop. "Something went wrong with the pacel. We barely made it out."

"What happened to her?" One of the soldiers eyed Maggie.

"Doctor Wilhelm pulled her from her pod when things started to go badly wrong," Alden said. "We're to take her back to his laboratory and wait for him."

"Do you think anyone made it out?" the third soldier asked. Fear had etched lines in his young face.

"I have no idea." Bertrand stepped out of the cart, seizing Maggie's arm and dragging her from her seat. "Until we know differently, we have to follow Doctor Wilhelm's instructions."

"What if she's what caused it?" the young soldier said. "What if she started the fire?" He reached for his blade.

The rods around Nic's neck whirred to life, forming sharp prongs, which he pointed at the soldiers.

"Certainly, you can't believe one girl could do any damage to the pacel." Sweat dripped down Alden's brow.

"We don't have time for this." Maggie pulled her dagger from the folds of her skirt. "I destroyed the pacel, and I'll kill all of you if you don't step into the cart right now."

Two of the soldiers paled, but the young one wrapped his fingers around the hilt of his sword.

"Don't," Maggie warned, letting flames dance along her fingertips. "Get in the cart, and you might get to live."

"Do as she says." Bertrand aimed the tip of his sword at the young soldier's throat.

"Now!" At Maggie's shout, the three men climbed in.

Bertrand placed a hand on the cart, growing the metal to encapsulate the men.

"Tell me the fastest way out of here, and he might leave you air holes," Maggie said.

"Out this door, turn right, down the long hall, and through the gate at the top of the stairs!" a soldier screamed as the flowing metal covered the men.

"Shall we?" Bertrand said.

Nic rolled to the door, wrenching it open.

The *rumble* of falling rocks chased them out into the hall.

"What if he lied?" Alden turned right into a long hall with polished marble floors.

"Then it takes us a little longer to get out," Maggie said.

"I doubt he lied," Bertrand said. "Miss Trent appears to have climbed from the depths of Hell to destroy the world. It takes an exceptionally brave man to lie to a demon."

A high scream echoed from up ahead. Maggie lifted her skirts, running faster as other panicked voices joined the chaos.

A woman ran into view far ahead of them, cutting out of another corridor. Jewels clung to her long silk skirts. She tripped on her hem, falling face first onto the ground as more people bolted from the same corridor the woman had fled.

"We have to get out!" a round man with gold woven into his hair shouted. "They'll destroy the whole city."

The crowd barely dodged around the woman on the ground. None of them bothered to stop and help her.

"You'd be better off here!" A man in a red suit chased the crowd. "I assure you all, the bank is secure."

No one stopped to listen.

Maggie leapt over the fallen woman on the heels of the crowd. She couldn't stop to help the woman. Couldn't risk anyone looking too closely at her and raising an alarm.

Alden ran next to Maggie, carrying Nic as they tore up the stairs and through the open gate.

The lobby was beautiful. Windows surrounded the domed ceiling. Gilded mosaics covered the walls. High desks behind barred windows took up one half of the room, and panicked patrons filled the rest. The crowd had stopped in the middle of the space. No one seemed willing to move toward the doors to the outside.

Maggie couldn't blame them—the sounds of chaos devouring the streets carried in through the closed doors. Screams of panic and fear and the shattering of glass cut over the frightened murmurs in the bank.

Alden set Nic down and took Maggie's hand, leading her to the door.

"Oh dear."

Maggie didn't have to look behind to know what Bertrand was muttering about. Soldiers stood in front of the door, their swords drawn to stop anyone from entering.

"Any ideas?" Maggie whispered.

"None that won't involve more fighting," Bertrand said.

Maggie scanned the room, not knowing what exactly she was searching for until she found it. Piles of ledgers on the desks behind the bars.

Hiding her hand behind her back, she formed a tiny bolt of lightning. Taking a breath to steady her aim, she tossed the bolt at the papers. A tiny flame took hold.

"Fire!" Maggie's scream echoed off the walls. "Fire! Let us out, there's a fire." She ran toward the door, trusting Bertrand, Alden, and Nic to follow.

The terrified screams of the people behind her were enough to make the soldiers turn around.

"Let us out!" The round man charged toward the door, darting between soldiers and reaching for the lock.

"Sir, we can't—" a soldier began, but there was no stopping the crowd.

Two women turned the heavy lock and thrust the doors open. A hand grabbed each of Maggie's as the crowd carried her out of the building.

She should have glanced behind to be sure it really was Bertrand and Alden who were holding onto her, but she couldn't look away from the street.

A pillar of fire soared into the air, towering over the high buildings surrounding the blaze. Sparks danced in the flames, like tiny bits of magic celebrating their freedom. Pandemonium had taken over the streets. People ran in every direction. Intets sped through the chaos, threatening to crush someone every second.

But it wasn't only purra who raced through the streets. A pack of people with gold marking their wrists charged toward the flames, carrying sticks, fire pokers, carving knives, and whips.

"It's happening," Alden said, stepping up to stand beside Maggie. "The Convocation said when the pacel was destroyed, the magicians would rise up. I thought we'd forgotten how to be brave."

A dozen soldiers charged down the street, chasing the magicians.

"We need to help them." Maggie started forward, but Bertrand blocked her path.

"We need to get out of the city," Bertrand said. "Alden, which way to the gate?"

Nic tapped his chest and started down a curving street.

"We can't just leave," Maggie said.

"We can and we must." Bertrand wrapped an arm around her waist, hauling her forward.

"The soldiers will kill the magicians." Maggie fought to pull away, but Alden added his weight, dragging her by the elbow.

A girl Maggie's age ran past with a heavy crate in her hands, tags glinting on her wrists.

"We have to help her," Maggie said.

The girl raised the crate over her head and threw it through a shop window. Screams mixed with the sounds of falling glass.

"No, we do not." Bertrand redoubled his grip.

Maggie forgot to fight as a tagged boy leapt into the shop through the broken window, wielding a plank of wood.

"I am very certain that, as of this moment, we have harmed no one who could be declared innocent," Bertrand said. "This city is descending into chaos, and the lines of what one might consider right are about to become irrevocably blurred. We accomplished what we set out to do, and we must allow the rest to be out of our hands."

"But what if the purra win?" Maggie asked as they left the curving street and ran onto the main thoroughfare. "What if what we did doesn't even help?"

"We've balanced the scales, Miss Trent," Bertrand said. "The rest is for those who will be here to establish a new order."

"That can't be the answer," Maggie said. "To come in and cause chaos, then leave and hope it all turns out all right?"

The gate loomed up ahead. A crowd had piled in near the small door as thousands tried to flee the city.

"You've done enough, Maggie," Alden said as they stopped at the back of the throng. "The two of you have accomplished more in a day than we've managed in a century. There will never be anything we can do to thank you enough."

Shouts carried from the gate. The crowd wanted the wall lowered.

"There is something you can do," Maggie said. "You can come with us to the Siren's Realm."

"Come with you?" Alden said.

"Yes." Hands shoved Maggie in the back, ramming her into the person in front of her. "We need you. I think we may even have been sent to find you. There's a sickness going through the Siren's Realm, and we need a doctor. We came here to find help, and you're it, Alden. We helped you, now you come to the Siren's Realm and help us."

"Maggie, I'm not even a real healer," Alden shouted over the rising screams from the front of the throng. "I might not be able to help."

"You can." Maggie laced her fingers through his. "I know you can. It's what you wanted anyway. Please."

"Damn." The unexpected word pulled Maggie's attention back to Bertrand. "Nic, find us a way through."

Nic's arms sprang to life, jabbing and slicing at the legs of the people in front of them, clearing a path forward.

"What?" Maggie strained to see over the crowd as they kept close on Nic's tail. "What's wrong?"

A scream of pain sounded from the outside of the crowd, followed closely by another.

Maggie craned her neck, peering between people. Alden's hands found her waist, steering her forward.

Men and women wielding tarnished swords and shields descended upon the crowd, slicing away at those unlucky enough to be left on the outskirts of the evacuation.

"Stop!" Maggie shouted over the screams of those around her. "Leave them alone! We're trying to get out!"

There was no way for the sword-wielding magicians to hear her. Arrows flew down from the top of the wall as the soldiers guarding the gate joined the fray.

"Miss Trent!"

She'd fallen behind the others, the path Nic had made for them closed in front of her.

"Lower the gate!" Maggie screamed, squeezing between purra as the hoard pushed toward the wall. "Bertrand, lower the gate! Go!"

Bertrand nodded as the crowd swallowed him.

Magic. A bit of magic and they'll clear out of your way. How many could be trampled to make you a path?

She shouldered her way toward the front of the crowd, moving one slow step at a time. Her skirt tore as a man behind her fell.

He clawed at the fabric, trying to save himself.

"I'm sorry," Maggie whispered as the crowd carried her farther forward.

She would never make it through the door. A barricade of people blocked the gap. Maggie shoved to the side, cutting an easier path away from the exit.

"Don't let me down, Bertrand."

CHAPTER 25

*A*n intet blocked her path. A family crowded in on top. Perched on their padded seats, towering above the bedlam.

The man holding the flower shaped wheel screamed, "Out of the way. Out of the way, or I'll drive right over you." He inched forward as the people in front of him tried to squeeze out of his path.

"No!" a woman screamed in front of the intet.

Maggie didn't have time to see the woman's fate as she disappeared below the wheels.

Maggie grabbed the side of the intet, hauling herself up onto the seats.

"Get down!" A finely dressed woman jabbed a sword at Maggie.

Maggie batted the sword away and leapt to the front of the intet. The man tried to push her down, but she'd already grabbed the wheel. His knuckles hit her cheek, but she'd done her damage. The flower wheel was nothing more than a puddle of metal on the ground.

Leaping toward the wall, Maggie dove into the crowd. The sea of bodies held her in the air for a moment, her feet unable to reach the ground.

As Maggie's feet found the street, several things happened at once. The wall of the city gave a lurch, and the grand gate began lowering into the ground. The crowd surged backward, away from the wall, as shouts of relief carried across the masses and a piercing *caw* sounded from the valley

Maggie pushed her way forward as the gate lowered, ignoring the pain in her limbs as she was stomped on, shoved, and hit. The gate moved quickly, dropping out of sight.

Another, undeniable *caw* sounded as the gate slid away. Three rammocs swooped through the gap in the wall, their greedy beaks open wide.

Screams cut through the throng while, as one, the crowd turned to run back into the city.

"Bertrand!" Maggie screamed. She'd almost reached the wall. Fifteen more feet, and she'd be free of the city. "Bertrand!"

A rammoc swept down, seizing a gold-clad man in its talons.

"Bertrand!"

A man twice Maggie's size rammed into her, knocking her backward, but she couldn't fall. There wasn't enough space.

The crowd dragged her back toward the city.

"Bertrand." Maggie had no air left to shout.

Cold metal wrapped around Maggie's wrist, dragging her forward. Nic's whistle throbbed in Maggie's ear as he poked and scratched the shins of every person in their way as he hauled her toward the side of the wall.

"Miss Trent!" Bertrand shouted from a hollow one story up in the wall. He lay on his stomach, his hands reaching down for Maggie.

Jumping up, she caught his wrists. Weight tore at her shoulders as Nic latched onto her ankles. Another set of hands joined Bertrand's.

"We've got you!" Blood trickled from Alden's nose.

The metal of the wall scraped against Maggie's chest as they hauled her up into the niche.

"Good work, Nic." Alden pulled the intet from Maggie's ankles.

A wave of warm air blasted Maggie's back as a *growl* shook the air.

Maggie flipped over, expecting talons to tear her back. But the thing rocketing past wasn't a rammoc but a flying intet. Golden light flickered under the four wings of the machine. A man with a golden box attached to his wrist sat astride the seat. The golden needle in the box spun wildly, and his face lit with joy as he aimed his crossbow at the rammoc.

"We need to move." Alden lifted Maggie under her arms.

Two more intets flew past.

A rammoc soared high over the sniffers and dove into the city.

"We have to stop them," Maggie said.

Bertrand started toward the blackness at the back of the niche. No, not a niche, a hallway that cut through the wall arching down toward the ground.

"Bertrand, we have to stop the rammocs."

"The sniffers can do that." Alden kept a hand on Maggie's back, pushing her down the corridor.

The floor rumbled as metal slid into place, closing the gap in the wall they'd climbed through.

"We have to stop the magicians from hurting civilians. They can't just attack everyone," Maggie said.

"They can, and they are," Alden said.

"But it won't help," Maggie said. "Rioting won't help. It'll only cause more harm."

The tunnel leveled out and cut sharply away from the city.

"Many revolutions look rather like riots at the start." Flames flickered to life in Bertrand's hand, lighting their way as they raced through the tunnel.

"Then we have to go to the Mira." Maggie's words echoed into the shadows. "We can get to the Convocation, tell them we destroyed the pacel, and they can come protect the city."

"The Convocation is filled with magicians too old and too timid to do anything," Alden said.

"Lara then."

"Lara hasn't been aboveground since infancy," Bertrand said. "She would do more harm than good."

"Ellic then!"

"I'm sure he's already leading a group trying to seize the palace," Alden said. "We did warn him of our plans. I'm sure he won't waste the opportunity."

"Opportunity?" Maggie batted Alden's hand off her back. "We just blew up a building with people still inside. Now there's a street war in the city and rammocs are flying in for the feast. We have to go back and do something."

"We lit the fuse, Miss Trent. The fire did not stop at the edges of the pacel."

"What we did—people are dying back there. Because of us." Maggie's mind raced through all of it. How many had died when the pacel exploded? How many would die on the streets? How much blood coated her soul?

"Miss Trent," Bertrand said. "You were tied to the pacel. You know better than either of us the evil of that machine. Do you believe it needed to be destroyed?"

"I—of course it did." Maggie tore her fingers through her hair. The cuts and blisters on her hands screamed with pain.

"Was there another way to end the power of the pacel?" Bertrand asked.

"No!" Maggie shouted. "There was no other way."

"Then we need to go." Bertrand started down the corridor.

"That doesn't excuse what we're leaving behind," Maggie spat.

"You said it yourself, Maggie." Alden reached for her hand. "They were feeding us to the pacel. It was genocide. The purra never would have stopped until they'd killed us all. You gave the magicians a chance to fight back. The valley burned once before, and civilization regrew. If the valley has to burn again to give the next generation a chance to rebuild a better world, then let fire reign."

Maggie didn't fight as Alden took her hand and led her through the tunnel.

"Good intentions can't wash away guilt," Maggie said. "If Histem burns, we're the ones who lit the match."

"The pyre was lit long ago, Miss Trent. The building of the pacel did that, a slow burning and torment of magical people. We fought fire with fire and had no other choice."

"You can stomach that?" Maggie asked. "You can live with jumping out of a land not knowing who's going to survive the chaos and fighting you've left behind?"

Bertrand stopped, rounding on Maggie. "Yes, I can. I am a wizard, not a god. I do only what I can, and short of seizing control of this world to rule over it ourselves, we have done all that lies within our power. So unless you are prepared to wet your hands in a bloody coup, then we are done here. There are other matters to attend to, or have you forgotten the blackness in the Siren's Realm?"

Maggie opened her mouth, but no words came. When Bertrand turned to run down the tunnel, she followed, still searching for words.

There has to be something. A way to stop the fighting. A way to block the rammocs from the city. To help find someone good to lead.

More death would come first. A long fight to seize power from the Regent. If they were lucky and the magicians won, then a longer struggle to build a new government. Rebellions from the purra. Power grabs within the ranks of magicians. Vicious punishments for civilian purra. Lack of laws for governing the use of magic.

Fire would purge the valley, and they couldn't wait the years it would take to see what new society would grow.

I hate you, Bertrand Wayland.

The tunnel arched up toward the surface. Nic rolled ahead, tapping on the door that angled overhead like that of a storm cellar.

It took Bertrand only a moment of magic before the tumbler on the lock clicked. He swung the door up and open.

Dim light from the setting sun peered in from above. Bertrand held his sword aloft as he climbed to the surface.

"Take Nic up." Maggie stepped aside, watching Alden lift Nic through the door before climbing up himself.

You could run. Forget the Siren's Realm and help form a new world.

"Maggie." Alden reached down through the door.

She took his hand and climbed into the open air. They were on top of a grassy hill, the strip of trees leading to the Mira on one side, the ruins of the great estate on the other. The cries of the rammocs echoed in the distance. Maggie turned toward the sound. The fires in the city had spread, reaching toward the palace in the east.

Eight rammocs flew around the city. More intets had taken to the sky, aiming at rammocs and people fleeing the city alike.

"How did you find this path?" Tears cut through the blood on Alden's face.

"I asked a soldier working the gate," Bertrand said. "Ordered him to drop the wall and told him I'd been sent on a mission on the Regent's orders. I needed the fastest path out of the city to lure the impi out."

A rammoc dove into the city—an explosion of fire rose to greet the beast.

"We should go before one of the rammocs comes for us," Alden said, though he didn't move.

Two rammocs dove at one of the flying intets, ripping the

metal wings off and letting the scraps fall into the trees below. Smoke carried up through the branches.

"This way." Bertrand ran toward the ruins.

In a minute, the hill blocked Histem from view. Only the smoke darkening the sky gave any sign the world had gone mad.

And we caused it.

Maggie didn't argue as Bertrand weaved between the rocks of the ruin, stopping every now and then before twisting away between another set of rocks she hadn't noticed before. They were laid out in a pattern as though the stone had once formed well-protected corridors.

Bertrand stepped around a low wall and stopped, gazing down.

A gaping hole led deep into the earth. The walls near the surface were smooth, as though someone had deliberately dug into the ground, but farther down jagged rocks cut into the tunnel where the earth had been violently cleaved apart.

"Jump toward the center if you can," Bertrand said. "Try not to be afraid, and don't fight the constriction. The first time in is by far the worst, I assure you."

Nic tapped his chest.

"He wants to come, too," Alden said, his eyes fixed on the endless darkness.

"I'm not sure how that will work for you, little fellow." Bertrand tented his fingers under his chin, his face infuriatingly calm. "You seem quite sentient to me, which would make you a magical being. Were it my choice, you would be able to make the leap the same as the rest of us. However, the Siren's ways are unknowable."

"He'll jump the minute we're gone," Alden said.

"Then I would suggest you aim for the center as well." Bertrand looked up to the sky for one more moment before turning to Maggie. "We should not linger."

He turned toward the pit and jumped, disappearing into the darkness. A faint flash of green carried up from far below.

Nic rolled backward as far as the walls would allow, then barreled forward, flinging himself into the pit.

"I would prefer to go next." Alden's voice crackled as he spoke. "I'm afraid if it were only me on the ledge, I might never jump."

"We'll go together." Maggie took his hand. "If you end up in the dark, don't panic. Ask the Siren for some light, and then ask to find me."

"Ask the Siren?"

"It'll work, I promise you." Maggie stepped up to the edge. "Just ask for what you need and get to me as quickly as you can."

"Maggie," Alden said, "can you look at me?"

She looked into his terrified eyes. After a moment, lines of contentment creased the corners. He nodded.

"Jump on three." She didn't wait for him to speak. "One, two"—she tightened her grip on his hand—"three."

They leapt into the darkness.

The stench of damp decay lasted for a split second before the void took them. Alden's hand disappeared from Maggie's grip, but there was no air in her lungs to call his name. The black pressed around her, numbing her.

For a moment, Maggie wished it would last forever. A void without need for thought, without threat of consequences. The darkness could be cherished, could be her salvation.

The void didn't care. It spat her out onto the streets of the Siren's Realm.

"Miss Trent." Bertrand stood over her, his shadow blocking the setting sun. "Are you all right?"

"Alden." Maggie pushed herself to her feet. The skin on her hands had healed. The flakes of gold pressed into her flesh had disappeared. Her bloody and burnt dress was the only sign of what they'd done in Histem. A shock of relief flipped in Maggie's heart. She could pretend it had never happened.

It did happen. You fought and killed. Pretending can't erase reality.

"Where's Alden?"

"He and Nic didn't arrive with you," Bertrand said. "We can only assume the Siren has created her usual welcome."

Shouts carried over the tents, a raucous chorus of voices the likes of which Maggie had never heard in the Siren's Realm.

"The blackness." The words fell from Maggie's lips.

She and Bertrand charged toward the noise.

CHAPTER 26

The tents of the Siren's Realm had no shadow of the blackness clinging to their bright canvass. A gentle breeze swayed the fabric as Maggie and Bertrand bolted past. The scent of sea air filled Maggie's tired lungs. The Siren had healed her skin, but not the terrible fatigue that pulled at every bit of her.

Bertrand turned down a wide lane of bright blue tents, then onto a narrow alley of tents with sparkling red thread marking their seams.

The sounds of the roaring crowd found distinction as they neared the fountain square. Music cut under the cheers. Bright, happy music that spoke of days in the endless light, not of death and decay.

Maggie ran faster, bolting past Bertrand as the platinum fountain came into view.

Half naked men and women swam in the sweet waters that surrounded the Siren's feet. Carts selling ale, wine, fresh bread, and sweet meats had trundled into the square. A band of six musicians stood in front of the fountain, playing an exuberant tune. Dancers filled the square, leaving a wide swath of open ground in front of the musicians.

"What's going on?" Maggie asked.

Bertrand didn't say anything. He walked into the square, heading straight for the fountain, his shoulders tense as though preparing for battle.

A woman in bright green, sheer silks spotted Maggie's dress. She didn't back away or scream in horror. She tipped her head to the sky and laughed. The blithe sound sent chills racing down Maggie's neck.

"I do beg your pardon." Bertrand stepped in front of a man who hopped by on one foot, trying to tug off his sock.

"There's no line." The man pulled the sock free. "You can splash in if you like. The Siren will care for us all."

"Why is everyone celebrating?" Bertrand said.

"You went down a wine hole, didn't you?" The sockless man snorted. "The blackness has been lifted. Two long weeks with no one new falling ill. The Siren has forgiven us for whatever those she took did to offend her." He clapped Bertrand on the shoulder. "Rejoice! The Siren's will has been done."

The man ran past them, skirting the open area in front of the band, and dove into the fountain.

"The Siren's will will be done," Bertrand murmured.

Maggie opened her mouth to speak, but the patch of bare ground caught her eye.

"We should find Alden if we can," Bertrand said.

A slab of stone, polished to shine, had been placed in front of the fountain. The musicians stayed behind it, and the crowd skirted the front, avoiding stepping on the words that had been etched as though by the Siren herself.

Lest we ever forget the price of transgression.

The Siren's will will be done.

Two long lines of names were listed below. Maggie read each of them, trying to find a memory of a face that matched.

The centaur Ramis

Verna the silk vendor

The vice around her chest loosened as she neared the bottom of the second list. Her friends had been spared.

Luric the drunk

Mathilda the food seller

Maggie's knees buckled. Arms caught her before she hit the ground.

"Miss Trent." Bertrand's voice echoed from far away.

"We abandoned them." The words shredded her soul. "We left them to die."

The dancers parted, letting Maggie through, clearing the way for the person who carried her.

"We abandoned them!" Maggie shrieked, pummeling Bertrand's chest and tumbling from his arms.

"Miss Trent." Bertrand reached for her.

"We left them all trapped here to die!"

The dancing didn't stop, nor did the music and laughter. But the dancers moved away as Maggie shouted, leaving her and Bertrand standing isolated amidst the celebration.

"We were supposed to help them," Maggie said. "The Siren guided us to that stitch so we could save them!"

"The Siren's ways are unknowable."

"Mathilda was my friend! I saw her every day. She worried about me, she probably came looking for me, and now she's dead. And we just left!"

"Miss Trent—"

"And for what?" Maggie shouted at the sky. "You really needed us to blow up a bunch of magic antiques? You wanted a doctor for next time? What the hell do you want?"

"It is not wise to question the Siren."

"Why not?" Maggie spat. "Her will will be done? She'll punish me for my transgressions? Mathilda was wonderful. She worked hard, she didn't do anything wrong."

"We can't know—"

"We trusted the damned Siren. We asked her to lead us to help, a way to protect people—"

"The Siren does not grant all requests. If she wanted to end the lives of those who have fallen, we could have fought her will for a hundred years and never won. I asked for mercy for the masses but above all a way to protect you. I wanted to protect you from the blackness, she let us leave for the duration."

"What?"

"We found Alden, and I had a twinkling ounce of hope she might have intended for more lives to be saved. That there was a way to dissuade her from killing. I had no way to know her mercy was only meant for us."

"So we get to be safe and everyone else can suffer? You wanted to protect me, so we slipped to Histem? No matter that my friends were here, dying. I went with you so we could stop the blackness."

"There is no stopping the will of the Siren!" Bertrand shouted.

The dancers moved farther away.

"None of us are strong enough to stand up to her will." He stepped closer to Maggie, his words barely audible over the music and laughter that filled the square. "If I thought for even a moment that we could stop the blackness by staying in the Siren's Realm, I would have fought for a cure until my final breath. If there were the slightest chance that we could reason with, fool, or defeat the Siren, I would have trusted no one but you at my side.

"But a battle with her is a battle that cannot be won. We saved a people from enslavement and extinction rather than stand in the street and helplessly watch people suffer. I would have thought my choice fit your preference."

"You don't get to think about my preference." Heat curled Maggie's fingers, but the magic stayed trapped beneath her skin.

"You don't get to decide that running away to other worlds is more important than staying with my sick friend."

"We didn't run away. We made a difference."

"No we didn't! The magicians might have a shot at being in charge now, but it doesn't matter. They'll hurt the purra. The purra will rise up and torment the magicians all over again. It's all just an endless cycle of bloody death. You say we can't stop the Siren's will. Nothing we did in Histem made any more of a difference than trying to fight her."

"Miss Trent, that is far from true."

"Death, blood, darkness, it all just comes back. There's no stopping it or fighting it. It's all just death gnawing away at everything."

"Miss Trent, I beg you not to believe that." Bertrand stepped forward.

"Don't." Maggie stepped back. The dancers swerved away from her as though they could scent the contamination of blood and smoke clinging to her soul. "I'm done. I'm done with you. I'm done with adventures. I'm done trying to help and making everything worse."

She stepped into the crowd.

"Maggie, please."

"Stay the hell away from me, Wayland."

The revelers parted as Maggie left the square, striding alone into the Siren's sunset.

Maggie's adventure continues in The Girl Cloaked in Shadow. *Order your copy now.*

CHAPTER 1

The sun peered in through Maggie's window, casting light across her bed. Dust motes swirled through the air, caught in the breeze off the Endless Sea. The rhythmic splashing of the waves tried to lull her to sleep, but she kept her eyes open, watching the specks float aimlessly through the air.

A shadow flickered past the window as a bird landed on top of her stone home. The gull's *caw* set Maggie's teeth on edge.

"Shut up."

At her murmur, the shutters swung closed, blocking out the sunlight and muffling the bird's call.

She rolled onto her back, staring up at the dark ceiling.

The waves kept up their steady hushing, like the sea itself whispered in her ear.

Get up, Maggie. Life is waiting outside these walls. There are a thousand worlds you've yet to explore.

The words of the waves didn't pull her from her bed. She didn't move until the pangs of hunger grew too strong to be ignored.

She kicked aside her blanket and dug through the dark for her fishing net.

A chill damp clung to the ropes of the net as she shoved open the door. The afternoon sunlight bored into her eyes, sending sparks zapping through her vision.

The flat rock that supported her home reached only five feet out over the sea. Maggie walked over the edge and dropped into the water, not bothering to take a breath before the plunge.

The waves swayed her body, dragging her closer to the sea floor. She didn't fight the current. Her toes touched sand as she drifted away from the shore.

The burning in her lungs told her to kick up. Her legs didn't seem to care to try. A fish the size of her head swam a loop around her, pausing for a moment to take in Maggie's limp figure, before settling itself in her net.

The Siren's will will be done.

Maggie kicked off, breaking through the surface of the water with a gasp.

A whirring *chirp* sent the gull who had perched on her house flying with an indignant *screech*.

"Hi, Nic." Maggie swam toward the shore, letting the heavy net drag behind her.

The silver bot rolled to the edge of the ridge above her roof, clicking at her and giving a shrill whistle.

"I was just catching lunch." She stopped at the edge of the rock that was her porch, tossed her net up, and climbed the slope that dipped into the Endless Sea.

Nic gave a dull *clunk*.

"I know it's closer to dinner," Maggie said, "but this is when I'm eating, so deal."

She had never been able to understand the exact words the little robot said, but there was no mistaking the judgmental tone of his *hiss* and *beep*.

Nic stared at her with his singular eye as she pulled the fish from the net. The late afternoon sun glinted off his upside-down teardrop-shaped head, which balanced precariously on his teardrop-shaped body. A ruffle of metallic arms lay dormant around his neck.

Maggie dropped the fish next to a mound of stones, ignoring Nic's eye watching her. She knelt and blew a long breath into the center of the rock pile. Fire instantly crackled to life. A tingle itched Maggie's fingers as the Siren took her payment for the flames.

Nic tinked his spindly arms together.

"I didn't ask for your opinion." Maggie stepped into her house, ignoring the mess that took up the tiny space, and grabbed her knife from the wooden table.

A *scratch* and a *thunk* sounded from outside as Nic landed on the ledge.

Maggie leaned out the door, glaring at Nic's back as he rolled toward her fish.

"Did I invite you down?" Maggie asked.

Nic grabbed the fish, lifting the floppy mass to be level with his eye.

"What do you want with a fish anyway?" Maggie said. "It's not like you eat."

The metal arms around Nic's neck sprang to life, slashing and clawing at the fish.

"Hey! I just caught that."

Before Maggie could think of how to rescue her meal from the whirling arms, Nic tossed the fish onto the flames.

"What are you…" Maggie's anger simmered away as she looked down at her cleaned and prepared lunch.

Nic whistled.

"I could have done it myself." Maggie sank to the ground, letting the dancing flames dry her clothes as they cooked her meal.

Nic raised his arms in a way that nearly looked like a shrug.

"And helping me with a fish doesn't excuse you coming down here without asking. This is my home. You live with Alden and"—she couldn't bring herself to say Bertrand's name—"and there's no need for you to come and check on me."

Nic stared at her.

"Alden sent you, didn't he?"

Nic purred.

"Alden!" Maggie shouted.

A bird somewhere out of sight squawked its displeasure.

"Alden, are you hiding up there?" Maggie lay back on the rock, staring at the overhang that was the roof of her home.

"I'm not hiding." Alden stepped into view, twisting the cuff of his pale blue shirt. "I was simply enjoying the view while you and Nic had a little visit."

"You sent a robot—"

Nic hummed in indignation.

"—to make sure it was safe for you to come down?" Maggie shut her eyes tight, the undeniable sense that she shouldn't have gotten out of bed stealing her will to argue with Alden.

"It's not that at all." Alden spoke over the clacking of stones as he climbed down to Maggie's rock. "I didn't want to be rude by overwhelming you with visitors."

His shadow fell across Maggie.

"I've brought food," Alden said, his voice swinging up hopefully.

"I have a fish." Maggie pointed to the flames.

The scent of the charring meat cut through the tang of the sea air.

"You need to eat more than fish, Maggie." Alden took Maggie's wrists, pulling her to sit up. "It's not healthy. I know these things—"

"You're a healer." Maggie opened her eyes wide enough to glower at Alden.

"Exactly." Alden let go of Maggie's wrists.

Nic rolled up behind Maggie, blocking her from lying back down.

"Look at the wonderful things I've brought." Alden reached into his bag and pulled out a spiked purple fruit, holding it out to Maggie as though it were a prized treasure.

"No?" He said after a long moment. "That's all right, I have more."

He reached back into the bag, presenting a basket of bright red berries, a sweet roll, and a box of chocolates.

"I thought you were trying to take care of my health?" Maggie bit the insides of her cheeks, stamping down the instinct to smile as Alden presented a glass smooth truffle.

"There is more to health than diet." Alden took Maggie's hand, placing the truffle in her palm.

Nic rolled toward the house. A *bump* and a *clatter* sounded as soon as he disappeared through the door.

"Don't break anything," Maggie called after him.

"Eat, Maggie." Alden sank to the ground, taking a moment to arrange his gangly limbs. His dark hair puffed up with the wind, flying in a dozen different directions. "You'll like it."

Maggie nibbled on a corner of the truffle. Deep sweetness flooded her mouth. A tiny thread of the knotted anger that had settled in her chest weeks ago unraveled.

She placed the chocolate back in the box. "You don't have to bring me food, Alden. I can take care of myself."

Nic rolled back out of her home, carrying the two plates and forks she owned. She had gotten a second plate in case Bertrand ever…

Rage flared in her lungs. She snatched the truffle back up, tossing the whole thing into her mouth.

"I would never think you incapable of anything," Alden said. "But you're my friend. One of the very few I have in the Siren's Realm. There is no illness here for me to cure. There is no battle for me to fight. The Siren provides for everyone's needs. I am useless here. Let me at least do a tiny thing to take care of you."

Maggie watched as Nic reached into the fire and pulled the

fish free, placing a portion onto each of the plates before handing them to Maggie and Alden.

"Thanks, Nic," Maggie said.

Nic purred.

"Fine, you can worry about me." Maggie kept her eyes on her plate. "But only because it gives you something to do, and no wasting magic on me."

"You could never be a waste, Maggie."

"The magic you brought into the Siren's Realm is all the magic you've got." Maggie dug into her fish with her fork, watching the meat flake into pieces, like the fish was meant to be nothing more or less than tiny bites for a person to eat.

"I have plenty of magic," Alden said. "I spent a whole lifetime in Alondra not being able to use any of it, I have enough stored inside to be able to pay the Siren's price for a very long time."

"What about Nic?" Maggie set her plate down, unable to look at the ill-fated fish any longer.

"He's not drawing magic from me." Alden rubbed the flecks of gold embedded in his wrists. "I can feel it when I pay people for things in the Textile Town, or even when I pay for something I've asked the Siren for. A tingle as the magic is pulled away from me, and a microscopic void forming where the magic used to live. Nic never pulls magic from me."

"Then how are you still running, buddy?" Maggie looked to Nic.

Nic turned his eye up to the sky.

"It seems to me the most likely answer is he's feeding off the ambient magic in the air."

Maggie looked away as Alden took a bite of fish.

"The Siren's Realm is created by magic, consistently altered by magic, powered by magic. It's as though the air itself is breathing power into him."

"At least the Siren is helping someone," Maggie said.

Alden gave a tiny gasp and looked up to the sky. "Maggie, you shouldn't say such things."

"Because the Siren will hear me?" Maggie leapt to her feet, energy like she hadn't felt in days coursing through her body. "Because then the almighty Siren will know I think she's nothing more than a thieving, murdering, little—ow!"

Nic jabbed her in the shin with one of his many arms.

"I will kick you into the ocean." Maggie rubbed her shin.

Nic rolled to the far side of the flat rock.

"Maggie," Alden said, unfolding his limbs as he stood, "I know how upset you are."

"Upset?" Maggie growled. "Upset! The Siren decided to let a plague sweep through her perfect realm, and now my friend is dead."

"Losing someone you care for is a great—"

"And you." She pressed a finger to Alden's chest. "You're living with the traitor, which makes you no better than he is."

"You think I'm a traitor?" Alden tipped his head to the side, something between hurt and confusion filling his eyes.

"No." Maggie's chest deflated as the anger rushed out of her, leaving her even more exhausted than before. She sank down onto the rock. "But I don't know why you put up with him."

"I know you blame him," Alden said slowly. "For convincing you to leave the Siren's Realm when the blackness was taking people, for helping to free my people—"

"Don't." Maggie waved a hand at the fire, extinguishing the flames. "Just don't."

Alden picked at his fish, tearing it into tiny pieces. "Bertrand Wayland aside, you can't hide out here."

"I'm not hiding."

"When was the last time you left this rock?"

Nic cocked his head to the side.

"When I left the Siren's Realm." Maggie grabbed a chocolate from the box. "When we went to Alondra and found you."

"You haven't left at all since you've been back?" Alden's eyes widened.

She popped another truffle into her mouth and looked out over the sea. There was nothing new or interesting in the waves, but staring at their shimmering surface was better than seeing the worry in Alden's eyes.

"People die, Maggie," Alden whispered. "That doesn't mean you get to stop living."

"People die, but you still have to eat breakfast." A coarse laugh rattled the knot in Maggie's throat. "My mother taught me that a long time ago."

"Then let's go find breakfast." Alden grabbed Maggie under the arms and hoisted her to her feet. "Her shoes please, Nic."

"But it's dinnertime, and my clothes are wet."

Nic rolled into her home.

"Nic, don't. I've already eaten," Maggie said.

Nic tossed her boots through the door. They landed limply at her feet.

"You haven't eaten enough." Alden crossed his arms in a way he seemed to believe was intimidating. "I'm the healer here. A long walk and some good food, that's what you need."

Maggie glared between Nic and Alden, the urge to throw both of them into the Endless Sea ebbing the longer her friends stared at her.

"Fine." Maggie pulled on her gray leather boots. "I'll agree to go into town. But If I see Bertrand and decide to kill him, you agree to stay out of my way."

"Perfect." Alden beamed at her. "I've got an excellent adventure in mind, and there's no worry of running into Bertrand at all."

"Has he decided to lock himself in the dark as penance for all the damage he's done?" Maggie climbed up to the overhang, not needing to look to know where to place her hands.

"He's gone on one of his adventures," Alden said. "I haven't seen Bertrand in more than a week."

CHAPTER 2

The sounds of the Textile Town carried to the very edge of the beach. The chatter of voices and *clatter* of wheels set Maggie's teeth on edge.

She stopped with her toes still on the sand and looked toward the rocky mounds that took over the sleepy beach. If she ran full out, she could make it to the rocks. From there, it would be easy to outpace Alden and Nic. She'd be locked safely in her house before they could drop from the overhang and onto her stone porch.

And you'd have to do all this again tomorrow.

Maggie stepped from the sand onto the packed dirt road.

That's the trouble with having friends. They won't leave you alone.

"That wasn't so hard, was it?" Relief softened Alden's face.

Nic gave a crackling *whirr*.

"Thanks, Nic." Maggie didn't fight the tiny smile that curved her lips.

"This really is going to be a remarkable evening." Alden lifted Maggie's hand, looping it through his elbow. "At least, I hope it will be a remarkable evening. I'm not really sure what you're used to."

"Hiding in a stone house?" Maggie let Alden lead her down the lane.

Bare sea grass surrounded the first stretch of road, swaying gently with the evening breeze.

"I mean before your little rest from the world," Alden said. "Before I came to the Siren's Realm."

"Well, before I met you I was here," Maggie said, "living on a rock, selling fish for magic, being an idiot who thought there might be meaning to all this."

Nic whistled.

"Fine." Maggie rolled her eyes at Nic. "And before here, I was at home on Earth, living in an awful Academy that was basically a prison for kids nobody wanted to deal with."

Heat pressed on the corners of Maggie's eyes.

Alden gazed down at her, a crease forming between his eyebrows.

Tents cropped up on either side of the street, low and made of plain canvas with their flaps tied shut against the setting sun.

"I suppose," Alden said, "that means your bar for a fantastic evening is set remarkably low."

"I guess. Avoid blood and dying and you've pretty much got it in the bag."

"Excellent." Alden sped up his pace, his long legs covering so much ground Maggie had to trot to keep up. "I had been worried you wouldn't be impressed. From what the others I've met have told me, things of this sort weren't normal before the dark time, but if your world held such wonders, then you might not be interested at all."

"Interested in what?" Maggie asked.

Alden didn't answer as he hurried down the road. The tents surrounding them grew wider and grander as they neared the heart of the Textile Town.

Every jewel tone Maggie could imagine had been used in the wishes to the Siren that built this part of the city. Intricate patterns of everything from soaring birds to words in languages Maggie couldn't read had been stitched into the canvas.

"Has the city been redone?" Maggie asked. "The tents weren't so colorful before. I mean, there were colors, but not like this. Not so—"

"Bright and new? There has been quite a bit of new textile created throughout town." Alden turned onto a narrow side lane.

Pale pink wildflowers that matched the surrounding tents covered the ground.

Maggie hesitated, not wanting to crush the blooms, but Alden plowed forward. The flowers had a bounce in them that gave an involuntary spring to Maggie's step.

Nic growled as he rolled behind them, his three wheels fumbling on the flowers.

"You okay?" Maggie asked.

Nic glared.

"Sorry you hate the flowers," Maggie laughed. The shaking of her chest tensed foreign muscles, sending a pang into her lungs.

"Nic doesn't like anything that bothers his wheels, and the roads are becoming more and more interesting by the day. Everyone seems intent on having a welcoming and delightful home. From what I've been told, the massive renewal of the Textile Town began when the dark times ended. Whether in gratitude for being left alive or a desperate need to prove to the Siren they are good stewards of her realm, I don't really know."

"And the Siren's just letting people redecorate?"

They veered onto a wide road filled with people all moving in the same direction.

"I suppose she must be," Alden said. "It keeps happening, and all magic works by her will."

"By the Siren's will," Maggie whispered.

A tent four stories high came into view at the end of the road, in a place Maggie had been a hundred times before.

"That's the market square," Maggie said. "Why is there a giant tent in the market square?"

"They did work quite quickly. It wasn't there this morning." Alden steered her through the crowd, cutting around others who, like Maggie, gaped up at the enormous, violet tent.

"Is it going to be there forever?" Maggie asked.

"No idea. I suppose not. None of the market shops mentioned moving locations when I visited for breakfast."

"Then why did someone put up a giant tent?" Maggie squinted at the fabric.

Golden embroidery sparkled in the red glow of the setting sun. The stitches were laid out in a careful pattern, but she couldn't quite tell what they were meant to be.

"They put up the tent for the festivities," Alden said. "I really hope you'll enjoy the evening. I've got us box seats and everything."

"Box seats?"

As the sun faded, the embroidery grew brighter, sparkling in the twilight.

Dead ahead, where people were filing into the violet tent, a lion with the tale of a scorpion marked the canvas. A woman with wings stitched to her back flew on one side of the great beast, while a unicorn galloped on the other.

They reached the front of the queue of people waiting to enter the tent. Centaurs with gold and silver ribbons wound through their manes flanked the entrance, collecting tickets as people passed.

"Alden, what are we going to see?" Maggie asked.

"A fantastic assortment of wonders only visible in the Siren's Realm." Alden patted his pockets. "I've been looking forward to it for days. Ever since the notices were posted. I purchased seats for us straight off, but Nic thought it best I surprise you. Not give you a chance to overthink coming."

"Smart, Nic."

Thick golden ropes tied back the flaps of the tent, letting the light from the hundreds of lanterns that filled the space spill out onto the street.

"Meat fer sale!" The familiar call came from within the tent. "Don't want to watch the spectacle hungry. Get yer meat. Finest roasted leg in the realm."

"Gabriel!" Maggie shouted, pushing forward in the crowd.

A troll rounded on Maggie. "Wait your turn." If the troll's glare hadn't been enough to turn Maggie back, the stench would have done the job.

Alden took Maggie's hand, drawing her back to their place in line. "We'll happily wait." Alden sounded like he had a terrible head cold. "Won't we, Maggie?"

"Right." Maggie coughed.

"This way if you please." A woman in a thick veil took the troll's ticket, leading him away from the crowd.

The throng gave a collective gasp of relief as the stink of the troll subsided.

"I know the meat seller," Maggie said as Alden handed their tickets to a centaur. "His name is Gabriel. I need to see him."

"This way, please." A girl of no more than fourteen beckoned them forward. A long, red braid trailed down the girl's back. Her skin shimmered as she moved, as though someone had rubbed silver dust all over her.

How did you get here? What brought a child to the Siren's Realm?

The questions balanced on the tip of Maggie's tongue as the girl led them around the wide, open space at the center of the tent to a set of sweeping stands. Waist-high walls separated the area into private sections of individual chairs.

"Here you are." The girl bowed them into a box.

Two wingback chairs and an empty table waited behind the gate.

"Will this do?" The girl turned to Alden. "We have other seating arrangements."

With a clap of her hands, the two chairs disappeared, replaced by a sofa just wide enough for two.

"I really don't think—" Maggie began.

"There are also privacy options." The girl clapped again.

The three walls not facing the open center of the tent turned opaque. A fainting couch took the place of the love seat.

Nic gurgled a trill.

"We-we're fine with the chairs, thank you." Alden blushed to the roots of his hair.

The girl clapped, and the chairs reappeared.

"The Compère wishes only for his guests' enjoyment." The girl bowed and backed out of the booth.

"Thank you." Maggie clicked the gate shut behind the girl. "Who is the Compère?" Maggie whispered to Alden, her gaze sweeping the vast space.

The tent had been laid out in quarters. The portion that housed their booth held the most private seating options. Some guests sat in seats much like Maggie and Alden's. Others had turned their walls dark, shielding themselves from the crowd.

To either side of them were stands with benches laid out in rows. Along the front stood a line of centaurs, their heads barely lower than the seats behind them.

Behind a shimmering patch of air along the far wall, a pack of wide and strangely scattered chairs held an array of trolls. Tables had been laid out, filled with everything from sweets to barely-cooked meat, which the trolls ate with abandon.

"To keep the smell in." Alden followed Maggie's gaze. "It was quite the selling point, believe me."

"Wine?" A woman in red silks strode past their booth, holding a decanter in one hand and a glass in the other.

"Would you like some?" Alden asked.

"I just want to talk to Gabriel," Maggie said.

She scanned the other vendors moving throughout the seated

spectators. Some sold cakes and candies, others offered paper pamphlets.

"Excuse me." Alden opened the gate of their booth.

"Wine, sir?" The woman in red winked at Alden. Her gaze slid over Maggie, and a smile curved her lips. "Or perhaps some companionship?"

"Actually, I was hoping you might be willing to send over the meat seller," Alden said. "Gabriel is his name."

"Meat with no wine?" The woman pouted. "That doesn't seem right at all. Better not have him come this way."

"Fine." Alden held out his hand. "I'll buy the wine if you send over the meat seller."

"Excellent." A glass cyclone filled with wine, and two glasses swirled into existence on the table. "Gabriel will be with you directly."

"I could have just gone to look for him," Maggie said. "You didn't need to buy any wine."

"I like wine." Alden sat in one of the wingback chairs. "And besides, this is a night for commerce. I have magic to spend. The wine seller needs to earn. It's the way of things. Now, would you like some wine or not?"

"Fine." Maggie sank into a chair.

Alden picked up the decanter. The swirling of the wine didn't stop as it poured into the glass. The liquid spun ceaselessly, creating its own vortex like a storm caught in a cup.

"I didn't know we were going somewhere fancy." Maggie took the glass Alden offered. "You should have warned me."

"Why?" Alden held his nose to his glass before taking a sip. "Aren't you having fun?"

"The wine lady looked at me like I was homeless."

"You look perfect just as you are."

"I could have worn clean clothes, or, I don't know, brushed my hair." Maggie held her nose over her wine. Her mouth watered at the warm scent of honey, fruit, and oak.

"The Compère won't care if your clothes are still damp," Alden said. "We're here for a night of fun, and a few tangles in your hair won't interfere."

"Yeah, well…" Maggie studied the storm in her glass. "I feel so wrong drinking this."

"Would you rather a white?" Alden asked.

"No." Maggie shook her head. Her hair had grown, falling down past her shoulders. The tangles tickled her bare skin, and goose bumps prickled her arms. "Back home, my drinking this would be illegal. I'm too young."

"But you were in a battle to save your world from an evil wizard." Alden wrinkled his brow. "You nearly died fighting him. You thought you had died when you came here."

"Yeah." Maggie sipped the wine. A hearty sweetness flooded her mouth.

"So you were too young to have wine but not too young to fight an evil wizard?"

"I never said it made sense. It's just the way it works."

"If there is ever a chance," Alden said, "I would love to see your world. A place where there is so much magic, and the non-magical people haven't even noticed. What a wonderful world it must be!"

"Maybe." Maggie shrugged. "I never got to see all that much of it myself. And I don't know if I'd want to go back even if I could ever find the right path."

Nic cocked his head at Maggie with a whistle.

"Too much time will have passed," Maggie said. "Everyone I knew will be gone."

"That is both the blessing and the horror of the Siren's Realm, I suppose. You can leave and find a thousand magnificent places, but you can never return to any of them. Not as you knew them before. Once you've passed through a stitch, the opportunity to change your path within a world is utterly gone."

Maggie took Alden's hand. Her fingers closed around his without thought.

"Do you wish you had stayed?" Maggie asked, the weight of knowing she had asked Alden to come to the Siren's Realm pressing on her chest.

"No. There was nothing left for me in my world. Only I sometimes wish I had been born to a different world, where seeking the Siren would never have occurred to me."

As one, the lanterns in the tent dimmed. A rush of whispers fluttered around the stands as a bright light burst into being at the center of the space, beaming down on a figure shrouded in swirling red.

Order your copy of The Girl Cloaked in Shadow *and continue the adventure.*

ABOUT THE AUTHOR

Megan O'Russell is the author of several Young Adult series that invite readers to escape into worlds of adventure. From *Girl of Glass*, which blends dystopian darkness with the heart-pounding danger of vampires, to *Ena of Ilbrea*, which draws readers into an epic world of magic and assassins.

With the *Girl of Glass* series, *The Tethering* series, *The Chronicles of Maggie Trent*, *The Tale of Bryant Adams*, the *Ena of Ilbrea* series, and several more projects planned for 2020, there are always exciting new books on the horizon. To be the first to hear about new releases, free short stories, and giveaways, sign up for Megan's newsletter by visiting the following:

https://www.meganorussell.com/book-signup.

Originally from Upstate New York, Megan is a professional musical theatre performer whose work has taken her across North America. Her chronic wanderlust has led her from Alaska to Thailand and many places in between. Wanting to travel has fostered Megan's love of books that allow her to visit countless new worlds from her favorite reading nook. Megan is also a lyricist and playwright. Information on her theatrical works can be found at RussellCompositions.com.

She would be thrilled to chat with you on Facebook or

Twitter @MeganORussell, elated if you'd visit her website MeganORussell.com, and over the moon if you'd like the pictures of her adventures on Instagram @ORussellMegan.

Ice and Sky

Feather and Flame

Guilds of Ilbrea

Inker and Crown